"GAYLE CALLEN IS WONDERFUL."

Cathy Maxwell

WHO IS THIS MAN?

The Duke of Thanet may have hired her as a governess to his six-year-old son, but there is something . . . different about the devilish rogue standing before her today. He seems to study her with an intensity she never noticed before, and he is certainly more charming than the last time they encountered each other. Was there always an alluring glint in his dark eyes? But the duke has a notoriously scandalous reputation, and Meriel will not let herself succumb.

Masquerading as the duke was not the simple solution Richard O'Neill had envisioned. When his ailing half-brother, the real duke, asked him to protect his young heir from a greedy enemy, Richard agreed. But he never thought he'd be attracted to the inquisitive governess, or that each moment in her intoxicating presence would tempt him beyond all reason. And letting down his guard could prove dangerous . . . especially to Richard's own heart.

By Gayle Callen

The Duke in Disguise • The Lord Next Door
A Woman's Innocence • The Beauty and the Spy
No Ordinary Groom • His Bride
His Scandal • His Betrothed
My Lady's Guardian • A Knight's Vow
Darkest night

If You've Enjoyed This Book,
Be Sure to Read These Other
AVON ROMANTIC TREASURES

Duke of Scandal *by Adele Ashworth*
Portrait of a Lover *by Julianne MacLean*
Promise Me Forever *by Lorraine Heath*
Scandal of the Black Rose *by Debra Mullins*
She's No Princess *by Laura Lee Guhrke*

Coming Soon

Tempting the Wolf *by Lois Greiman*

Gayle Callen

The Duke in Disguise

An Avon Romantic Treasure

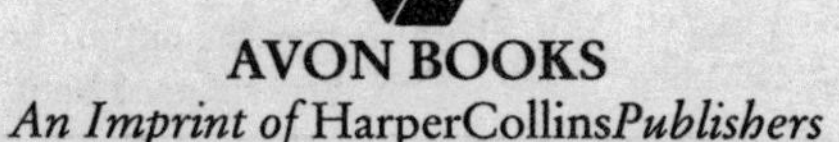

AVON BOOKS
An Imprint of HarperCollins*Publishers*

This is a work of fiction. Names, characters, places, and incidents are products of the author's imagination or are used fictitiously and are not to be construed as real. Any resemblance to actual events, locales, organizations, or persons, living or dead, is entirely coincidental.

AVON BOOKS
An Imprint of HarperCollins*Publishers*
10 East 53rd Street
New York, New York 10022-5299

ISBN-13: 978-0-06-078412-6
ISBN-10: 0-06-078412-1
www.avonromance.com

First Avon Books paperback printing: July 2006

Printed in the U.S.A.

10 9 8 7 6 5 4 3 2 1

To my son, Jim,
now off on your own
and exploring the world.
May every goal you pursue
bring you the same happiness
you've brought me.

Chapter 1

Ramsgate, England
1844

Meriel Shelby stood on the edge of the cliff, the wind swaying tall grass against her skirt, and looked out over the glistening North Sea. Watching the sun sparkle off foam whitecaps on the waves, she could imagine the bend of land off to the north, hiding the mouth of the Thames. She felt peaceful, alone, away from Thanet Court and the strangers she now worked for. But she knew she couldn't stay away long, so she turned and started back down the narrow, well-worn path. Little Stephen, the future Duke of Thanet, would be with his nurse, but it was time to resume his studies for the afternoon.

Meriel had never imagined that she would one day be forced to earn her living as a governess. She'd been a child of wealth, whose father earned his success as a banker to the nobility. Not quite a gentleman, of course, but she hadn't really seen the difference. She'd been educated and trained as a lady, meant to be the bride of a wealthy man—preferably a peer, if her mother had gotten her way.

Practical Meriel had understood the need for a husband and was not against the concept. She had always planned to make a logical decision on a man that she had much in common with. If love happened after that, then she would have been fortunate.

But all those plans dissolved with the death of her father, and the revelations that he'd died penniless and that her mother had known of their precarious finances.

Meriel's emotions varied wildly, from grief to the clutch of anger that never quite went away, and disappointment in her own ignorance. Why hadn't she recognized the signs of imminent trouble? Her parents' betrayal was a bitterness that still clouded her every judgment and left her with a heavy guilt that should not be hers to bear.

Her childhood home had been bought by a distant cousin, who would soon return and take possession. Meriel and her sister Louisa had secured positions as a governess and a companion, but their wages had not stretched as they'd all hoped. Her sister Victoria had been forced to sell family heirlooms to feed their mother, who was so devastated by her fate that she had to be coerced from her bedroom.

But a beacon of hope had come only last week—Victoria was getting married. It was a shock to think that her shy sister had been proposed to by a viscount! Their mother would have a place to live. It eased the burden on Meriel, who had been sending home as much of her meager salary as she could these past months. It had been a long struggle to this point.

She had lost her first governess position due to the wife's jealousy. Meriel had since learned to hide her golden curls with a severe hairstyle, mask her blue eyes with glass spectacles, and dress as plainly as possible. Luckily, her new position had no duchess to critically oversee her. That was one of the reasons she'd been glad to accept it.

Little Stephen had been alone but for the servants. His father, the Duke of Thanet, spent most of the year in London, the center of every gathering, socializing into the night, sleeping away half the day. Perhaps it was good that Stephen was not exposed to that, she thought wryly.

The grass swishing past her skirts gave way to a trim lawn overlooking Thanet Court, which was set lower than the cliffs. The house sprawled across the grounds, a living thing, three stories tall, with a turret housing the grand staircase, and hundreds of windows glittering in the sun. Meriel had grown up wealthy, but Thanet Court was like a palace to her. She'd gotten lost almost every day the first week of her employment.

Starting down the hillside, she remembered her naiveté when she'd first begun her new position. She had always admired her own governess, who'd filled Meriel with a love of learning. Mathematics had made the world seem a logical place, and she had appreciated the orderliness of it. She wanted to pass that on to her student.

Instead she'd found a six-year-old boy who'd been allowed to roam his estate like a wild thing. His mother had died at birth, leaving him with an absent father and longtime family servants who coddled him with their love. Meriel had expected resistance—especially when Stephen had informed her in a well-rehearsed sentence that his title was the Marquess of Ramsgate—but he was polite and inquisitive, and over the last several weeks, she thought she was making progress acquiring his trust.

Then they received word that the duke was returning to Thanet Court for an extended stay as he recovered from a recent illness. The servants did not openly say what he suffered from, but their urgent whispers were filled with the word "consumption." Stephen had seemed sad and worried, and Meriel had felt a maternal instinct to protect him as her parents hadn't protected her.

She was halfway down the hill, almost into the formal gardens, when in the distance she saw someone riding up to the estate. Shielding her eyes with her hand, she squinted, but all she could see was a man riding with quiet precision. He avoided the portico that sheltered the grand entrance to the mansion, and instead guided the horse alongside the building, heading for the servants' entrance. Yet the man rode like no servant she'd ever seen, and he was certainly dressed far too fashionably.

Then he pulled the horse to a stop and glanced up at the building. Without his hat shading his face from the sun, Meriel recognized him as the duke himself, whom she'd met when he interviewed her two months before. She'd thought him an arrogant, idle, handsome man, with little interest in his son. But he'd certainly been a man cognizant of his high status in the world.

He could not possibly have ridden all the way

from London alone, a journey of several days if he didn't change horses. Where were his carriage, his coachman and valet, his outriders?

Instead the duke seemed to hesitate, and he turned his horse back toward the front entrance and rode up beneath the portico. Before he could even dismount, several servants spilled out of the door as if they'd been waiting for him. After a groom took his horse, the butler escorted him inside. Meriel was left to stare after him, puzzled by his behavior.

Putting aside her curiosity, she hurried back through the garden to the servants' entrance, knowing that Nurse Weston might need her help should Stephen's father wish to see him. The nursery was above the master suite, with its own private staircase to connect parents to children. As far as she knew, no one had ever come up that way to see Stephen. The nursery had a washroom and several bedrooms for the nurse and children. The schoolroom was down a little corridor within the nursery, with Meriel's own bedroom next door. The bedroom was not as large and airy as her own in London, but it had a beautiful view of the grounds and orchard, with a distant glimpse of the blue sea.

She was just about to go looking for Stephen when his nurse knocked on her open door.

"Miss Shelby?" Nurse Weston said, folding her

plump hands beneath her bosom with a practiced gesture.

She spoke with the formality that Meriel was all too familiar with. Meriel was not considered a servant, so the other servants behaved awkwardly around her.

"Yes, Nurse Weston?"

"His Grace is waiting to see you."

"To see *me*?" she asked in surprise. Whyever would the Duke of Thanet want to see his child's governess the moment he returned home after a long absence?

The nurse betrayed a touch of impatience that surprised Meriel.

"His little lordship is getting changed as we speak, Miss Shelby. His Grace would like you to escort his son to him."

"I had assumed you would do such a thing, Nurse."

Again there was a flicker of impatience that made Meriel feel like a fool.

"He doesn't want to see *me,* Miss Shelby, not when he hired you personally. You're so pleasing to the duke's eye, but perhaps not so smart about such things, eh?"

Her reluctant sympathy made Meriel's stomach tighten, and she couldn't help thinking, *Not again.* "I don't understand why such a thing as my appearance should matter. I am his son's governess."

"He likes the women servants to be comely." The woman tried to hide a smirk, but didn't quite succeed.

Meriel eyed the departing nurse suspiciously, realizing that the woman was definitely pretty regardless of her plumpness. Meriel certainly didn't want to attract the duke's attention, so the plain brown gown with the grass-stained hem remained on. She sat at her dressing table, and instead of fixing her wind-blown hair, she loosened a few more curls to scatter untidily over one ear. If she was going into battle, she needed her armor as dented and unappealing as possible. She wanted to keep her position—but she did not want the attention of the duke.

Stephen met her in the nursery corridor, dressed in a clean shirt and trousers, dragging his frock coat behind him. The little boy had dark eyes and dark hair with a lock that always wanted to stand up at the crown of his head. She smoothed it down fondly, and he ducked away, unable to hide his eagerness. He was still young enough to think that this time, his father would pay more attention to him. She understood how he felt; her childhood had been filled with such disappointing moments.

"Miss Shelby, my father has come!" Stephen said, his face tilted up to her, his eyes shining.

She smiled and helped him into his coat.

"You'll be on your best behavior, won't you, my lord?"

"Of course!"

But she knew Stephen. Like all little boys, he couldn't sit still for long. Whenever she turned away for a moment, she often found him on his knees examining a bug or picking at a scab.

"How long has it been since you've seen your father?" she asked, as they walked down the long corridor to the grand staircase.

"I can't remember," he said, practically bouncing beside her, then running his finger along a table they passed.

"Keep your hands to yourself, my lord." She caught a vase as it tottered.

When they reached the ground floor, Meriel hesitated. "Why don't you lead the way to your father's study?"

Stephen beamed with importance, and she was glad he was still too young to realize she didn't remember the way. She'd been at Thanet Court for only five weeks, and the duke's study was not a room she'd visited.

She caught Stephen before he could barge through the closed door. "Please show your consideration by knocking, my lord."

"But why?" Stephen said. "Mrs. Theobald doesn't make me."

The housekeeper and all the other servants

were unintentionally trying to turn Stephen into a regular little peer, arrogance, entitlement, and all.

"Mrs. Theobald loves you and always looks forward to your visits," Meriel said, "but adults have business that children cannot be privy to. You must always knock."

"Oh very well," he grumbled. He knocked quickly and danced in his little boots as he waited.

A man's voice called for them to enter, and Meriel felt an unfamiliar worry. The duke had hired her; she was confident that she could prove she was a valuable employee. But what if he wanted certain other . . . needs met?

Stephen opened the door, and to her satisfaction, he entered at a walk instead of a run. The room had long, tall windows that cast sunshine across the floor. It took her a moment to see the duke's desk in a corner, surrounded by bookshelves and glass cabinets. The last time she'd met the man, he'd seemed very bored with the need to interview a mere governess. He'd been talkative, but so easily distracted by anything on the desk, or an everyday item he'd never noticed in the room before. He'd been only a man she needed to impress; titles had never overawed her. And then he'd been recently ill. She'd warned Stephen to be prepared for this.

But now something was different. The duke had obviously recovered. Indeed, he was a picture of good health, as he lounged to one side in his leather wingback chair. His head rested against the back, his posture as casual as she remembered it. He had black, close-cropped hair, but gone were his muttonchop sideburns and his mustache. His face looked strangely bare—masculine cheekbones above a mouth thin and sensuous.

Sensuous? Where had *that* come from?

His dark eyes seemed to study Stephen with an intensity that she would never have thought him capable of. It vanished a moment later, leaving her to question if she'd really seen it.

Why did she feel so . . . off-balance? She'd met the duke before; other than his facial hair, nothing had changed. But now she was nervous, and staring at him too much, and she wanted to fidget. The room seemed too hot.

"Stephen, it is good to see you," the duke said, rising to his feet.

She'd once thought his gracefulness a vain, practiced art, but now it seemed very much a part of him.

What was wrong with her?

The duke came around the desk and stood in front of them. Meriel had to look up at him. She was short in stature, which made him not all that tall for a man, but he seemed . . . taller, powerful, broad through the shoulders, stocky through the chest. He was dressed as immaculately as before, in bright patterned London colors, a man who obviously took pride in the clothing that adorned him like the brushstrokes necessary to a masterpiece.

She wanted to groan. Since when had she become a secret poet? She was a woman with a head for figures: mathematics was her specialty. She taught literature only because it was expected of her. Words were not something that called to her soul.

But she found she wanted to . . . describe the duke. Luckily, his attention was for his son.

Stephen stared up at his father, and Meriel found herself touching the boy's shoulder. He remembered to bow then, but he still looked up at the duke with curiosity. How long had it truly been since they'd seen each other?

"Hello, Father," Stephen said, wariness making his voice sound even higher than normal.

Meriel was glad to put all her concentration back on her pupil, where it belonged. He would need her comfort when his father dismissed him. Mrs. Theobald had warned her about the duke's disregard.

To her shock, the duke knelt on one knee to look in the boy's face.

"You are well, Stephen?"

"Of course, Father." The little boy was tense, his fidgeting gone.

"I see you've begun your studies. I hope you've been behaving for your governess."

"Yes, Father. I like her."

They discussed her as if she wasn't there. Even after all these months, it still took Meriel a moment to remember that she was almost a servant now.

"She likes numbers, just like I do," Stephen continued, his words rushing faster and faster as if he might be stopped. "We go on long walks and we even find things in the woods, like birds' nests and beetles and flowers. Miss Shelby knows *everything*."

A blush swept from her chest up to her face as Stephen's praise caused the duke to look up at her. Under his regard, she tried to remind herself of his poor reputation, of his preference to look at pretty servants. But his black eyes, fringed with more lashes than a man had a right to, trapped her within his gaze. She couldn't look away, couldn't remember to feel affronted by his regard.

"Miss Shelby is an accomplished teacher," the duke said softly.

He got to his feet and moved away, and she breathed a sigh of relief. He looked out the window with a restlessness that made her feel more at ease.

Stephen followed him and began to talk about their studies, his reading and writing and the simple history she'd begun to interest him with. He had a good mind, and she knew she could teach him much, if only he could focus better. He'd spent so much of his young life in the outdoors that she tried to set at least one lesson outside each day.

But although his father looked out the window as if the grounds interested him more than his son, they spoke together for several minutes, both of them used to doing the speaking. They each gestured with their hands. Meriel found herself backing away to sit in a corner of the room, not wanting to disturb this small amount of time Stephen had with his father.

To her dismay, there was a part of her that knew when the duke was looking at her. Never before had she met a man who could captivate her attention, who could make her know deep inside that he was man.

She had thought she was learning to conquer her traitorous emotions. Her heart had betrayed her where her parents were concerned—she hadn't seen the truth until it was too late. She'd vowed that only sound logic would rule her life. But her reaction to the duke confirmed her worst fears. She was once again leading with her emotions, rather than her intellect. It was a weakness she could not afford. She would conquer it.

Chapter 2

It was difficult to keep Stephen interested in addition and subtraction that afternoon when Thanet Court seemed to be coming alive with the duke's homecoming. The servants bustled everywhere, as if preparing for a party instead of just one man. Stephen sat at his desk, his head cocked toward the corridor, listening for the next interruption, until finally Meriel agreed to take him for a walk about the house, as long as he promised to behave himself.

He led her to his favorite place, the kitchens, where he was allowed to taste all the evening's confections. Servants bustled from the pantry to the washroom to the cellars, and all had a kind word for him.

Meriel stopped the housekeeper, Mrs. Theobald, when she was hurrying through. Though constantly busy with the immense household, the older woman always made one feel just as important as the master. It made her beloved by the servants, and had set Meriel at ease from the first. Mrs. Theobald kept her white hair tidy under a neat lace cap, and her ever-present apron over her black uniform was always spotless, although she worked as hard as anyone else.

"I don't have much time, Miss Shelby," the housekeeper warned her apologetically.

"I only want to know if I should prepare Stephen for dinner with his father."

"No, His Grace never eats with his son. It just wouldn't do."

"But the boy is six now. Surely he needs to learn what is proper behavior in a formal situation. He can't learn that nearly as well by eating with me in the nursery."

But Mrs. Theobald could only apologize and move on to her next task. When Meriel took Stephen upstairs for his meal, she resolved that she would have to speak to the duke herself.

Once again, speaking with her employer seemed like an intimidating task. She didn't want to be alone with him. Many of the nobility seemed to think that they could behave as they wished. She had heard stories over the years of abused governesses who could say nothing against their employer because they feared losing their position.

And now she was one of them.

Yesterday, she'd walked to the post office to send money home—a pitiful sum it had been, too. She had thought herself capable of helping her mother—she could not afford to lose a *second* job.

Two days passed, and the duke remained elusive. Meriel watched Stephen grow more dejected. She kept reminding the boy that his father's recovery would be slow, but inside she was working up the anger to insist on a meeting with the duke.

That night, dinner was a lonely affair as usual. Nurse Weston went down to the servants' hall, but Meriel was never invited to join in the camaraderie. She ate her meals with Stephen, and though he was a good-hearted boy, she missed adult conversation. She missed intelligent conversation—she missed her sisters.

Her heart gave a painful lurch, and she put down her fork as her appetite faded away. They had spent their whole lives together. Meriel had always thought that even when they all married, they'd be together in London much of the time.

But Ramsgate seemed like the end of the world, situated as it was on the southeastern edge of England. Meriel walked to the window and looked out at the sea. Home was many miles in the opposite direction. She had already cleared a few days' holiday with Mrs. Theobald to attend her sister's wedding. But for now, letters would have to do. She kept them in her desk, treated them gently so they wouldn't tear, and read them over and over again until she knew them by heart.

She turned to retrieve her letters from her desk, and saw that Stephen's chair was empty, his food half eaten.

"My lord?" she called to the empty room, wondering if he was hiding again.

She searched the cupboards, then walked down to his room. "Stephen?" she called outside the washroom.

He was gone.

She should have known that he would not be able to quiet his curiosity, now that his father had shown a small interest in him. He was a boy full of questions about his parents, from his absent father to his deceased mother. Meriel could answer few of them, so she should have known that Stephen would take the first opportunity. Standing at the head of the private staircase that led to the master suite below, she prayed Stephen had not dared to use it. She had heard Nurse Weston reminding him over and over that it was for his father only.

Meriel walked down the grand staircase to the dining room first. The large double doors were open, and several footmen were clearing away the dishes from the head of the table. The duke had eaten alone and was thankfully gone.

The two footmen, so identical in height and build, stopped what they were doing to look at her suspiciously.

"Robert," she said to the one whose name she remembered, "have you seen Lord Ramsgate?"

"No, Miss Shelby."

He was polite, but she sensed an underlying suspicion, as if he silently accused her of losing the boy.

It wouldn't be the first time. She'd spent much of the first week looking for Stephen everywhere, and she thought she knew all his hiding places. Thank goodness it was night—or she'd be looking for him near the fake castle ruins in the garden where he often pretended to be a ghost.

She left the dining room and searched the conservatory, especially in the back, where high ferns blocked her view. She tried the music room beneath the piano, and the library beneath both globes. She managed to avoid most of the servants, especially Mrs. Theobald, who would understand immediately what Meriel was doing.

How could she have allowed the boy to escape so soon after the duke's arrival?

Finally, she had no choice but to head to the drawing rooms. She assumed the duke had not yet gone to bed, so Stephen was probably following him about.

She heard the murmur of voices as she crept softly along the marble-floored corridor, using the carpets when she could. With her head bent, she strained to listen, but all she heard was the clink of a glass being set down. How could she just walk in and ask the duke if he'd seen his son?

She froze when a footman left the blue drawing room. He saw her at once and paused, but she put a finger to her lips and begged with her eyes. He turned away from her down the corridor. She sighed with relief.

"Miss Shelby, is that you?"

The duke's deep voice made her jump, as if she was doing something wrong. She lifted her chin and stepped into the doorway. He was leaning a shoulder against the carved white mantel, the empty hearth beside him. Two Irish wolfhounds lay at his feet. The duke's waistcoat was checked red and gold, standing out in a room decorated mostly in blues and whites. Even the paintings clustered on the walls seemed to be landscapes dominated by variations of blue skies.

"Good evening, Your Grace," she said.

He straightened and lifted his glass from the mantel. "Are you looking for Stephen?" He glanced toward the windows. "Stephen, perhaps you should show yourself now."

Meriel held her breath for an endless moment, but it didn't take the little marquess long. He stepped out from behind the draperies near the tall windows. The boy was disheveled, and there was a tear in his coat, but he was doing his best to look contrite.

"Forgive me, Your Grace," Meriel said. "I'll take Lord Ramsgate back to the nursery."

The duke laughed. "When he's gone to all this trouble? Stephen, I surely can't be interesting enough to spy upon."

Stephen's head lifted a bit. "I-I've never seen your dogs pay so much attention to you."

Meriel frowned, wondering what the boy meant.

The duke smiled as he looked down at his pets, who watched him with adoration, their heads cocked, their ears perked. "I think they missed me. Did you miss me, Stephen?"

The little boy stared at his father, his dark brows lowered in puzzlement. "Father, I can't remember how many months have passed since I saw you, so I can't really miss you."

Meriel's stomach flipped over with dread. She

was obviously failing to teach the boy proper courtesy.

But the duke only laughed again and took a sip of his drink. "Then we'll have to get to know one another all over again. Miss Shelby, do come in and make yourself comfortable."

She tried to retreat to her usual window seat, but the duke would have none of it. He bade her sit on the sofa beside Stephen, and he took a chair opposite them. The dogs settled on either side of the duke, then put their heads down again. Only their eyes continued to stare, as if they couldn't let their master out of their sight.

Stephen swung his feet together in rhythmic bumps. "You don't look sick, Father."

Meriel silently agreed, chastising herself again for noticing far too many other things about the duke's appearance.

"I'm getting better, my boy, but I find myself still tired though my long journey was several days ago. If I were truly recovered, even exhaustion would not stop me from finding a party to attend tonight."

"You're with Miss Shelby and me."

The duke smiled, and his gaze caught Meriel. She noticed the whiteness of his teeth and the darkness of his eyes. The first time she'd met him, he'd made her feel her place as his inferior. But now there seemed to be no distance between them except the width of a low table. She felt uncomfortable—vulnerable.

"But you don't mean people like us," the boy continued. "You want to be with ladies."

The duke's toes tapped on the floor, and Meriel understood from whom Stephen had inherited his restlessness.

Again the duke laughed. "Ladies make a party amusing," he agreed, "but as long as I'm not alone, I enjoy the company."

"Miss Shelby is a lady," Stephen said.

Meriel wanted to close her eyes and groan. They were both looking at her now, Stephen with innocence, the duke with knowing amusement. She wished she could tell him not to look at her that way, that she was in his employ. He was crossing the line into a dangerous sort of flirting—at least it seemed so to her.

But to a man fond of ladies, perhaps just looking at a woman seemed tame. She would tolerate it as much as she could for her family's sake.

"I agree that Miss Shelby is a lady," the duke said. "Ladies are raised to be so accomplished."

She stiffened warily.

"Miss Shelby, surely you can entertain us at the piano to alleviate our boredom."

That was something she could do. She almost hurried to the grand piano that took up a corner of the room. She left behind the sound of Stephen chattering on about the music lessons she was giving him. She simply put her fingers on the keys, closed her eyes, and tried to be swept up in the music. Her sister Victoria was the true musician of the family. Victoria had concentrated on her musical studies with the same fascination that Meriel had had for mathematics. But a lady learned music, and Meriel had always learned whatever she was supposed to.

When she heard a third voice, she stopped playing and opened her eyes.

Nurse Weston stood in the doorway. "Your Grace, shall I take Stephen to his bed? The evening is growing late."

Meriel rose to her feet with relief.

"Of course," the duke said. "But Miss Shelby, do continue your playing. I find it quite soothing."

Nurse Weston shot her a worried look that could have shouted, *I told you so.*

Meriel sank back onto the bench.

"Good night, Miss Shelby!" Stephen called, giving her a wave from the doorway.

"Sleep well, my lord." She was a little annoyed with him—after all, it was his fault she was trapped "entertaining" his father.

"Are we still going down to the shore tomorrow?" Stephen asked.

"Of course," Meriel said. "I have several special lessons planned for the afternoon."

When the sound of Stephen's chattering voice had faded down the corridor, the room became very silent. Meriel did not look at the duke, but simply began to play again. She was concentrating hard and did not realize that the duke had moved until he spoke right at her side.

"Excellent technique," he said.

She jumped and hit the wrong note.

"Forgive me for startling you." He leaned his elbows on the piano, drink in hand, a smile in his voice, but not on his face. "Can you play and converse at the same time?"

"Perhaps."

He was far too close for comfort. It wasn't right to be alone like this with him—but she was only a woman in his employ, not someone he need worry about compromising.

"So you're taking Stephen to the shore," he said.

"Your son enjoys biology and geology, Your Grace."

"No need to be defensive, Miss Shelby. I know you would not neglect his studies." He looked toward the window, now closed by draperies for the night, as if he could see the sea beyond. "My own governess thought that learning from books was enough."

"That is a shame, Your Grace." She kept her eyes on the sheet music, not wanting him to see the twinge of sympathy in her eyes. She would have thought the childhood of a duke's heir to be perfect.

"Where are you from, Miss Shelby?"

She wasn't surprised that he'd forgotten, though she'd informed him of that when he'd first interviewed her. "London, Your Grace."

"Did you always want to be a governess?"

She couldn't stop her wry smile, but she didn't dare look at him to see if he noticed. "No. After my father's death, we had financial troubles."

"Forced to a life of servitude, then," he said.

She stiffened. "I consider myself a teacher, Your Grace. Since I was taught well, I enjoy being able to share a love of learning with my pupil—your son."

"But what had you wanted for your life?"

His voice was soft with an intimacy that made her uncomfortable. He was between her and the door. Did he realize what he did? Or was he just a bored man who occupied himself with whomever was at hand?

She stopped playing and gave him a cool look. "Do you require such intimate knowledge of every woman in your employ, Your Grace?"

He stared at her for a moment, and behind that playful look she sensed . . . what? His eyes were black, and could hide many secrets. But he suddenly straightened and stepped away from the piano.

"Forgive me, Miss Shelby. I have attended so many gatherings that for a moment, I forgot I was not at another one."

"We certainly did not move within the same social circles, Your Grace. You would never have met me."

He nodded, and again his gaze became unfocused and distracted, as if he was thinking of something else.

Or forcing himself to think of something else.

"Your Grace, might I retire for the night? Your son and I begin our lessons at eight o'clock."

He smiled. "There are people awake at such an unseemly hour?"

"Little boys," she said, almost tempted to return his smile.

"Then I shan't keep you any longer. Good night, Miss Shelby."

She walked sedately to the corridor, not knowing if he watched her, but feeling as if he did. Only when she was out of eyesight did she lengthen her strides.

She would make sure Stephen never came upon his father alone again.

Chapter 3

After the governess had gone, Richard O'Neill collapsed into a chair, leaned his head back, and closed his eyes. He was only three days into his ridiculous masquerade as the duke, and already he felt as if he'd made a thousand mistakes. He was lucky that the duke's longtime servants expected him to behave in an eccentric way. It was hard to master the duke's personality, when he'd always considered himself so radically different from Cecil Irving, the Duke of Thanet. The ability to talk constantly was more difficult than he'd imagined.

And the flirting! God, how he hated to subject

the poor governess to one of Cecil's worst traits. But if Richard was going to be convincing as the duke, he had to notice everything in skirts.

Not that it was difficult to notice Miss Meriel Shelby. He was fascinated by the obvious lengths she went to, to disguise herself. Though she tried to hide her beauty behind lifeless colors and drab hairstyles—and those spinster spectacles!—her radiance still peeked through like the sun from behind rain clouds. She had the profile of a cameo: pert nose, a delicate mouth, and a chin that strained not to rise defiantly into the air. Her hair, bound tight to her head, wanted the freedom to cascade in curls across her shoulders like the rays of the sun. Petite in stature, she displayed the well-rounded curves of a woman.

And her eyes had looked on him with such directness, he'd been able to see their deep blue color behind the spectacles. They had reminded him of the depths of a forest pond, still water hiding what was beneath.

It was almost easy to adopt the duke's distracted air, since all Richard seemed capable of doing was thinking about Miss Shelby. Such rare beauty was normally seen at the center of a drawing room, surrounded by adoring men.

Far from where he usually stood at parties. He was always the man talking business in the corner. Maybe that was why his luck with women had not been good. He had been too busy to pay them the attention they deserved.

But now he was pretending to be the Duke of Thanet, and no woman could be safe from him.

Even the poor governess.

The trick would be to flirt—and not follow through. Because of course he would be seeing a lot of the governess. This would be the hardest part of the masquerade. Cecil had always ignored his son. Oh, he'd treated Stephen well, given him the best of everything—except his attention. This was normal among the *ton*.

Richard knew all too well how it felt to be an ignored child.

Somehow he would have to convince the staff that he'd had a change of heart about Stephen. Perhaps illness had made the duke see how important his son was to him. But the little boy who'd walked solemnly into the study had seemed so . . . hopeful. Richard didn't remember what it was like to expect goodness from people with such childlike trust, as this boy still did. Richard would not turn him away.

Stephen *was* important—he was the heir. And no one at Thanet Court knew of the rising danger to him.

Richard had always prided himself on being

focused on his work. He'd already had the staff investigated—even the new governess.

Because he must consider Stephen his work now.

As usual, Richard awoke at dawn. He started to sit up, then fell back on his elbows as he remembered where he was—who he was.

The room was still gray with shadows, but the opulence was unmistakable, from the velvet bed curtains hanging above him to the intricately carved furniture centuries old. The ceiling was painted and frescoed, and the fireplace mantel was held up by statues of nude women.

He wondered how much the succession of duchesses had appreciated *that*.

His mind was abuzz with everything he wanted to do today, especially putting an advertisement in the London papers to hire a new valet. To Mrs. Theobald, he'd explained the absence of Cecil's valet by claiming that the young man had fallen in love and quit to follow the girl north.

Richard couldn't begin his day until noon, which was Cecil's usual time to rise. He must have been more exhausted than he thought, because he ended up falling back asleep. When he next awoke, the sun was streaming in the tall mullioned windows. By the clock, it was ten. In the silence, he heard the faintest patter of feet overhead. Though it had been many years since he'd been to Thanet Court, he remembered what was over the master suite—the nursery.

Miss Shelby had already been at her lessons for several hours. He wondered if Stephen was as poor a student as his father. Not that the duke was unintelligent—he just hadn't cared about the world beyond his own little kingdom, or even how to run it properly.

Richard flung back the covers. The duke would just have to awaken early today.

He ate a solitary breakfast, waited on by two footmen. Then he surprised the steward in his office. Jasper Tearle was obviously unaccustomed to the duke questioning him, but Richard was not a man who could ignore what he was in charge of, even temporarily. He spent the rest of the morning pretending to be bored while looking over the account books. He asked questions as if he were ignorant, and couldn't really study everything as he wanted to. With an estate of this size—and all the other property—there was no reason for Cecil to be running out of money.

During his solitary luncheon, he was considering how best to drop in on Stephen's seashore lesson without looking like he was following the boy—which he was—when the butler announced a visitor.

"Who is it, Hargraves?" Richard asked. He resisted the urge to rise to his feet. Instead he lounged back in his chair and waited with an assumed indolence he was far from feeling.

A woman breezed in and said, "It's your long-ignored neighbor."

Richard smiled, though inside he cursed his bad luck. Miss Renee Barome. Her brown hair haphazardly tumbled down her back from the wind, and her riding habit was wrinkled and dusty. Why couldn't she be married and gone? Renee had once known Richard O'Neill as well as she knew the Duke of Thanet.

"Good afternoon, Miss Barome," he said, giving her a leer worthy of Cecil.

She sank into the chair at his side. "Oh please, Cecil—you sound like your brother."

Richard inwardly stiffened, but on the outside he laughed and rudely slung one leg over the arm of the chair.

She picked up a spoon and helped herself to a taste of his pudding.

"You're so upset that I didn't visit you immediately that you have to insult me, fair Renee?" he asked.

"So now it's an insult to be compared to your

brother?" She gave him a sideways look. "Last I knew, he was a rather successful fellow."

"Ah, but without the title, how happy can he be?" Richard grinned.

Renee laughed. "I imagine he makes himself happy, just as you do. It's been some time since he haunted this part of England. When did you last see him?"

"Months at least. Maybe years. One loses track."

"Not you, Cecil. You never succumbed to the pressure to let your brother go."

He waved a hand. "I was young then. Now he's far too stuffy for me. But must we talk about him? Surely there is gossip to be had. We always had fun making fun."

She sighed, and her pleasant expression faded into worry. "You haven't changed, Cecil. Even illness can't make you into a serious man."

"I'm still far too young for that."

"But feeling better?" she asked with concern.

Renee had always had a hopeless crush on Cecil, and it saddened Richard to see that she still cared a bit too much. Though a gentlewoman, she was not polished enough for Cecil's taste, possessed not enough wealth and breeding. But it would have done Cecil good to marry her.

"So news of my illness spread even to this remote outpost?" he asked.

"Of course. The neighbors were quite worried."

"You mean *you* were worried. I'm not sure the other neighbors cared—unless it interfered with my hosting the annual Thanet masquerade."

She finished his pudding and sat back. "You would have to be on your deathbed to escape that. Have you set a date?"

Richard rose to his feet. "I'm still thinking about it. Care to accompany me for a ride, Renee?"

When she brightened, he felt guilty. She was the one person he would not flirt with. He wanted to ask if she'd found someone to love her as she deserved, but he suspected from her behavior that she had not.

But he needed an excuse to see Stephen, and she would do well for that.

Renee glanced at the dogs. "Are they coming with us?"

"No, although they have developed a new fondness for me. It must be because I could have died."

"Cecil!"

He concealed his worry, and hoped that the dogs' newfound affection wouldn't be his undoing.

The well-trained horses were led easily down the narrow path that cut into the side of the cliff. Richard walked in front, holding the reins of both horses. Renee walked behind. The day was just cloudy enough to give relief from the hot sun. Below Richard, the rocky sand stretched out to the North Sea, and people strolled by twos and threes, taking in the sun. It was easy enough to spot Stephen and his governess. Their heads were bent together as they examined something on the ground.

Feeling relieved, Richard pretended he wasn't purposefully looking for anyone, as he waited for Renee to catch up to him. She smiled and took a deep breath of sea air. When he linked his hands and offered to boost her back into the saddle, she gave him a surprised look but accepted, shaking her head. Probably another thing Cecil wouldn't do. His brother would have brought a groom for such things.

Renee rode sidesaddle, and he wondered when she'd finally acquiesced to it. He mounted his own horse, and she quickly challenged him to a race. They galloped off down the beach away from his intended target, but now that he knew Stephen was all right, he would bide his time.

She beat him to the designated outcrop of rock—Cecil always had a poorer seat than he had—so Richard cheated and started back before she did. He let the exhilaration of the sun and sand and the feel of the horse pounding beneath him take away his constant worries. He and Renee were both laughing, neck and neck, when he pulled up a bit too near his governess. Miss Shelby caught Stephen's shoulders and pulled him against her, wearing the wary look of a mother lion. He liked her dedication. If he hadn't lost his hat in the surf, he would have doffed it to her. She was dressed in another drab gown, but the wind tossed the skirt this way and that so that he glimpsed her white lace petticoats.

So . . . her undergarments weren't as plain as her outer garments. He felt a thrill of challenge he shouldn't be feeling. A normal duke should never pay too much attention to his servants.

But Cecil wasn't a normal duke—and Richard wasn't the duke at all.

"Good afternoon, Miss Shelby," he said.

She gave a brief curtsy that he sensed was very reluctant.

"Your Grace," she murmured.

Stephen grinned up at him and pulled away from his governess. "Father! You ride so fast. Have you been taking lessons like I have?"

His expert riding had been a critical mistake, but one Richard could thankfully rectify. He gave the boy a conspiratorial wink and said, "I couldn't continue to let Miss Barome beat me in races, now could I?"

Renee was struggling to tame her hair, the last curl of which had lost its anchor in the salty wind. She caught it with one hand and gave the governess a frank, friendly stare, before looking down from her horse at Stephen. "Lord Ramsgate, I've spent my life outdoing your father on horseback. Since I have much more patience at my lessons than he does, I'll be faster again in no time."

"I can ride fast, too," Stephen said. "Bill the stable boy says my mother rode like the wind. Isn't that a funny thing? Miss Shelby says I take far too many risks."

Now that sounded like Cecil, Richard thought. "My manners are atrocious," he said. "Miss Renee Barome, meet my new governess, Miss Shelby." He saw Miss Shelby give a start at his possessive wording where she was concerned, and he felt a very male satisfaction. He had never thought teasing a woman the way Cecil always did could be enjoyable, but this was one thing he was learning. Yet he understood too well from personal experience not to take it any further. "Miss Shelby, Miss Barome is one of our neighbors."

The women exchanged good afternoons, while Stephen reached up to pet the horses' noses.

"C-could I ride with you, Father?"

There was a hesitancy in the boy's voice that reminded Richard of the uncertainty of his own childhood. He told himself that Cecil would not bother with his son's request, not when there were women to charm. But Stephen was the whole reason that he was there.

Grinning, Richard reached down. "Grab my hand in both of yours. Up we go."

He pulled the boy up in front of him and set off down the beach. To his surprise, Renee didn't follow them.

Meriel shielded her eyes from the glare and watched the duke ride away with his son, ignoring her own strange surge of pleasure as he moved. There was a recklessness to his gallop that felt like . . . freedom. What was it like to be at the top of the world, to do whatever one pleased? Once she had thought the days stretched out in endless pleasure before her. As long as she chose the correct husband, she could live as she wished. But all those dreams were gone. She was too logical to dwell on the sadness of that for long, because the past couldn't be changed.

Miss Barome dismounted and came to stand at her side. She, too, watched the duke and Stephen race away from them.

"It is good to see him take an interest in his son after all these years," Miss Barome said.

Meriel was surprised to hear the woman speak so freely. "He is the boy's father," she said hesitantly, uncertain of her place with a stranger.

"Maybe he's finally realizing that," Miss Barome

said. She glanced at Meriel. "I never thought that would happen. It gives me hope for Cecil."

Meriel reacted with raised eyebrows to the woman's familiar use of the duke's name.

Miss Barome laughed. "Forgive my insolence. I have known the duke since we were children. I didn't call him Your Grace then, so I can hardly start now."

"I did not mean to imply that it was my concern," Meriel said carefully.

"Of course you didn't, but if we're to be friends, you should know that."

Surprised, Meriel remained silent and wary.

Miss Barome held her hair out of her face and gave her another frank smile. "You'll discover that I make friends easily, Miss Shelby. More importantly, I am a good judge of character. You're new here, so you must not know many people. And you're a governess, which implies a certain solitude in a great house like Thanet Court. Am I correct?"

Meriel slowly smiled. "You're correct on all counts, Miss Barome. And I gladly accept the offer of friendship. It has been a lonely few weeks."

Miss Barome linked her arm through Meriel's, her horse's reins held in her other hand, and they both started walking in the direction taken by the duke and his son.

"You must come to my home for tea this Sunday," Miss Barome said. "I assume you don't teach on the Lord's day?"

"Again, you're correct. And I would be delighted."

The duke and his son rejoined them soon enough, and to Meriel's suspicion, the duke opened his saddle bag and spilled his provisions onto a blanket in the sand. Her first thought was that he'd planned for a private tryst with Miss Barome. But there was far too much food for just two people.

"I always travel prepared," he boasted, throwing himself down to lie on his side on the blanket while the ladies busied themselves serving him.

"Since when?" Miss Barome scoffed, unwrapping the paper from cherry tarts.

He shrugged and laughed. "Since Mrs. Theobald insisted."

Meriel couldn't stop watching him—curious about his response, of course, since his longtime friend suspected his motives—but also fascinated by a duke's easy relaxation in the sand on the seashore. He propped his elbow on the ground and his head on his hand, and his hair blew about. She kept telling herself that he was just her eccentric employer, but there was a rare presence about him that made him hard to ignore, and that bothered her. She didn't have the heart to pull Stephen away for lessons when his larger-than-life father was here.

She kept waiting for the duke to concentrate on Miss Barome, but his gaze lingered at some point on each of them. Just a momentary look, but when it touched her, she felt it like a physical force. Though she did not mean to—did not want to—she met his gaze for that brief moment, and it was like an electrical current shot between them. She hastily looked down at the wine bottle she was holding and almost dropped it.

Was this becoming a biology lesson that she'd never experienced before?

Stephen had finally eaten enough and wandered toward the surf. He asked her rather than his father if he could remove his shoes, but his father didn't notice. The duke was looking off down the beach, paying what seemed only a small amount of attention to Miss Barome's discussion of the newest Ramsgate residents. Miss Barome was leaning back on her hands, her face to the sun, her freckles practically darkening as Meriel watched.

And Meriel knelt primly, her bonnet still firmly in place, not daring to relax. She kept her attention on Stephen, who chased gulls, splashed through the surf, and collected shells to bring to her. The farther he roamed, the more the duke seemed to watch him.

Did the man not trust her to take care of his son? After all, she had Stephen's care most of the day.

As she was deciding whether to be offended, she saw the duke's gaze take in a lone man who walked down the beach toward them. The stranger moved with purpose, instead of the slow stroll of a sightseer.

Meriel wouldn't have even noticed the man, except that the duke's relaxed pose seemed suddenly . . . stiff. No longer did he glance at Miss Barome or Meriel herself. The smile on his face became fixed.

He slowly sat up, his forearm resting on one bent knee.

Miss Barome's eyes were closed with the bliss of the sun on her face, so she noticed nothing.

But Meriel looked between the duke, Stephen, and the stranger. The duke's tension had transferred itself to her, and she felt suddenly afraid, as if a dark cloud had moved between her and the sun.

What was wrong with her? There were many people walking the shore.

Softly, she said, "Shall I get your son, Your Grace?"

He shook his head without looking at her. "I'll go."

He rose to his feet smoothly and began to walk

toward Stephen. She had an irrational urge to follow him, as if he couldn't protect his own son.

Protect him from what?

The duke reached Stephen before the stranger did and squatted next to the boy. Stephen gestured down at something, but didn't notice that his father was watching the man instead.

Meriel's stomach clenched as the man came ever nearer. The duke put an arm about Stephen's shoulder and turned him to face the sea, as if pointing out the ship that lingered on the horizon.

But he was putting his own body between Stephen and the stranger.

Perspiration broke out on Meriel's face. She clutched her skirts with damp fingers. What was going on?

The stranger was now within yards of them. She came to her knees without realizing it.

And then the man nodded pleasantly at the duke and just kept walking.

The duke rose to his feet, glancing over his shoulder at the stranger, then leaning down to answer something Stephen had said. Meriel sank back on her heels.

As the man reached them, he called out, "Good afternoon, Miss Barome."

The woman shielded her eyes and smiled. "A good afternoon to you, too, Mr. Sherlock." She introduced Meriel to him and said, "I was just mentioning to the duke that Ramsgate now has you for a new grocer."

"How kind of you, miss," he said, bowing and smiling and looking so harmless. "Didn't know the duke was in residence."

"He'll be here indefinitely, Mr. Sherlock. I'm sure you'll see him in town."

When the duke made no move to leave Stephen, the merchant finally left without an introduction.

Miss Barome frowned at the duke and shook her head. "Cecil could have at least come meet the man. But then he never does think of those things. Rather self-absorbed is our Cecil—as I'm sure you'll see, Miss Shelby."

Meriel nodded, but her eyes were for the duke, who didn't seem to pay attention as Mr. Sherlock left them. She could almost make herself believe she'd imagined the whole thing.

But she hadn't. And she deserved to understand what was going through the duke's mind, if she was to spend so much time with his son. She would ask to make an appointment to meet with him. They could discuss Stephen's studies, and she could ask if Stephen could have dinner nightly with his father.

And she could ask why the duke sensed danger on a sunlit beach.

Chapter 4

Richard felt like a fool. Clearly the fears that Cecil had expressed to him had made him overreact to a simple stranger walking down the beach. Thank God that Renee had noticed nothing unusual about his behavior.

But Miss Shelby had. He had felt a connection between them from the moment they'd met, and it had only intensified. She knew damn well that he'd thought Stephen was in danger. He had kept waiting for her to question him, alerting Renee.

But she'd said nothing. Her face had gone pale, as if she'd understood the danger to Stephen.

She couldn't know anything of the sort.

But she'd gotten that impression from him. How was he supposed to convince her otherwise? He certainly could not have her on her guard, or soon she'd begin to suspect *him*.

He and Renee walked their horses back up the cliff path, following Stephen and Miss Shelby. When they reached the summit, he found himself wanting to put Stephen in the saddle with him, but it would be ungentlemanly of him to ride when Miss Shelby had no mount.

So instead he turned to Renee at the top of the cliff. "Let me see Stephen and Miss Shelby home, and then I'll ride with you to Ramsgate."

"You want to *escort* me?" she said, laughing with obvious disbelief.

He wanted to groan at his own stupidity. As if Cecil would ever think about such a thing.

And he noticed Miss Shelby's attention on him once again. Damn.

He grinned and patted Renee's horse on the neck as it nosed him. "Ah, Renee, you make a man want to protect you."

She laughed merrily and put him at ease.

"Cecil, just help me to mount. I'm hardly far from home."

She was still laughing and shaking her head when she wheeled her horse away from them. "Remember to come for tea on Sunday, Miss Shelby!"

"I will!" the governess called.

For a moment, Miss Shelby didn't hide herself behind a governess's stern expression. He watched the smile that warmed her face, made her eyes as carefree as a cloudless summer day. She was younger than he imagined; he saw that at once.

And she was so beautiful that it made him ache.

He had to stop this romantic nonsense. He had one mission here, nothing more. And then it was back to his life in Manchester.

He hefted Stephen into the saddle and led the horse down through the tall grass, walking at Miss Shelby's side. They were quiet for several minutes, and he glanced over his shoulder to see that the boy's head was drooping toward his chest, and his eyes blinked heavily.

Meaning only to alert Miss Shelby to Stephen's behavior, he touched her arm.

And she jumped as if he'd sprung from a hiding place to scare her.

He wanted to apologize, but had to resort to Cecil's grin instead.

Her face flushed red. "Yes, Your Grace?"

He nodded toward Stephen, whose head bobbed with the rhythm of the horse.

Her expression softened. "He's had a tiring day. Do you think he'll fall off?"

He wanted to say that he'd watch over Stephen—but then he remembered who he was supposed to be. "Just wanted you to keep an eye on him."

The warmth in her eyes cooled. "Of course, Your Grace."

He hated feeling like a cad—but that was Cecil. And he sensed that it was best to keep Cecil between the governess and him like a barrier.

"Your Grace," she said, "there are several things I'd like to discuss with you about Stephen. Might I make an appointment to meet with you?"

"Talk with my secretary," he said with forced indifference. "I'm sure there's an hour somewhere in my schedule."

She damn well knew he had the time, and that he was putting her off as if he didn't care about his son.

Not *his* son—Cecil's.

The next morning, Stephen and his nurse went to play with his shuttlecock outside, leaving Meriel a free hour for her scheduled meeting with the duke. She went down to his study, but of course he was not there. He was almost fifteen minutes late, and even then he looked surprised to find her waiting for him. There was a frozen moment between them, when she realized that she simply enjoyed looking at him, regardless of his flaws. She was so disappointed with herself.

He stared at her, and his two wolfhounds stood on either side of him, the height of his waist, and stared as well. She didn't get a menacing feeling from the dogs, but they were as large as colts, and therefore intimidating.

"Ah, Miss Shelby," he said.

He started around his desk, then seemed to think better of it and sat in a more comfortable chair near the hearth. The dogs gave him a questioning look.

"Victoria, Albert, lie down."

The dogs merely wagged their long tails, but did not obey him.

Meriel covered her mouth and pretended to cough, or she would have laughed aloud. Until the duke's arrival, the dogs had usually remained at the kennels, and she had never heard anyone speak their names. "You named your dogs after our queen and her husband?"

He shrugged and waved a hand indolently. "The irony appealed to me. And as you can see, they listen to me as well as the queen does."

He repeated the command, pointing to the floor, and both great dogs reluctantly lay down. Then the duke lolled his head back in the chair and looked at her.

She had never before met a man so . . . casual. His very posture emitted decadence. But then again, her meetings with men had mostly been at formal parties or the opera or museums. Safe ground.

She never felt safe around the duke.

Except yesterday, on the shore. For some strange reason, she had had no doubt that he would have attempted to protect them all—and succeeded.

She was granted a few extra minutes to compose herself when a maid—Beatrice, Meriel thought—brought in a tray with coffee and biscuits. The girl was pretty and blond. Meriel remembered Nurse Weston's comment that the duke hired servants based on attractiveness.

Although Meriel felt certain that Beatrice had passed by just minutes before and seen her in the study, the tray contained only one cup.

The duke didn't notice its absence until after the maid had left, and he was raising his cup to his lips.

He arched a brow. "You did not receive coffee, Miss Shelby?"

She shook her head. "It is of no importance, Your Grace. I came to discuss your son."

She could have sworn his shoulders tensed imperceptibly. Was he worried about something?

She had to stop reading hidden meanings into everything he did.

"Your Grace, I know Lord Ramsgate's mother died at his birth, but little else. What am I permitted to say to him about her?"

"Anything you'd like, Miss Shelby. We were very young when we married, both but nineteen. It was rather freeing to make those kinds of choices for myself."

She frowned. "If you don't mind my asking, then yours was not an arranged marriage, but one of love? Stephen would want to know this, of course," she hastily added.

The duke smiled in such a wicked way that she felt her face heat with a blush.

"I certainly *felt* myself in love," he said.

But later concluded he wasn't? she wondered.

"Marguerite was a gentle soul who relished the opportunity to have a child," he continued. "I am saddened that Stephen will never know a mother's devotion."

Now he sounded like a man who would never marry again. Blast her curiosity, which could never be appeased.

"Thank you for giving me permission to discuss his mother with him," she said. "He is growing older, and is ready for what life can teach him. He is six years old now, Your Grace. It is time for him to begin to learn his manners around his elders. As a future duke, much will be expected of him."

He cocked his head, an amused smile quirking

his lips, and she remembered she was speaking to a man raised to be a duke. She flushed and continued to speak.

"Lord Ramsgate eats his meals with me in the nursery, and it is difficult to hold his attention to his manners. I request that he be allowed to begin eating dinner with you in the evening." He opened his mouth, but she rudely hurried on. "Of course, if you're expecting guests, he would remain in the nursery."

"This is not a problem, Miss Shelby. You might have asked me anytime, without making a special appointment."

"But I couldn't risk Lord Ramsgate overhearing, just in case you turned down my request."

He sipped his coffee. "I see."

She hadn't anticipated his easy acquiescence and felt a bit lost in her rehearsed speech.

"Miss Shelby, of course you understand that you will be joining us."

She tensed. "That's not necessary, Your Grace. I'm certain you and your son will do fine without me."

"But who will guide him in his manners? You certainly can't count on me. I eat as I wish, and no one has ever corrected me, because I'm the duke."

"And you're saying you don't wish that to happen to your son?" She spoke hesitantly, not wanting to offend him.

He cocked his head. "Correct. There are times when one wishes to . . . blend in more."

She didn't know what to say to that except "I understand, Your Grace. Of course I will accompany Lord Ramsgate to dinner."

The duke petted his dogs and drank his coffee, but he still managed to watch her far more than she felt was appropriate. And every look made her self-conscious and flushed. But she could not possibly berate her employer as if he were a student.

Why did he make her feel so nervous?

"Did you have any questions about your son's studies?" she asked awkwardly.

"No."

That stopped her. She clasped her hands together and nodded.

"He is making good progress, Your Grace, settling into his first routine well."

"He was rather wild the last time I was home."

"He is a very inquisitive, active child," she assured him.

"And it is your job to tame him?"

He was laughing at her now.

Coolly, she said, "No, Your Grace, but I can teach him to guide his enthusiasm. You saw how he behaved on the shore yesterday. He once would have run off without giving us a thought. He is learning to ask permission."

The subject of their picnic on the shore made

the duke's smile fade a bit, and she knew it was time to take a chance.

"Your Grace, yesterday I could not help noticing your tension."

"I was not tense, Miss Shelby," he said mildly.

But as if reacting to something in the room, Victoria the wolfhound lifted her head and looked at her master.

Meriel found herself childishly wanting to point out that even the dog noticed.

"Your Grace, when Mr. Sherlock approached us, you were obviously worried."

He set down his coffee and rose to his feet. She wondered if he was trying to intimidate her, for he came closer and stared down at her.

"Miss Shelby, have you ever been a member of a noble household?"

"No, Your Grace."

He seemed about to say something of a serious nature—and then it was as if a light went out behind his eyes, hiding what she wanted to see there. His irreverent grin was back, along with the leering way he looked at her.

"Then you've not perchance made a study of how a nobleman behaves?"

She blushed again, far too easily of late. "No, Your Grace."

"Then you don't really know what I was thinking, do you?"

"No, Your Grace." She lifted her chin, beginning to grow angry because he was mocking her, and she was unable to stand up to him.

"So you understand that I don't need to explain myself to you, my son's governess."

"Of course, Your Grace," she said stiffly.

He smiled, and she realized with shock that he was no longer staring into her eyes, but at her mouth. She'd allowed herself to be kissed several times, and she knew what that look from a man meant.

Long ago, when she was still the center of attention among her own class in London, she had responded with anticipation—from curiosity's standpoint, of course. She had been kissed, and though it had been pleasant, the experience had been disappointing.

Now, as she looked at the duke, all she could do was be stunned by the pure feeling of anticipation that swept over her, through her, even though she still burned from his mockery. Appalled, she realized she wanted to taste him.

She backed away quickly. She would not let this happen. A man like the duke would take advantage of her and then release her from his employ.

"Will Stephen be joining you for luncheon, Your Grace?" She prided herself on how normal her voice sounded.

"I have an engagement elsewhere," he said.

His lazy smile was gone, and she could not allow herself to be stared at a moment longer.

"Then I wish you a good afternoon," she said, then escaped.

All afternoon, Meriel was torn between pride that she'd stood up for Stephen, and anger directed at herself for not realizing what having dinner with the duke every night would mean for her. She would have to suffer his attention and devise ways to distract him without jeopardizing her employment.

Dressing for dinner was an exercise in futility—what was she to wear? Her best gowns were far too lovely for a governess to wear—especially a governess who was trying to stay unnoticed. She certainly would not allow the duke to think she was deliberately attracting his attention.

She finally chose a black silk gown that she had worn to her father's funeral and dressed it up with a simple cameo at her throat. From now on, this would be her only evening gown. The few beautiful gowns she hadn't wanted to part with remained concealed at the back of her wardrobe. She wore her hair in the plain, severe style she now favored, pulled back off her face, with not a curl showing.

Beatrice the maid had stopped by earlier to tell

Meriel when the duke expected her for dinner. Her attitude had remained cool, and Meriel hadn't bother to ask why. How could the servants be upset that Stephen needed to have dinner with his own father?

When she finally collected Stephen—looking adorable in his miniature frock coat and trousers—and went down to the dining room for dinner, the duke was being waited on by his footmen. The first course was already being taken away. Every click of silverware echoed in the cavernous room that could easily seat fifty. Beatrice the serving maid was bent near the duke, wiping crumbs from the tablecloth. The girl didn't meet Meriel's gaze.

The duke finished chewing and regarded Meriel with amusement. "So punctuality is not one of Stephen's lessons?"

Stephen, uncomprehending, stared between them.

Meriel felt her face redden. "Your Grace, we are five minutes early."

"You are almost a half hour late, Miss Shelby."

He did not seem angry, which was even more frustrating, because *she* was angry—angry with herself for believing the innocent-looking Beatrice, whose pretty face was flushed with excitement as she hovered near the duke.

Meriel bit her lip. So now was she in some sort

of contest with a maid for the duke's attention? Shouldn't Beatrice care that it was *Stephen* she hurt more?

Stephen gripped her hand tighter, his happy face collapsing slowly into worry. "Father, did I do something wrong?"

"Of course not, Stephen," the duke said. "Miss Shelby did."

She flinched.

"But you have missed only the first course. Come eat with me."

For the first time, Meriel wanted to flee a room because of embarrassment. She'd always prided herself on being punctual and prepared for any situation. She refused to let a jealous maid control her actions.

Chapter 5

As Stephen sat at his elbow, and Miss Shelby sat on the other side of the boy, Richard watched her consternation fade into a quiet resolve. He had seen the governess glance at the maid, and knew that his dinner instructions must have been deliberately altered. He wanted to just let the whole thing go—but he was Cecil now.

He forced a smile. "Beatrice, have you been naughty today?"

The girl blushed and smothered a giggle behind her hand. Her triumphant gaze landed openly on Miss Shelby. The governess ignored her, nodding to Robert the footman, who set a plate before her. Miss Shelby then turned to Stephen, reminding him of the proper utensil and guiding the placement of his napkin.

She was a cool one, Miss Shelby. And so obviously intelligent that for a moment this afternoon, looking so closely into her deep blue eyes, he had considered telling her that a duke's heir might always be in danger—from the next heir. But that was his secret for the moment, his and Cecil's. He could not have an inquisitive, worried governess nosing into where she didn't belong.

And then during their private meeting in the study, he'd really lost his mind. He'd wanted to kiss her. Her lips had become all he could think about. And she had sensed it, he knew. Which was maybe a good thing. She should be on her guard with him. He wanted to tease her, occasionally humiliate her, but he did not want to care for her. There was too much at stake.

"So what did Miss Shelby teach you today?" Richard asked Stephen.

The little boy at first started talking with his mouth full, but with only a glance, the governess was able to remind him of his manners.

"I learned about India, Father," he said after swallowing. "Miss Shelby even has a scarf from there!"

Richard glanced at Miss Shelby.

She continued to watch her pupil with fondness. "My father used to travel when I was young," she explained. "That was one of the gifts he brought me."

"Are you well traveled, Miss Shelby?"

"London is such a big city, Your Grace. Though I explored, there is still so much left to see."

"So you are not well traveled," he said, driving the point home in a way that made him want to wince.

A faint blush colored her cheeks. "No, Your Grace."

"But my guess is that you had always planned to."

She looked directly at him with her clear gaze.

"Before your unfortunate financial difficulties," he continued, hating himself for hurting her.

"Of course, Your Grace," she said. "Every woman has plans for how she'll live her life."

He smiled. "With her husband, of course."

Stephen looked between them uncertainly. "Are you married, Miss Shelby? Then why are you a miss?"

She gave her pupil a fond smile. "No, my lord, I am not married. The duke was simply teasing me as a way to pass the time. Witty dinner conversation can make a simple dinner so much more interesting."

To Richard, her tone subtly conveyed the fact

that his conversational skills were wanting. He was amused and impressed by her daring. Bantering with the lovely Miss Shelby could be far too distracting.

Hargraves the butler opened the double doors from the corridor and stepped inside. "Your Grace, you have unexpected guests."

The resigned tone of his voice let Richard know this was not an unusual event.

"The visitors are Lord Yardley and his sister, Lady Parthenope Dean, and Lady Lawton. Shall I have them wait in the blue drawing room until you have finished dinner?"

Richard wanted to tell them all to go home. He vaguely remembered Yardley, and that he had a sister, but Lady Lawton was a stranger. He'd hoped that the need for Cecil to recuperate would have kept people away for a while yet. But then Cecil's friends were hardly the type to respect rules—unwritten or otherwise.

Richard waved a languid hand. "Tell them I'll be there when I'm finished with dinner, Hargraves. They won't mind waiting. Provide them with whatever refreshments they'd like."

But as they were finishing the main course, loud voices erupted in the corridor, and the doors were thrown open by a red-faced, laughing man. It had been at least five years since Richard had seen Yardley, and it was obvious that a life of dissipation had not been good for him, as evidenced by his too-tight waistcoat and his bloodshot eyes.

"Thanet!" Yardley called, then stumbled and grabbed the door handle for support.

Hargraves pushed past him. "Your Grace, forgive this interruption. Lord Yardley would not wait any longer to see you."

"Been waiting too long," Yardley said, slurring his words together. "The brandy's fine, but me poor sister needs someone to entertain her."

The two women giggled from where they gathered behind him, and Richard forced himself to smile as if he were pleased by the interruption.

Yardley swung an arm around the neck of a plump woman. "This is Lady Lawton, Thanet."

"Your Grace." She managed a passable curtsy.

"We been spending time together," Yardley said. "Poor thing's husband up and died on her last year."

Richard watched with disgust as Yardley waggled his eyebrows in an exaggerated manner, as if Miss Shelby wouldn't understand his vague sexual references. The governess was speaking in a soft voice to Stephen, who looked bewildered, but resigned.

As if his father routinely abandoned him.

Richard would have to do the same thing.

Yardley grabbed his sister's elbow and tugged

her forward. She was obviously embarrassed and tipsy and hopeful, all at once.

"Thanet, you remember me sister, Parthenope? Finally out of the schoolroom, she is."

Richard felt strangely old looking at the young girl. But of course he was five years older than Cecil. Inwardly he sighed even as he grinned.

The footmen waited with dessert. Richard motioned them forward, and as they began to serve, he said, "Miss Shelby, you and Stephen enjoy your custard." He looked at the boy. "I promise we'll have a longer dinner tomorrow night."

Stephen shrugged and dug into his dessert. Miss Shelby left hers untouched, her eyes downcast and her face devoid of expression.

"Why don't you bring your pretty friend," Yardley said, eyeing Miss Shelby lasciviously.

The other two women pouted.

Miss Shelby's formidable gaze took in Yardley, and before Richard could speak, she said, "I am Lord Ramsgate's governess, my lord."

"You don't say?" Yardley said. "Means you need a night off, I think."

She drew in a deep breath, but said nothing else.

Richard grinned at her. "Nurse Weston could escort Stephen to bed, Miss Shelby. You seldom get a chance to converse with adults. We'd be happy to have you join us."

Meriel wondered if her skin was as fiery red as she imagined, from both anger and humiliation. She could not believe that the duke would ask her to *socialize* with him—in front of his own son, no less! It was one thing to be invited to a family event, since she was a member of the household. But this was going too far. Luckily, Stephen was too young to realize the lewdness of Lord Yardley and his friends.

But deep inside, a restless, dark part of her soul imagined being with the duke as she used to be, a young woman of potential, of fortune, whom men had wanted for a bride—not a conquest. "You are kind to offer an invitation, Your Grace," she said, "but I must decline. I had already promised Lord Ramsgate a tour of the portrait gallery."

"Won't it be too dark to see much?"

Stephen grinned. "Miss Shelby promised a lesson on my ance—ancest—"

"Ancestry," she corrected.

"Ancestry," the boy repeated dutifully. "But I'm looking for ghosts."

The three uninvited visitors hooted with laughter at that, but Meriel noticed that the duke only smiled.

"Let me know if you find any," he said to his son.

He looked back at Meriel and gave her a short

bow that provided even more amusement to his friends.

"Have a good evening, Miss Shelby," he said.

"Thank you, Your Grace."

Meriel had done her research before attempting to speak with Stephen about his ancestors. In the library, she had studied several history books written about the centuries-old Thanet dukedom, and even questioned Mrs. Theobald about the most recent duke, the grandfather who'd died before Stephen was born. All it proved to Meriel was that such power and wealth could corrupt easily. It was up to her to help Stephen be a better man.

Not that she thought the present duke was exactly corrupt, she realized as she escorted Stephen through the immense house to the portrait gallery. The duke treated his servants—especially the women, she thought dryly—well enough, and she had yet to hear any complaints about him. He was seldom in residence for more than a few days at a time, so the household usually moved through each day undisturbed. But she sensed an eagerness connected to his visit that she didn't quite understand, especially among the maids, if Beatrice was any example.

She tried to examine her feelings. Would Meriel herself be eager to see him again after his inevitable departure? He brought uncertainty and arrogance—and sometimes amusement, she admitted reluctantly. Tonight she imagined him with those rude, drunken people who disgusted her.

But *he* didn't. Was she beginning to think of him as *above* the everyday sins he committed? Maybe that made her no better than the lovesick Beatrice. A man was surely the sum of his actions, not what Meriel *hoped* he could be. She didn't know why she wished he were a better man—except for Stephen's sake, of course.

They reached the portrait gallery, which stretched the length of the house on the first floor. There were windows on either side, overlooking the front drive, as well as the inner courtyard to the rear. But the windows were dark now except on the courtyard side, where the lights of the far wing of the house glittered. Mrs. Theobald had seen to the candles being lit, but Meriel also carried an oil lamp to hold up near each portrait.

Between the windows were several dozen portraits, some ten feet tall (mostly the dukes themselves). Others were of a more moderate size of three or four feet—duchesses and children, and even the occasional wolfhound. Sadly, Stephen's mother had died young, before she'd had a chance to pose. Meriel would have to see if her family could provide Stephen with a portrait of her.

She took Mrs. Theobald's advice and started

two-thirds of the way down the gallery with Stephen's great-grandfather, who'd commanded a battalion in the colonies. As Stephen grew older, she would eventually work their way back through his older ancestors. It was a good way to study history.

And of course, look for ghosts. Stephen was still hopeful, and it was difficult to keep his focus on her voice, when he kept peering behind each drapery or statue.

She had begun to discuss Stephen's grandfather when the duke appeared out of the shadows near their end of the gallery. Meriel gave a little start, and inside her heart kicked into this new rhythm that seemed only inspired by him. Why was she so drawn to him, a man she should have no respect for?

Stephen broke into a smile and ran toward his father. Then he stopped awkwardly to bow. But Meriel knew he'd wanted to throw himself into his father's arms. Even after only a few days and some meager attention, the boy thought the duke could be more to him.

She glanced behind the duke, but there was no sign of his visitors.

"Hello, Father."

"Hello, Stephen," the duke said. He smoothed back his son's unruly hair. "Are you paying attention to Miss Shelby?"

"Oh yes! I learned about soldiers and battles. Did you know my grandfather fought against the French? And my great-grandfather against the Americans?"

The duke smiled at Meriel. "You certainly picked the correct history to hold a young boy's attention. No discussion of the fever that wiped out half the household two hundred years ago? Or the younger son who fled to the colonies and became an American?"

"I thought we would start small, Your Grace," she murmured.

"Did you see any ghosts?" the duke asked his son.

Stephen's shoulders slumped. "None. I thought the darkness would help, but it doesn't. Have you ever seen a ghost here, Father?"

Meriel watched the duke lift his head and gaze down the length of the gallery. There was a faraway look in his eyes.

"When I was your age, I used to wonder if there were ghosts in Thanet Court," he said softly, his deep voice containing an unexpected rumble. "I kept thinking I saw one out of the corner of my eye, but I never really did."

There was an awkward silence, and she realized that the duke wasn't even looking at the portraits. Of course, he'd spent his life looking at them.

"Did your guests leave, Your Grace?" she found herself asking, though it was none of her business.

He actually seemed relieved at the change of topic. "Yes, they did. They had not heard of my recent illness, so I had to explain that I tire easily."

Not that he looked tired, she thought, wondering why such a popular man would send his guests home. He was full of vitality and strength. His dark hair and eyes became part of the shadows, conquering them. If there were any ghosts, his mere presence would make them retreat with envy.

The poet inside her was struggling to get out again, she thought with disgust.

"Father, we're going to talk about *you* next!" Stephen said.

"Then I arrived at the right moment. You'll need personal commentary on my life and times."

But there was no ten-foot-tall painting of this duke, only a smaller one of him as a boy about Stephen's age. He was sitting on a garden bench, surrounded by foliage, wearing a mischievous grin that hinted at exuberant thoughts.

"There's no dog in your portrait, Father."

"No, my father's dogs didn't like me very much. Maybe I teased them too much."

Stephen nodded. "*Your* dogs seem to like you just fine, not like when you were last home."

Meriel frowned, but before she could think of a tactful question, the duke began to speak.

"I'm supposed to sit for my new portrait, but I just can't seem to find the time." He glanced back at the one on the wall with a thoughtful look. "This one will do just fine for now. Have you had a portrait done?"

Stephen shook his head. "Nurse says I can't sit still long enough. Maybe I can have mine done with you!"

"Perhaps" was the duke's only answer.

At that moment, a new light appeared at the far end of the gallery.

"It's not a ghost, Miss Shelby," Stephen said. "It's Nurse Weston."

It wasn't until the woman came closer that Meriel could see that Stephen was right.

"And how did you know she would come?" Meriel asked him suspiciously.

"I knew Father would join us. He likes your lessons. And those people who came during dinner didn't seem like any fun at all."

Meriel couldn't even look at the duke, who was being discussed as if he wasn't there. But he said nothing, just watched in amusement.

"Good night, Miss Shelby!" the little boy said as he ran to his nurse. "Good night, Father!"

Meriel caught the disapproving expression that the nurse tried to hide.

"Wait, Nurse Weston," Meriel called. "I'll join you." She certainly didn't want the other servants to think that she looked for ways to be alone with the duke.

She turned to wish the duke a good night, but he said, "I'm not finished with our conversation, Miss Shelby. How else will you discover more details to teach my son about his family history?"

She watched Nurse Weston and Stephen walk away down the long corridor, feeling very alone. When they were finally out of sight, she slowly turned and looked up at the duke. There was something very intimate about being in a dark place at night with a man. Perhaps because she'd usually had a chaperone, she'd had no idea how safe they made her feel.

She was so very aware of him looking down at her. The connection between them seemed to pulse and shimmer with a life of its own, drawing her forward though she was unwilling.

"Your Grace, this is highly inappropriate," she said firmly. She might be risking her position, but she could not continue to allow the duke to take such liberties with her.

He raised a black eyebrow. "It is inappropriate to make sure that you teach my son correctly?"

"It is inappropriate for you to keep maneuvering

to be alone with me. And you should never have asked me to join your guests tonight."

"But you're not a servant, Miss Shelby. I assumed you wished to be treated as one of the family."

She took a step away from him. "That is kind of you, Your Grace, but your methods are . . . unusual."

"Then I will refrain from being unusual."

But he wasn't leaving, and she didn't know how to insist on her own retreat. So instead she looked at the painting of him.

"Is there something I should know about your portrait, Your Grace?"

Chapter 6

Richard watched how the shadows highlighted the beautiful curves of Meriel's face as the lamp gleamed across her pale skin. Her black dress made her vivid hair stand out like gold hidden in a cave. It was so easy just to look at her, to forget about his worries and bask in the pleasure of her.

But she was obviously uncomfortable being alone with him. If he continued to stare at her, he knew she would flee. And he didn't want her to go. Only when he was with her did the loneliness inspired by this old house recede. He didn't know what it said about him that a strange young woman, suspicious of him, could somehow bring him a moment's peace.

He forced himself to look at the portrait of his brother, Cecil, which had been painted eighteen years ago. What could he tell her about it, except that as a child, he'd stood nearby and watched it being painted day after day?

"The setting was in the conservatory," he began slowly.

She looked up at the portrait in surprise. "I wouldn't have guessed that, Your Grace."

"The artist captured the sun well, but at the time, I was not very cooperative. I was seven, and when they'd tried to paint me outdoors, I kept escaping. So the conservatory it was."

She hesitated, her gaze fixed on the image of his brother. "You had a devilish smile, Your Grace."

"I'm sure I was thinking up terrible mischief. It's what I did best."

He looked down at her as she held the lamp up high. She was close enough to touch, and in that moment, his vaunted control almost deserted him. Never had he felt a woman's presence in such an overwhelming way. No wonder he'd let work rule his life—he'd never found anyone who drew him like Meriel Shelby did.

"I still enjoy mischief," he said softly.

Her reaction was swift. With a start, she stepped away and lowered the lamp.

"I'm sure you quite put out your governess," she said.

"I did. It's amazing I learned anything at all."

She glanced quickly back at the portrait, and seemed to study it a long time. "Your Grace, I already told your son about the military exploits of your father and grandfather. Did you ever give thought to serving?"

Richard himself had not had the money to purchase a commission when he was younger, and by the time his inheritance began to pay off several years later, the government needed him more for his prowess guiding industries to success.

Remembering to play Cecil, he said, "There haven't been any wars that needed me."

She cleared her throat. "Your Grace, the British army in India has been fighting in the border countries for several years."

"Oh, *those*. But they're not true, *declared* wars, are they?"

"Well—"

"I became the duke at such a young age—seventeen—that after that it was unthinkable that I abandon the running of all these estates. After all, who would do all the spending that so many people need to keep their employment? We dukes play a very important role in our country's economy."

She stared at him as if she were trying to

decipher his words, and he breathed a silent sigh of relief.

From somewhere nearby, a feminine voice called, "Your Grace?"

Richard was glad Stephen wasn't there—certainly the boy would have thought it was a ghost, instead of Clover, one of the upstairs maids. She was a redhead, statuesque and sturdy, as pretty as the other maids that Cecil must have enjoyed looking at. The girl walked toward them, and he saw her glance at Miss Shelby. The maid wasn't at all good at schooling her features, and a flash of distaste and anger marred her prettiness.

Miss Shelby lifted her chin as if she had nothing to be ashamed of. And she didn't—but it must look otherwise, and it was his fault.

"Yes, Clover?" he said, knowing his tone sounded short.

"I've turned down your bed, Your Grace."

"I'm awaiting a new valet," he explained to Miss Shelby.

She nodded coolly but didn't respond.

"Is there anything else I can do for you, Your Grace?" the maid asked.

Richard winced inwardly, knowing how that must sound. "Nothing, Clover. And tomorrow, please send up a manservant to prepare my room instead."

She flinched, dropped a curtsy, and fled. He

knew he was handling everything badly tonight.

Miss Shelby finally spoke. "If there's nothing else then, Your Grace, I'll bid you a good night."

He wanted her to stay; there were ghosts haunting this corridor, but they were only inside him.

"Sleep well, Miss Shelby," he said, and watched her retreat down the gallery.

When he was alone, he looked back at the portrait of Cecil and let himself be swamped by old memories.

In the conservatory, it had been very easy for Richard to hide in the ferns and watch as Cecil, the future duke, was being painted. Cecil had thrown a tantrum demanding that Richard pose with him, too, but the duchess had coldly refused. She had come to the sitting the first few days, so Richard had had every reason to remain out of sight. But after she grew bored and stopped attending, Cecil had used his antics to coax Richard from hiding. Soon, the little boy refused to pose unless his brother was there, making him laugh.

There were no portraits of Richard O'Neill—there never were in cases like his. He was a bastard, the old duke's firstborn son by an Irish maid. Cecil had been young and still innocent of how his own place in the world would alter him. Later, Richard's little brother had insisted privately that they would share the portrait, since the brothers looked so alike.

It was *that* little boy that Richard wanted to help, not the indulgent, arrogant man Cecil had become. The strength of those childhood memories had been what made Richard finally agree to this mad plan.

Richard was at Thanet Court to protect Stephen while Cecil was recovering from consumption. Cecil had almost died, and the doctor in London had insisted that silence and peace were most needed to recover. But Cecil had insisted that he couldn't rest unless he knew that Stephen was safe from the machinations of their cousin Charles.

Cecil had confessed that he'd accepted a loan or two from Charles, who was next in line to the dukedom after Stephen. Consequently, Charles had begun to make more insistent demands that he officially be named little Stephen's guardian, should something happen to Cecil. Cecil had been certain that if he looked too weakened by illness, Charles would push the matter, using it as leverage to stay close to Stephen. Richard had wanted Cecil to go to the police, but Charles had been careful to issue no real threat.

It was the thought of Stephen that had swayed Richard to Cecil's cause. He'd never met the boy before this week, but he knew what Stephen must feel like, with no parent to look out for him—the same as Richard had often felt when he was that age.

What might happen if Charles felt he could control Stephen? Richard well remembered that Charles's own servants feared him. There had been a rumor, never substantiated, that Charles had tormented a child or two on the estate when he was young.

Yet Richard's motives for accepting his brother's plan were selfish, too. Some part of Richard was still that boy hiding in the ferns, spying on the life he'd never have, the one he'd thought he no longer wanted.

The next afternoon, Meriel found her laundry waiting for her—wrinkled. So now even the laundry maids were angry with her? Did all of them really think the duke would notice anyone but a woman of the nobility?

Maybe they didn't care about marriage—maybe his attention was enough.

Not for Meriel. She had no illusions about the kind of husband she could attract now. And she was not the sort of woman to accept the crumbs of a man's attention.

Even if he was a darkly handsome duke who made her think about sin. The kind of sin a man and woman committed together.

Meriel started down to the laundry rooms carrying three of her gowns. She seldom moved freely among the servants, and she finally realized what she had never noticed. All the young women were pretty, some truly beautiful. Straight teeth, flowing hair, and stunning figures, enough so that Meriel felt like one of the plainer women there.

She went to the housekeeper's suite first and found Mrs. Theobald at her desk, absorbed in the household accounts.

The older woman gave her a friendly smile, even as her glance took in Meriel's burden. "May I help you, Miss Shelby?"

"I'm sorry to bother you, Mrs. Theobald, but the gowns I sent down to the laundry have returned . . ."

She paused to lay the gowns across a chair, and Mrs. Theobald finished the sentence for her.

"Severely wrinkled," the woman said, frowning. "What could have gotten into the laundry maids?"

"So others have had the same complaint?" Meriel asked.

"No, Miss Shelby, only you." She looked apologetic, and even vaguely guilty.

"Do you know why, Mrs. Theobald?"

"I might have overheard a thing or two," the housekeeper said, without any embarrassment.

Meriel waited.

Mrs. Theobald finally sighed. "You are a threat to the maids, Miss Shelby, but then anyone new in the household is."

Meriel sank into a straight-backed wooden chair. "How could I be a threat? I'm simply the governess."

"You're a new pretty face to distract the duke."

Meriel opened her mouth to object, but the housekeeper quickly went on.

"It's not your fault that the duke likes to look at beautiful women. It's no one's fault." She eyed Meriel's plain garments. "You can try to disguise your features, but they aren't easily fooled. The girls down here have decided that since you're constantly with the duke's son, you have an unfair advantage over them."

"An unfair advantage— How would I even use such a thing?"

For the first time, Mrs. Theobald seemed embarrassed, and she looked away. "It makes little sense, I know, but handsome girls grouped together always feel like they're in competition with each other."

Meriel felt distinctly that the housekeeper wasn't telling her everything, but how could she accuse her of lying?

"Do you have any suggestions?" Meriel asked. "I can't wait around wondering if I'm going to be poisoned someday."

Mrs. Theobald looked at her aghast. "Oh, don't worry about that! These are mostly good girls, whose fine features have given them ideas they shouldn't have. But they won't *hurt* you."

Meriel would reserve judgment on that.

"Leave the gowns with me," Mrs. Theobald said. "I'll have a word with the laundry staff."

"Thank you, Mrs. Theobald."

Feeling disgruntled, Meriel went back to finish Stephen's lessons in mathematics.

After spending the morning with Mr. Tearle, pretending that Cecil was finally interested in his faltering finances, Richard decided to involve Stephen in the training of the two wolfhounds. If the boy was familiar with the dogs and their commands, the dogs could be used to guard Stephen when Richard wasn't available. From what Richard understood, the dogs didn't like Cecil, so his brother hadn't bothered with them. They seemed to like Richard, and everyone at Thanet Court had noticed. It was time to have the dogs trained, so at least their devotion to Richard could be controlled.

He found the boy and his governess on their hands and knees in a remote corner of the garden, their faces bent near the earth, heads close together as they talked. For once, Victoria and Albert stayed behind Richard, cocking their heads in curiosity.

Richard squatted down beside Miss Shelby and Stephen.

"What's so interesting?" he asked.

They gasped and bumped heads and fell on their rumps. Richard got another glimpse of lacy petticoats, before Miss Shelby came to her knees, holding her skirts down around her thighs. They were face to face, and he saw at once that her immaculate hair had begun to come down in disarray. A curling lock hung over her eyes, and she blew up at it to no avail. Her eyes, so blue, were naked to him, no longer hidden behind glass. She had long, delicate lashes, and even the curve of her eyebrows bespoke grace.

"Where are your spectacles, Miss Shelby?" he asked in a soft voice.

Stephen chimed in. "She didn't need them to see the ants, Father. They have a nest right here, and it looks like a hill. Do you want to see?"

He regretted that he could no longer look at the world from a child's innocent point of view. But he was already straying from Cecil's boundaries.

"Another time, perhaps," Richard said, his gaze sliding back to Miss Shelby.

She slid her spectacles back onto her nose and rose regally to her feet. From below he had the perfect view of her breasts, corseted so immovably within her dark blue gown.

She frowned at him, so he stood up beside her.

"Did we have an appointment I did not know about, Your Grace?"

"No."

Victoria and Albert trotted past him, and put their snuffling noses down near Stephen's. The boy laughed and put his arms around their necks.

"But I made a decision that Victoria and Albert need more training than I can give them," Richard continued. "I thought Stephen should come with me to talk to the huntsman. You, of course, may come as well."

He saw the indecision she didn't bother to hide.

"I'll accompany Stephen, Your Grace. We can finish our studies afterward."

"Will you accompany me, too?" he asked, enjoying the playfulness that he'd once thought didn't come naturally to him.

"If I must."

"Ah, your reluctance wounds me, Miss Shelby."

She looked up at him over her spectacles. "I'm sure you have plenty of other ladies who would never wound you. A Lady Parthenope comes to mind."

"Lord Yardley's sister?" He grinned down at her. "You are a natural flirt, Miss Shelby."

She looked down at Stephen, who scratched

the hounds' ears and watched his father and governess.

"I do not flirt."

"Then call it a natural ability to excel in drawing room conversation. Surely you did much of that before your . . . unfortunate circumstances."

"Converse in drawing rooms?"

"Converse with men—and women—in drawing rooms."

She shrugged and leaned over to wipe the dirt and leaves from her skirts. "I attended my share of dinners and parties."

"Do you miss them?" he asked, knowing he was going beyond playfulness.

She could have answered flippantly, but she gave it some consideration. "I miss the companionship of a busy social life. But that could be summarized in one sentence. I miss my sisters more."

She did not look at him, just continued to watch over Stephen, who rolled around with the dogs.

"How many sisters do you have?"

"You already asked me that at our first interview," she said crossly.

He liked that she wasn't afraid to speak her mind to a duke.

"You cannot expect me to remember such a detail from months ago when you were a stranger to me."

"A stranger you were hiring to teach your son!"

"Well, yes, so humor me and answer again."

"I have two sisters."

When she said nothing more, he said, "And their names? Their ages?"

She sighed. "At twenty-four, Louisa is two years older than I."

So Miss Shelby was young—eight years less than he. He was feeling older by the minute.

"She went off to be a companion to an elderly woman. Victoria is four years older than I, and I just received word several weeks ago that she is to be married to Viscount Thurlow."

"I don't know the man," he said thoughtfully, "but I've heard him speak in the House of Commons. He's quite the politician."

Suddenly, she met his gaze, and in her own he saw worry.

"Are you speaking with honesty, or with sarcasm?" she asked.

"Honesty. Why?"

"She only just met him." Her voice lowered and slowed, as if it were pulled out of her. "I worry that she is only doing this to save our mother from poverty."

"And if she is, then she's a good daughter. Are you not attempting to do the same thing?"

Miss Shelby closed her eyes for a moment.

"Perhaps you're right. I guess I shall discover his character when I attend their wedding."

It was his turn to frown. "I did not know of your request for a holiday."

"I discussed it with Mrs. Theobald. I thought such a thing beneath your notice."

"My son is not beneath my notice. When is the wedding, and how long will you be gone?"

"I leave in four days, and I'll be gone for four. I assure you, Stephen might be glad for the holiday from *me*."

She was attempting to lighten his mood, but he could see her worry. A man in his position could selfishly refuse her permission to go.

And he was tempted.

What if she didn't return? Her sister would be a wealthy woman. Surely Viscount Thurlow would provide for his new sisters by marriage. Miss Shelby could once again have all of London at her feet.

"I'm sure Nurse Weston can keep Stephen occupied while you're gone," Richard finally said.

She didn't bother to hide her relief. "Thank you, Your Grace."

"But until then, you're at my beck and call."

She took a step away, suspicious yet again.

"Stephen and I have been invited to an assembly in Ramsgate."

She looked at the boy dubiously, as he found a

new patch of mud to play in. "Lord Ramsgate, we are with your father. Do behave."

The boy sat back on his heels guiltily, but continued to look at the mud with longing.

"Yes, Stephen will be attending," Richard continued. "There will be a separate party for the children, and I need you to watch over him. If you have nothing appropriate to wear, I'm sure Mrs. Theobald—"

"I can find something, Your Grace. I will not embarrass you."

She folded her lips together primly, and he knew she was offended.

"I would not be embarrassed if you attended dressed as you are."

She gave him a disbelieving stare, then said, "But of course. I'm the governess."

"You misunderstand me quite deliberately once again, Miss Shelby. I simply meant that your handsome looks make any gown passable."

He wasn't giving her too much of a compliment, not really. But the faintest blush rose up her neck and overtook her cheeks.

That was the response he wanted.

"Now that that's settled," he said, "let us go visit the huntsman."

Stephen jumped to his feet. "The huntsman? Will you hunt a fox today, Father? I could go with you. My riding is no longer so dreadful."

"And who claims you're a dreadful rider?" Richard asked.

"Why, you, Father."

If Stephen had kicked him, it couldn't have hurt more. What kind of a fool was Cecil? Miss Shelby pointedly looked off to a distant corner of the garden, as if leaving Richard to sink or swim alone.

"Then I did not make my meaning clear, Stephen," he said, trying not to sound too gentle. "I meant you were having a dreadful time that particular day, and we all have those."

"Oh," Stephen said brightly.

"But we're not riding today. Victoria and Albert have become quite willful of late, and some training is in order. Would you like to work with the huntsman to train them?"

Stephen's answer was plain. He called the dogs by name and began to run toward the kennel, situated back behind the stables.

"You'll still accompany us, Miss Shelby?" Richard asked.

"If you don't mind, Your Grace, I have changed my mind. I have letters I should write."

"To your sisters?" he said, wondering what he'd done to drive her away.

"And my mother."

"Then go ahead."

She left him standing in the garden, and he

watched the sway of her hips, and the disciplined way she held her shoulders before she disappeared past the fountain. Did she carry herself differently when she was free from the worry of finances? And however did such a lovely woman not have dozens of men clamoring to marry her, even without a dowry? He was tempted to have someone investigate further, but he chastised himself. He was not here to pursue a governess; he was here to see to his nephew's safety. His priorities back in place, he followed Stephen toward the kennel.

Yet his mind betrayed him by imagining Miss Shelby at the assembly. Even though she would be taking care of Stephen, there would be men there who would want to dance with her.

But *he* couldn't.

Chapter 7

Two days later, Meriel used her free time during the afternoon to lay out her evening clothes for the assembly that night. The sedate gown of deep purple, with a respectable neckline, had been crushed during the move, and she hadn't bothered to have it ironed.

To prevent more unrest, Meriel was trying to keep quiet the news that she was attending, so she could hardly ask Beatrice or Clover to take the gown to the laundry. She would just have to ask the laundress herself. Surely the woman would not refuse her request.

It was a several minutes' journey back to the

servants' wing of the house, where the corridors were narrower and darker. She passed the occasional footman or scullery girl, but no one questioned her. She had to cross the entrance to the servants' hall on her way, and she held her breath, hoping that luncheon was long finished.

A woman's voice called, "Miss Shelby?"

Meriel closed her eyes and came to a stop. It was not Mrs. Theobald. She turned about and looked into the hall.

There were several long tables with benches on either side. The ceiling rose high above, and on either end were massive hearths that would fit in as well with the decor in her own father's drawing room. Beatrice, Clover, and two other women that Meriel couldn't place were just rising from the table with plates in their hands.

"Did you wish to speak to me?" Meriel asked, not knowing to whom she was directing her question.

Beatrice coldly eyed the gown Meriel was carrying. "Back to the laundry again, are you?"

Clover snickered behind her hand.

Meriel simply nodded.

"What do you need such a fancy dress for?" Beatrice demanded.

This was the question she'd been dreading. "I'm to accompany young Lord Ramsgate."

Beatrice reddened with obvious anger, Clover's

mouth dropped open, and the two other women fell to whispering to each other.

"*You're* attending the assembly?" Clover demanded.

"There is a children's reception in the next room. I will be overseeing Lord Ramsgate there."

"But you're attending the assembly," Clover said again.

"I will be working," Meriel pointed out.

Beatrice strode toward her, leaving her dishes forgotten on the table. "But you'll be escorted by His Grace."

"He is my employer, the same as he is yours," she said patiently.

"But you'll be escorted by His Grace!" Beatrice fairly shouted it like an accusation.

"It's not fair!" Clover said to the other two women.

"It is not my wish to attend," Meriel said, wondering if she could turn her back and walk away.

"He can't have chosen her!" Beatrice said to the others. "He's been in London so long he hasn't picked one of us in ages!"

Meriel was stunned that the woman was near tears. "He has not chosen me for anything other than as governess to his son."

"And she's stupid, too!" Clover cried, aghast. "Everything's going wrong. He's never waited this long to choose one of us!"

Meriel stared uncomprehending between them, and was relieved when the voice of sanity in the person of Mrs. Theobald spoke from the doorway.

"Girls, what is going on here?"

"Has he chosen *her*, Mrs. Theobald?" Beatrice demanded as spokesman for the group.

The housekeeper's lips formed a thin line as she glanced at Meriel with a surprising amount of guilt. "He has not chosen anyone, girls. I am always the first to know."

This seemed to mollify them. With their noses in the air, they marched past Meriel without saying another word.

Meriel stared at the housekeeper in the silence that followed, waiting for an explanation. When none came, she said, "Mrs. Theobald, what do they worry I've been chosen for?"

The older woman sighed. "Come to my office for tea, Miss Shelby."

Meriel didn't want tea. But she wanted answers, so she accompanied the housekeeper across the corridor to her sitting room. Mrs. Theobald closed the door behind her and poured them each a cup of tea from a tray on her desk. The account books of her station were lined behind her on shelves. A table and several chairs were grouped on the far side of the room, where Meriel knew she often hosted the upper servants for dessert. Meriel had never been invited.

Oh, she knew Mrs. Theobald would not deliberately hurt her. The woman was only thinking about Meriel's position as governess, one above the other servants. But Meriel would have enjoyed having an occasional conversation that was not about Stephen.

Mrs. Theobald sat back in a cushioned chair next to Meriel and released a deep sigh. "Miss Shelby, His Grace has certain . . . peculiarities, all of which are tolerated because he is a duke."

Meriel nodded, feeling worry begin to seep in to squeeze her chest.

"Have you noticed how lovely most of the female staff are?" the housekeeper asked.

"How could I not?" Meriel said dryly. "Nurse Weston said I was hired for the same reason, although I find that very doubtful. I am well qualified to be a governess—"

Mrs. Theobald interrupted. "I have no doubt that you are, Miss Shelby. But it is true, His Grace prefers to look upon beauty in his household. There is a purpose to this of course, one that is morally reprehensible. But he is so generous about it that none of the girls mind. In fact they almost . . . compete."

"Compete for what?" Meriel demanded, losing her patience.

"Every month or so, the duke chooses a new mistress from among the staff, either here or in another of his homes."

Meriel stiffened and simply stared at the housekeeper, who watched her closely.

"Are you saying . . . he deliberately chooses a member of his own household and demands that she . . . satisfy his needs?" She felt sick to her stomach that she had not suspected the duke of such depravity. While she'd been trying not to fantasize about him, he'd been sizing her up as a potential conquest.

"There is no *demand* involved," Mrs. Theobald said. "The maids understand very well what will happen. When the duke chooses a woman, she is treated like a queen for that month, showered with gifts, and in the end, given a sum of money that she could not hope to earn in her lifetime. Of course, she is then released from the household, but none of the women have minded."

"Are you saying that it's acceptable because he pays them like they are prostitutes?" Meriel said, aghast.

The old woman put her face in her hands for a moment. "His father the old duke was the same. I regret that I take it for granted, but there is nothing I can do to change it. If His Grace treated the girls cruelly, I would stand up to him. But he doesn't. They experience more kindness from him than most have ever seen. Do you know how they'd react should I try to stop the practice? You've seen Beatrice's and Clover's reaction to *you*."

Meriel sat back and tried to rationally examine her own disappointment. Masters seducing their servants was nothing new—the fact that these women *wanted* to be seduced was something she couldn't imagine. She knew she'd been partly chosen for her features, but it seemed worse now that she knew he might act upon his baser needs.

She finally realized that she had thought this behavior beneath him. Had she expected him to be noble, when he'd shown her no such inclination? Why did she want him to be different from other sinful men?

Because she was attracted to him. Because the feelings she couldn't control told her he was worth her admiration.

And she'd been lying to herself, letting her emotions sway her judgment. He had shown her the kind of man he was over and over—forgetting about his son for months on end, maneuvering to get her alone, talking to her like she was an equal to ease her suspicion of him.

He was looking for a woman easily seduced.

And the way she'd been behaving, he could have kissed her and she might have believed she was special to him. She was the worst kind of fool.

"Miss Shelby?" Mrs. Theobald spoke in a hesitant voice. "Are you well?"

"I am." Her voice was back under her control, and she would make sure her silly emotions followed. "Thank you for explaining everything to me."

"Are you going to leave your position here?"

Meriel thought of Stephen, who'd seemed to blossom under her discipline and tutelage. How could she leave him with his father, a man who might very well hire the next governess because of her *bosom*, not her intellect!

Then she remembered the duke's strange behavior on the beach, when he'd acted as if Stephen was in danger. What if the boy truly was? She could not abandon Stephen.

"Mrs. Theobald, if he . . . chooses me, can I refuse?"

"It happened once before, Miss Shelby, and the duke accepted rejection with good grace. After all, there are so many eager young women to choose from," she added sadly.

"Did the woman lose her position?"

"No. Although I will admit that within the year, she found work at another grand household of her own free will."

"Very well then. I will not leave Thanet Court—except for my sister's wedding, of course."

Mrs. Theobald glanced at the wrinkled gown Meriel had laid across a chair. "I assure you that I had a conversation with the laundress—"

"This is a gown I haven't worn yet," Meriel interrupted. "I was wondering if the laundress wouldn't mind ironing it before tonight."

"Of course," the housekeeper said with a smile. "Allow me to take it to her."

"Thank you." Meriel hesitated, but it had to be said. "Mrs. Theobald, if the subject of me as a potential mistress comes up with His Grace—"

"We don't speak of such things, Miss Shelby."

"But if it does, make sure he understands that I will never be one of his household conquests."

"A governess is a lady above the rest of the household servants. Perhaps he would not consider such a liaison."

But Meriel saw how the duke looked at her, like a man who was . . . interested. She would not return that interest, even if her traitorous body wished otherwise.

Richard waited alone in the entrance hall, pacing beneath the vaulted ceiling and threading between marble columns. He found himself anticipating watching Meriel Shelby walk down the grand staircase to meet him. He wondered what she'd wear—certainly not a simple day dress.

As the minutes passed, he restlessly continued pacing, and the two footmen pretended not to notice. Finally, Hargraves entered and came up short.

"Your Grace, the carriage was brought around for you twenty minutes ago."

"I'm waiting for Miss Shelby and my son."

Hargraves hesitated. "I was given to understand that Miss Shelby and Lord Ramsgate are already in the carriage."

Richard frowned. "They didn't come through here."

"The carriage picked them up at the servants' entrance, Your Grace."

Richard felt like a fool, as if he were waiting on his escort for the evening. But all he did was grin. "Then that explains it. And I was trying so hard to be punctual, too."

The enclosed carriage was waiting in the great circular drive beneath the portico. Richard climbed up inside and found Miss Shelby and Stephen already seated with their backs to the front of the carriage, leaving him the best seat. That irritated him.

Stephen was almost bouncing on the bench. "Father, Miss Shelby said we were supposed to be gone already."

Richard glanced with amusement at Miss Shelby, who closed her eyes briefly.

"Your Grace, I was not implying that you were late," she began.

Stephen joined in. "I told her that the duke always has the right time. Isn't that right, Father?"

Richard relaxed back in his seat as the carriage departed. He was childishly glad the embarrassment had been handed off to Miss Shelby. He wouldn't even bring up the fact that he'd been waiting for her.

"Yes, Stephen, a clock has no meaning for a duke."

Miss Shelby looked out the window, and he thought her jaw muscles had clenched. She must know he was teasing, but she did not seem in a receptive mood.

"Stephen, I don't think Miss Shelby understood my joke," Richard said. "Certainly a duke needs to be concerned about the time. There are always so many meetings to attend, and I could never do business if I left people constantly waiting for me."

That was Richard speaking rather than Cecil, but Miss Shelby kept her silence and ignored him. Leisurely, he took the opportunity to study her. She was wearing a dark cloak that hid her from her neck to her toes. He was disappointed that she still wore her hair in the usual plain, severe chignon, but he could hardly command she style it another way. Of course, *Cecil* would have . . .

"Miss Shelby," he said, "no elaborate hairstyle for the evening?"

She coolly glanced at him. "Are the guests going to object to my appearance?"

"No, but perhaps I might."

Her tone became even more frosty. "Your Grace, if you plan to dictate my hairstyle from now on, we will have a meeting to discuss my response."

Where she would point out a corner of hell for him to reside in, he thought, not bothering to hide his grin.

It was less than a half hour's ride into town, and except for answering Stephen's questions about the fishing fleet and the royal harbor, Miss Shelby said nothing. Richard was getting the distinct impression that she was angry with him, but he wasn't certain why. There could be so many reasons, due to the way he was behaving. He found himself wishing he could be himself around her—but that would mean telling her the truth, and he would trust no one with that, certainly not a woman he'd met just days ago.

The assembly was being held in the public rooms above the Bull and Bear Tavern. The view overlooked the harbor, and Richard studied the fishing boats, their masts rocking gently in the twilight. Usually landlocked in Manchester, since he'd been home he'd found himself enjoying the sea air. Maybe he could just stay out here and avoid the crowds, all of whom knew Cecil. Or he could pretend that his illness had returned, instead of the true reason: that his nerves were telling him he'd never be able to fool so many people.

But these were locals more than Londoners, whose company Cecil usually preferred. Richard told himself that if Cecil's own servants didn't recognize the truth, why would mere acquaintances?

So he led Miss Shelby and Stephen through the public room of the tavern, nodding at the various greetings thrown at him by the men at the bar. Cecil was a popular man even with the locals. He felt himself begin to relax.

They ascended the stairs and were met at the top by a line of four matriarchs, forbidding women all, who presided over town events. Richard could not remember their names, but he thought he might once have been afraid of them when they'd visited his father long ago.

Now they were older, more stooped than he remembered, and still they peered at him from behind monocles and over fans. He found himself tensely waiting for the inevitable cry of "You're an impostor!"

"Looking healthy, I daresay, Your Grace," said one old woman with enough feathers in her hair to take flight.

He grinned. "Just being in your presence makes a man feel invincible, Your Ladyship."

He wanted her to titter with laughter, but the four of them regarded him sourly.

"Who's that cowering behind you?" said another woman, garbed in black like a perpetual widow.

Richard stepped aside, and Miss Shelby was put on display. Stephen held her hand. To her credit, she swept into a graceful curtsy.

"This is my son's governess, Miss Shelby," Richard said. "Miss Shelby, these are the great ladies who control all the social aspects of Ramsgate."

After that, they ignored Miss Shelby and peered at Stephen, who stared up at them wearing an eager smile.

"You've never brought your son before," said the woman in feathers.

"I didn't think him old enough before."

"Well, the children's assembly is through those doors."

Miss Shelby put a hand on Stephen's shoulder to guide him away. Richard wanted to follow, but how would it look for Cecil to care about a children's party, when he'd brought along a governess for that purpose? Instead, he wandered into the room beneath thousands of candles in the chandeliers, and found himself besieged by eligible young ladies and their mothers. Since they'd all been introduced to Cecil, they felt free to approach him. Luckily, they reintroduced themselves. He thanked God that everyone knew of his brother's forgetfulness.

He took turns dancing with them all, but he couldn't help thinking how insipid and silly they were compared to Miss Shelby. None of them spoke of anything more interesting than the weather, or gossip about the other assembly guests. He found himself glancing often through the open double doors to the children's party. There were flowers and streamers and the happy sound of children's laughter. Once he glimpsed Miss Shelby herself, and he almost stepped on his partner's toes, before he whirled her away from the door. Miss Shelby wore a gown of deep purple, like the sky an hour before sunrise. She didn't belong in that room. To her credit, she watched over Stephen while wearing a smile, when many of the other governesses strained to see into the main assembly.

When he felt he'd done his duty as a dancing partner, he discovered a card game in a third room. Just as he was about to enter, a man intercepted him.

Sir Lambert Metcalfe, a landowner from nearby Broadstairs, flashed him a friendly grin. "Thanet, how good to see you up and about. Come tell me what you're up to here in the country."

To Richard's surprise, Metcalfe took his arm and tried to steer him away. He eyed the man, showing none of his suspicions. "I'm feeling well enough for a card game. You still play, don't you, Metcalfe?"

Perspiration seemed to break out on the man's forehead as Richard watched. Metcalfe was actually *trying* not to look into the card room.

"It's crowded, Thanet. Let's have a drink together instead."

Richard forced a grin. "No, I'm in the mood for cards. Why don't you want me to go in there, Metcalfe? Worried I might win too much?"

The man's face reddened, and with a reluctant sigh, he pulled Richard into a corner of the room, where a tall column partially obscured them from the rest of the guests.

Metcalfe blotted his bald head with a handkerchief. "I didn't want to be the one who told you—good gracious, I certainly don't *believe* it."

Richard leaned back against the wall, trying for Cecil's languor, even though every nerve in his body seemed on fire with tension. "Just say it, Metcalfe. Whatever it is, I probably won't care all that much."

"Oh, you'll care, my boy—uh, I mean, Your Grace. Thanet."

He leaned in close enough so that Richard could smell the brandy on his breath.

"Thanet, there's a nasty rumor circulating that you cheat at cards."

Richard never let his pleasant smile die. In fact he started to laugh, causing more than one head to peer around the column at them. But he didn't feel any amusement as he wondered if this was a deliberate attempt to discredit Cecil. "Damn, Metcalfe, as if anyone could believe such a ridiculous thing. Why would I need to cheat at cards, when I'm already so good?"

And in his worry, he'd made a critical mistake; Cecil *wasn't* good at cards. He didn't have the patience or the discipline for it. But *Richard* did.

Metcalfe eyed him, looking as worried as if Richard had confirmed the suspicions. "You might not want to be showing the lads that, Thanet."

Richard wanted to take this lightly, but he couldn't. An accusation of cheating could be a serious blow to the dukedom—no one would ever trust Cecil again. Even young Stephen would carry the stain on his honor.

"So a man can't practice to improve his skills?" Richard asked lightly.

"I never thought you *wanted* to improve," Metcalfe said. "You always said what fun was money unless you were practically giving it away."

Cecil could be such a fool, Richard thought tiredly. Once again, he was going to have to take care of his brother's problems.

"Metcalfe, I can't be having my honor questioned—what I've got of it, anyway. Let's go."

"But Thanet—"

Richard swaggered into the card room, and he noticed that Metcalfe hung back. So the man could warn Richard, but not associate with him in too obvious a manner. Things were bad indeed. Cecil was not a man people hated—he didn't have enough principles to take a stand. Therefore, someone had to be deliberately making the duke look suspect.

Would their cousin Charles feel that this helped him somehow in obtaining Stephen's guardianship? Was this the initial salvo of a war?

First things first. There were several different card games going on at various tables. Richard made a decision on his plan of attack.

"Gentlemen, could I have your attention?" he bellowed, cutting through the raised voices. His grin was genial, his posture relaxed.

Several men gave him their immediate attention; he *was* a duke, after all. It rather annoyed him that a local baron didn't even turn his head.

Richard headed for the baron's table first, "accidentally" stumbling over the man's chair to distract him. The baron looked up, and his grimace faded when the Duke of Thanet peered down at him.

"Do I have everyone's attention now?" Richard asked.

The sound of voices finally faded away. Some expressions were friendly, others wary, some cunning, and more than a few looked disappointed.

"Gentlemen, it has come to my attention that someone has decided to spread a rumor that I cheat at cards."

There were looks of surprise, even approval. Several heads came together as a low buzz hummed throughout the room.

Richard spread his arms wide, his drink in one hand. "I have come to protest my innocence. I am available to play any who wish to attempt to prove me false. You can all watch me for signs of cheating. I am simply a man who decided to improve his card skills, because a duke should play better than his six-year-old son."

Several men laughed. One called out, "So the ladies aren't as distracting as they used to be, Thanet?"

Richard grinned. "I didn't say *that*. But you don't see any here now, do you?"

A whist player asked if he'd like to partner,

and Richard was in business. He won in whist, broke even in vingt-et-un, and in commerce his choices proved correct more often than not. The tension in the room eased, and Richard risked a glance at Metcalfe, who wiped his brow and nodded his approval. Crisis averted.

Metcalfe escorted him out of the room as news of Richard's triumph at cards spread. Richard was feeling a little cocky, a little too in control of the situation, so he thought nothing of seeing Miss Shelby on their side of the assembly. She stood demurely near the children's party, far too short to see much. He thought she might be standing on her toes, and he realized she must be looking for him.

There could be no good reason that she'd invade this room, much as he had fantasized about taking her in his arms for a waltz.

Richard started toward her.

"Who's that?" Metcalfe asked.

Richard hadn't realized that Metcalfe was still with him. The man was ogling Miss Shelby like she was fresh meat on market day.

"My governess."

Metcalfe yanked on his elbow, pulling Richard to a halt. "So she's the one you've chosen? I can see why."

Richard wanted to frown his confusion. Chosen for what? Instead he gave Cecil's usual disarming grin and hoped for the best. "I chose her to be my son's governess, yes."

Metcalfe elbowed him in the ribs. "You know what I mean. So you haven't chosen her? Then why's she here?"

"Because my son is here?" Richard elbowed him in return. "I don't see him with her. I'll be back."

Metcalfe leered in Miss Shelby's direction. "Take your time."

As Richard crossed the crowded room, he could perfectly see the effect that Miss Shelby's presence caused, as if a pebble had been thrown into a pond, and ripples spread outward. Men watched her with interest, while the women's dismay was palpable. Richard felt a sense of possession he wasn't entitled to, and he was relieved when Renee Barome stepped in front of Miss Shelby and began to talk to her.

When he joined them, Renee was looking about, trying to hide a frown. Richard's feeling of well-being vanished.

Chapter 8

Meriel breathed a sigh of relief when Miss Barome stood between her and the rest of the guests. She was feeling decidedly on display, and knew that everyone was appalled that a governess had dared intrude on the assembly.

"Miss Shelby," Miss Barome said, "I didn't know you were attending tonight."

"I am actually with the children's assembly, Miss Barome, but I confess that I have a problem." She felt her face redden with disappointment at her own gullibility. "Stephen asked for a glass of punch, and I only turned around for a moment—"

Miss Barome smiled. "And he disappeared. He's a clever boy. Shall I help you find him?"

"I don't wish to put you in such an embarrassing position," Meriel said. "He is my responsibility."

Suddenly the duke was looming over them, and Meriel jumped, because she'd been so distracted that she hadn't seen him coming. Perhaps it wouldn't be *she* who made the decision regarding her continuation as governess.

"Ladies," he began in his deep, unsettling voice, "is there something wrong?"

Meriel put aside her anger at his past conduct and tried to think of him as a concerned father, which he'd recently shown. In fact, he was looking at her with such a serious expression that her stomach felt uneasy. "Your Grace, I confess that Stephen took his leave of me once again."

Wearing a fake smile, he put his arm through Miss Barome's, as if they were having only a lighthearted conversation. In an overly loud tone of voice, he said, "Miss Shelby, they have run out of punch in the children's reception? Miss Barome, do show Miss Shelby where our refreshments are. I'll rejoin you ladies in a moment."

Meriel stared at him wide-eyed. Was he going to just *hope* Stephen would return? Miss Barome pulled her toward the punch bowl, and Meriel surreptitiously continued to watch the duke.

There was a tension about him, a stiffness in the way he held his shoulders that seemed out of character. It reminded her of the afternoon on the beach last week, when he'd seemed concerned about a stranger walking toward Stephen. No, "concerned" was the wrong word—he'd been visibly worried. What did he think was going to happen to Stephen at an assembly?

Now the duke moved from group to group, chatting, smiling—and searching. He swept his foot beneath tables while he continued to talk, and on the third try, his foot connected with something. He pulled his son out from beneath and held the boy up in the air in front of him. Stephen's hands were filled with tarts and his face was covered in jam. For a moment, Meriel glimpsed a relief in the duke's face that seemed too great.

"So there you are, my boy," the duke said a little too loudly. "Your governess will be most upset that I lost you when I was supposed to be watching you."

Several women gathered around him and chuckled, assuring him that he was a *wonderful* father.

Miss Barome cocked an eyebrow and shook her head. Meriel didn't know what to think. The duke had saved her, when he certainly could have left her alone and embarrassed. He brought his sticky son to her, and she gladly pulled the little boy to her side.

"Now Miss Shelby," the duke began.

Meriel braced herself.

"You will forgive me for losing him again, won't you?" he asked, a twinkle in his eye.

"You know there's nothing to forgive, Your Grace," she murmured, feeling confused. Once again, the tension in him had dissolved so completely that she questioned her own observations.

"Nobody lost me," Stephen said grumpily. "I was hungry!"

Meriel leaned down to speak near to his ear. "Next time, please tell me, my lord, so that I can escort you to the children's refreshments."

As they started back toward the other room, Stephen tugged on her hand, and she leaned back over.

"My father didn't lose me," he said in a quiet voice. "Was he helping us?"

Meriel looked over her shoulder at the duke, who was conversing with Miss Barome. "Yes, he was."

She squeezed the little boy's hand, and he grinned in return.

At the end of the assembly, Meriel led Stephen back to his father. She noticed that the crowd had thinned out as people said their good evenings.

Miss Barome joined them and smiled at Meriel. "The duke has offered me a ride home, so I'll be joining you."

"We appreciate the company," Meriel replied, and meant it. The more adults between her and the duke, the better.

Outside, the duke signaled for his coachman, and as they waited, Meriel couldn't help overhearing the conversation between him and Miss Barome.

"Cecil," Miss Barome said in a low voice, "I feel the need to warn you about a rumor that could damage your reputation."

"Let me guess," the duke said affably, leaning against the doorway. "They said I cheat at cards."

Meriel stiffened and kept Stephen distracted by asking him questions about the stars.

Miss Barome put her hands on her hips. "You know about this?"

"Metcalfe told me tonight. I promptly told them all that it was a lie, played anyone who cared to challenge me, and won enough that they believed my skills."

"But Cecil, you're terrible at cards."

"I've been practicing. Maybe that's where the accusation came from. Or maybe not."

"What do you mean?" Miss Barome asked in a softer voice.

Meriel casually leaned nearer, only half listening as Stephen chatted on about using the North Star for guidance. If they chose to speak in front of her, it was not her fault that she could hear them.

"Who did you hear the rumor from?" The duke spoke in a voice that sounded too serious to be him.

"Sir Dudley," Miss Barome said. "But I cannot credit him with the intelligence to deliberately harm your reputation."

"I agree. Doesn't he move within Rexford's circle?"

"Yes."

"Then perhaps it came from him."

"But why?" Miss Barome asked.

The carriage drove up before them, and the duke waited for Stephen to scramble up inside before next lending a hand to Meriel.

He turned to help Miss Barome, and Meriel heard him say, "Not sure, old girl. It didn't hurt me, so what does a harmless prank matter?"

But Meriel didn't believe he cared so little about a challenge to his honor.

Why couldn't she believe the worst about him? After they let Miss Barome off, the duke turned down the lamp so that Stephen could continue to watch the stars. Meriel answered questions from the boy, but mostly she sat on her bench opposite the duke in the darkness, where an occasional gleam from his eyes reminded her that he was watching her.

Not that she needed to see it to know it. Regardless of what she'd learned about him today, just being near him made her feel strange yearnings. She told herself he had been kind to her tonight because he wanted her impression of him to be favorable. As far as her physical impression of him, he didn't have to worry. Black and white evening clothes made him look dashing and elegant and handsome, and watching him dance with other women had made her feel her newly humbled position more than anything else had. In the past, *she* was the one every man had wanted to dance with.

Why could she not remember that he was a man who seduced his servants?

Because he was also a man who worried about his son, and spared his governess public humiliation. She told herself that he was only trying to soften her resistance.

When they arrived home, she saw Stephen up to his nurse, then took a chance and went back to look for the duke. She found him in the library, relaxing in a comfortable chair, his feet propped up as he faced the door—as if he was waiting for her.

As if he knew she'd come.

She stood in the doorway and linked her hands together, striving to look relaxed instead of nervous. "Might I come in, Your Grace?"

"Of course, Miss Shelby."

He said nothing else, only watched her, letting her make the next move. His cravat and stock were loosened, baring more of his skin.

Oh, why did she have to notice such things?

"I wish to apologize for my conduct tonight in regard to your son," she said.

He leaned his head back. "Your conduct? I heard you explain the stars to him in a way perfect for a six-year-old to comprehend."

"But I lost sight of him again, Your Grace."

"He is good at escaping, it would seem. I'm rather proud of the way his mind works."

She remained silent—confused, angry, grateful. These feelings conflicted within her, making her miserable. She should leave his employ, but instead she would only leave to attend her sister's wedding. Maybe the time away would help.

"I'll be leaving in two days' time, Your Grace."

He got so swiftly to his feet that she took a step backward.

"Leaving?" he said, stalking toward her, his usual pleasant expression gone.

By candlelight, he looked . . . dark and exotic and forbidden. And her insides churned in reaction to him.

"I have not terminated your position here."

She licked her lips and arched her neck to look up at him. He was far too close. "I am attending my sister's wedding. We discussed it several days ago."

He rocked back on his heels, hands on his hips, danger at bay for the moment. But she knew it was still there.

"I had forgotten."

He paused for an uncomfortably long moment, and she was almost about to escape when he spoke again.

"Your sister, the one who's marrying the viscount—she'll be able to take care of your mother now, won't she?"

She nodded, not bothering to hide her confusion.

In a softer voice, he said, "She would take care of you if you wanted her to."

Meriel stopped breathing as she stared up at him in silence.

"But you won't remain with her, will you? Stephen needs you."

A flash of anger took her by surprise. "Your Grace, I am offended at your presumption that I would abandon your son so easily."

And she was rather surprised at herself, that such a thought hadn't occurred to her.

But the viscount was rescuing her sister, and was being saddled with her mother. Meriel couldn't presume that he would accept sisters into his household as well.

And how could she leave Stephen? Every day the questions he asked filled her teacher's heart with joy. She loved sharing her knowledge with him. If she ever left him, she would have to make sure he was in capable hands other than her own.

Because she didn't trust his father. It all came down to that. Something was wrong in this household, and it wasn't just her worry about her physical reaction to the duke.

He cocked his head. "I didn't think you would abandon my son easily, Miss Shelby. But London is a city that lures people to remain."

"You think a *city* would induce me to remain, after I had given my promise elsewhere?"

"If not a city, then your family."

He was too close to her own thoughts. "No, Your Grace. I will be gone four days. That is my promise to your son."

Meriel excused herself and left him, striding angrily up through the mansion, wanting only her bed so that she could pound her pillow in frustration at the feelings she couldn't understand. Nurse Weston was just leaving Stephen's room in the nursery, and closed the door behind her.

"He had a wonderful time," the nurse said in a soft voice.

Meriel nodded.

"And did you enjoy yourself?" the nurse continued.

Meriel glanced at her with suspicion. "I watched over the children along with many governesses. I was working."

"I thought perhaps His Grace would . . ."

When she didn't finish, Meriel faced her and sighed. "Nurse Weston, whatever His Grace plans to do with one of the servants, it will not be with me. He has not chosen me for . . . for anything except as governess to his son."

Nurse Weston arched a brow. "I only seek to warn you, but His Grace most certainly is thinking about you."

This was too close to what Meriel saw in his eyes, so she only shook her head, remaining silent.

"Did you know he was waiting to escort you outside early this evening?"

"That can't be true—Stephen and I waited in the carriage for twenty minutes."

"And he was waiting in the entrance hall for twenty minutes—for you."

Meriel swallowed heavily and leaned back against the wall. "Oh, heavens. Why would he do such a thing?"

The nurse only shrugged, but her expression spoke clearly.

"Then it's a good thing I'm leaving for a few days," Meriel said. "Maybe he'll be so lonely that he'll choose someone else."

But Nurse Weston didn't look convinced.

After Miss Shelby had left for London, Richard thought Thanet Court seemed . . . quiet. He hadn't realized how much he enjoyed catching glimpses of her throughout each day. He buried himself in his subtle work to rebuild the finances of the estate, but that was difficult and tedious, when he kept having to pretend he wanted to learn what to do.

Stephen seemed unusually quiet the first day, and on the second, he reverted to the wild boy he'd been before Miss Shelby had begun to tame him. Nurse Weston came to Mrs. Theobald with her concerns, and she in turn came to Richard.

Richard stared at the housekeeper, who stood near his study door without coming fully into the room. There was a watchfulness to her that made him uneasy, and he'd been avoiding her as much as he could. Of all the servants, she'd been at Thanet Court the longest, and knew both Cecil and him.

"What would you like me to do about Stephen?"

he asked. "The nurse should be able to handle this."

"Your son is lonely, Your Grace, and lately he has enjoyed your interest in him. Surely that wasn't just because of Miss Shelby herself."

"No. I know I have not been the best father."

"Then have luncheon with him today. He usually eats with Miss Shelby, and I think yesterday's luncheon set him off to a bad afternoon."

Richard thought about his own childhood in this massive, lonely place. He had been the only child for five years—he knew what Stephen was feeling. Then why did he feel like he was making a mistake?

"Send him to the dining room then," he finally said. "Perhaps I can also find something for him to do afterward."

"Thank you, Your Grace," she said.

She used a cool, professional tone that he did not associate with her. Was she disappointed in him?

After she'd gone, Richard leaned back in his chair and contemplated Miss Shelby—Meriel. She had a beautiful Christian name, one you could almost put to music. He remembered the night of the assembly, how she'd looked in the library after everyone had gone to bed. Her silk gown had shimmered by candlelight, and her hair had gleamed like gold. Never before had he met a woman who made him almost stumble over his words, made him forget everything but the thought that he might not see her every day. She spoke her mind, not caring that he was a duke—that he was supposed to be the duke. He missed her presence as much as Stephen did.

Was he letting himself be distracted from his true mission, Stephen's protection? Right now, Richard was presenting himself as the target. After all, he was portraying the duke, and if Charles wanted to control Stephen, he would have to manipulate Cecil—Richard—first. Richard was certain that Charles's first move had been to discredit the duke's honor. What would Charles try next?

When Richard arrived in the dining room for luncheon, Stephen was already there with his nurse. The woman looked tired and exasperated, and much as Richard would have liked to give her time off, Cecil would never think of it. So the nurse had to stay.

"Stephen, what have you been doing since Miss Shelby returned to London?" Richard asked.

"She left me 'signments," he said glumly. "But only she knows how to make it interesting."

Nurse Weston rolled her eyes, and Richard smiled at her. She blanched and looked back down at her food, as if he would yell at her. Meriel would have understood the humor of the situation. Every sentence out of Stephen's mouth contained "Miss Shelby" somewhere. Richard noticed that the nurse was eating quickly, as if she couldn't wait to leave.

A selection of desserts was brought in on a cart, and Richard chose an apple tart as Nurse Weston turned to speak to the footman.

Stephen leaned closer to Richard and whispered, "You can't eat that."

Richard frowned down at his plate, his fork at the ready. "Why not?"

"Father, you don't *like* apple tarts, remember?"

Richard stared at the little boy, who glanced at the nurse, then went back to his food single-mindedly. Richard hesitated, a cold feeling of worry settling inside him. Stephen couldn't possibly know the truth about his masquerade . . . could he? Wouldn't he have said or done something before now, if he thought an impostor was pretending to be his father?

Richard had the footman take away his dessert, and the boy smiled. Maybe Stephen was just playing a game with him. After all, the boy seemed more restless and fidgety than he'd been since Richard had arrived as the duke. But he had to be certain.

"Nurse Weston, I've been meaning to take Stephen fishing at my favorite childhood place. Take the afternoon for yourself."

Both Stephen and Nurse Weston perked up. The nurse looked tired and hopeful, and the fact that she didn't hide her emotions testified to how exhausted she must really be.

Richard grinned down at Stephen, who was bouncing with excitement. "But Nurse Weston," Richard added, "find him some old clothes first."

Chapter 9

To stay true to Cecil, Richard made the poor nurse wait an extra half hour before he met them in the garden just behind the conservatory. After dismissing Nurse Weston, Richard allowed Stephen to lead him down the paths toward the stables. Stephen assured him that the stable boys would lend them poles.

It was a rare day of blue skies and warm temperatures, a kind of day Richard hadn't let himself enjoy in a long time. He'd always been too busy improving himself—proving himself. If only he didn't have the cloud of doubt about Stephen hanging over him.

When the head groom looked shocked to see the duke in his domain, Richard shrugged and said he was avoiding a tenant meeting. Stephen began collecting things for their fishing expedition. Soon, besides poles with string and hooks attached, they had a shovel to dig for worms, a couple of bottles of cider donated by the head coachman, and some biscuits from a stable boy, who promised rather forcefully that he hadn't stolen them from the kitchen.

There were many offers to go along and help, but Richard refused them all. He needed to be alone with Stephen. The two of them walked a long time before they left the formal gardens and entered the woods that bordered a stream.

"I used to play in here all the time," Richard said, following a well-worn path.

The temperature cooled as the sun winked at them from behind a bower of tree branches.

Stephen was literally skipping, his pole over his shoulder. "I'm not allowed to play in here by myself."

"I wasn't, either," Richard lied.

They reached the stream and followed it south for a dozen yards until the current slowed as it widened into a pool. Richard helped Stephen find worms and bait his pole, and soon the two of them were leaning against the broad trunk of a tree, their legs dangling between its roots where the water had washed away the earth.

The silence was peaceful, and Richard hadn't felt so at ease in at least a month—maybe not in years. He closed his eyes, ready to doze and wait for a fish to jerk his pole.

"My father would never take me fishing," Stephen said matter-of-factly.

Richard opened his eyes and looked down at the boy. "I'm taking you fishing right now," he said carefully.

"But you're not my father."

That proclamation shocked Richard, but Stephen seemed unperturbed as he dangled his legs over the tree roots and searched the water for hungry fish.

"Why would you say such a thing?" Richard asked.

"Because it's true. My father doesn't fish, and he doesn't like apple tarts, and he doesn't care what I study like you do."

Richard opened his mouth, but nothing came out. All his careful plans to protect the boy during Cecil's absence were crashing around him.

"Stephen—"

"Oh, it's all right, Father. See, I can still call you that, if you want. Why *are* you pretending to be my father?"

Richard sighed. "Because your father is still

very ill. He doesn't want anyone to know that he's getting better very slowly."

"Why?"

"Why am I here?"

"Why is he getting better slowly?"

"Some illnesses are like that, Stephen. They take a long time to recover from."

"I bet he doesn't want me to catch it from him."

"I'm certain he thought that." Richard hesitated, trying to find the right words. "Your father is a very powerful man, and if he looks weak, unable to take care of himself, there are some bad men who would try to take what is his, or maybe damage what is his."

Or hurt his son.

"So you took his place," Stephen said brightly.

"Yes."

"Are you the uncle he told me about?"

Richard felt a tightening in his chest, an ache for family that slumbered, but never quite went away.

"You look just like my father," Stephen continued. "I didn't even know you weren't him at first, until you started wanting to be with me."

"Stephen, your father is a busy, important man," Richard said softly, putting his hand on the boy's shoulder. "He trusts your nurse to take care of you, and he did hire Miss Shelby to teach you."

"But are you my uncle?"

"Yes."

"What's your name? I know he told me, but I can't remember," he added sheepishly.

Richard smiled and rubbed his warm back. "If I tell you, will you promise not to tell anyone else, not even your nurse or Miss Shelby?"

"I promise," he said solemnly.

"I'm Richard."

"Uncle Richard."

A bug must have flown into Richard's eye, because he found himself blinking at the unaccustomed sting of tears. He had forgotten he still had family who needed him. Richard was a bastard, whose parents had been dead almost ten years. His only brother had been more of a burden than a brother. But now there was Stephen.

"I can help you," Stephen said. His pole gave a shudder, distracting him. "I got a fish!"

They spent several minutes bringing in the trout, and Stephen insisted that Cook would serve it for dinner. Richard baited the hook again.

When they were settled back against the tree, Stephen said, "I really can help you, Uncle Richard."

"How would you do that?"

"Well I won't tell anyone who you are, of course."

"I would appreciate that."

"And I can tell you when you're doing something wrong, like with the apple tart."

"Ah yes," Richard said, smiling. "That's important."

"And with Miss Shelby."

"What about Miss Shelby?"

"My father doesn't talk to the servants much, but I can tell you like to talk to Miss Shelby."

Even a little boy knew that Richard couldn't stay away from Meriel. What must the other servants be thinking?

"I don't need help with Miss Shelby, Stephen, but thank you."

"How long can you stay?"

Richard shrugged and closed his eyes. "Until your father returns."

"Where is he?"

"Stephen, I can't tell you everything. Your father made me promise to keep his secrets. Just like you're going to keep mine, right?"

The little boy contemplated the water with a frown. "For as long as you need me, Father."

Richard closed his eyes, but he knew that dozing was no longer an option. How was a six-year-old going to keep this kind of a secret?

* * *

Two days later, Meriel returned to Thanet Court in time for dinner, and to her surprise the duke sent word that she join Stephen and him. She wanted to do nothing more than collapse in exhaustion from the dusty, loud train trip, but she dutifully washed and dressed. Stephen was waiting in the corridor when she left her room, and to her surprise, he hugged her about the waist.

She tilted his head back so she could see into his face. "And what were you up to while I was gone, my lord?"

He grinned to reveal a new gap.

"Why, you lost another tooth."

He nodded. "I did my 'signments, too, and I learned how to fish."

"That's something I always wanted to learn when I was young. Who taught you?"

"My father."

Meriel kept the surprise from her face. "How thoughtful of him. We'd better go so we don't keep him waiting."

As they went down the grand staircase to the dining room, Meriel knew she was nervous. She had been gone four days, and all she'd been able to think about was the duke. She hoped he'd turned his attentions to another servant, but when they entered the dining room, he lounged back in his chair and gave her a smile that made her heart pick up speed.

Oh God, she'd missed him. She'd missed how he made her feel like his sole focus with just a glance. She told herself he had lascivious reasons for looking at her so unprofessionally, but it didn't seem to matter to her traitorous emotions.

He made her feel . . . alive.

He was dangerous to her, and for the first time, she wondered if she'd be able to resist him should he pursue her. She hadn't even been able to speak of him to her sisters. He was a dark, guilty secret she carried within her.

"Did your sister's wedding go well?" the duke asked as she took a seat beside Stephen.

She would simply have to avoid the duke as much as possible. "Yes, Your Grace."

"You liked the bridegroom?"

She couldn't help stiffening. "That remains to be seen. As long as he continues to treat Victoria well, he will earn my blessing."

"He has to earn it, does he?"

She glanced at the duke, and that was a mistake. He was watching her with knowing eyes, as if he knew her misgivings, knew even that Victoria's husband had already lied to her once. Did all men mislead women?

"Your Grace, any spouse must prove his worth before earning a family's trust."

"It sounds like your sister trusts him more than you do."

Meriel shrugged. "I am not the one marrying him." She was not going to discuss her family with the duke. She had to trust that Victoria knew what she was doing. At least Mama would be safe, and perhaps the grief of Father's death would ease. Lord Thurlow seemed like a nice enough man; their marriage could become more than just pleasant someday.

Meriel had thought for certain that "pleasant" was all she'd ever need in a marriage, but since she'd met the duke, she'd begun to realize that there were emotions she might miss if she settled for just "pleasant."

The duke interrupted her thoughts. "London was as you'd left it?"

She frowned but kept her eyes on her own plate. "Yes, Your Grace."

There was an awkward silence.

Stephen looked between them. "Miss Shelby, why don't you want to talk to my father?"

She could feel the duke's eyes on her as he waited to hear her answer.

"I *am* talking, my lord," she said to the little boy. "But you will learn that sometimes one must keep to one's place. A governess and a duke are not social equals. You and I have had this discussion before, my lord."

The little boy continued to frown. "So I can't

talk to some people, like Bill the stable boy, or Mrs. Theobald?"

Meriel winced and risked an irritated glance at the duke. This was all his fault, but he wore the most innocent expression.

"My lord, of course you may speak to any of the servants," she said. "But they cannot be your closest friends, because it could be awkward for them. You shall be their employer someday."

To her surprise, the duke said in a low voice, "It is noble to want to befriend everyone, Stephen. But we are in a position where sometimes we don't know who our true friends are. And it is easy to get hurt if you're not very careful."

Meriel stared at the duke, who looked away as if he regretted speaking. What man hid behind the shallow, vain façade of the duke? Why did she catch glimpses, only to see him disappear? Sometimes he could be so thoughtful, and other times, as with his female servants, he could be . . . selfish.

"Father, no one pushes me down or hits me. They love me."

"Not that kind of hurt, Stephen," the duke said. "I mean when your feelings get hurt."

Stephen was watching everything his father did with a new hero worship. And it worried Meriel, because the duke could hurt Stephen the most. Did he cheat at cards as the rumor suggested, and maybe at other things, too? Would he blatantly have a mistress in his house, right in front of his son? She couldn't keep quiet any longer. She had to tell the duke how he affected Stephen, how the boy was old enough to understand a mistress for what she was—a woman to be used and discarded. If a father was going to be worshipped, he needed to be worthy of it.

After dinner, Meriel escorted Stephen up to bed and left him in the capable hands of Nurse Weston. Before Meriel could change her mind, she turned and went back down to the ground floor to confront the duke.

Chapter 10

Richard was contemplating another evening alone. He'd turned down a dinner invitation, but knew he was not going to be able to do that for much longer. He strolled into the library and looked at the thousands of books. In his old life, when he'd had an evening free from business meetings or social events—which were also all about business—he'd enjoyed the occasional novel.

But now he looked about the room, and all he could feel was exhausted. He had spent the entire dinner willing poor little Stephen to keep his secret. Every time the boy had opened his mouth,

Richard's stomach had clenched in worry. He would have to get used to this feeling, because Stephen would be spending every day with Meriel Shelby, a woman who could probably *sense* a lie.

As if thinking about her had magically conjured her, she appeared in the doorway, hesitating, one hand on the frame. He stopped his pacing and stared at her. She'd been gone four days. He was dismayed by how gladdened he'd been to see her again. Now it took him a moment to raise the façade of Cecil's smiling leer. Slouching into a chair seemed so difficult.

"Why, Miss Shelby. Did I call for a pianist?"

"No, Your Grace," she said solemnly. "I need to speak with you."

With a languid hand, he waved her in. He wanted to stand, to offer her a chair of her own, but he held fast to his masquerade.

"We need to discuss Stephen, Your Grace."

Richard crossed his feet on a low table, trying to act as if he didn't fear the worst. "Did we do something inappropriate while you were gone?"

"Of course not."

She bit her lip, and that gesture betrayed her femininity as no other way could. He found it intoxicating, arousing, and he was glad he'd kept his coat buttoned.

Lifting her chin and speaking in a firm voice, she said, "Might I speak freely, Your Grace?"

His interest only increased. "Of course."

"I'm worried about the effect that your mistress will have on Stephen."

He wanted to gape at her, but he settled for a raised eyebrow.

"Oh, I know you have not chosen one yet," she continued quickly. "But the servants assure me that it's only a matter of time, that you're usually as regular as a ticking clock. Surely you can see how frantically the women are preening for you."

Richard continued to smile, but inside everything began to fall into place: all the lovely servings girls, the maids fighting over the chance to be near him, Metcalfe at the assembly asking if Meriel was the one he'd chosen.

Good God, did Cecil choose mistresses from within his own household?

He shouldn't be surprised, he thought bitterly. Richard's own father, the last duke, had gotten his Irish maid pregnant, and Richard had been the result. The ducal power to abuse the helpless staff sickened him. Though the old duke had set his mother up in her own household, Richard remembered her loneliness and isolation. He had lived at Thanet Court, the only child for five years, and had not realized how his mother had felt, especially with the duchess's cruelty toward her. She had died when he was in his teens, still far too young.

And Cecil continued to contribute to this cycle?

What was Richard to do? He had to convince everyone that he was Cecil. By delaying in taking a mistress, had he already contributed to his own downfall?

"This is an unusual situation we find ourselves in," he said to Meriel. "I've never discussed a mistress with a lady."

"I am your son's governess, Your Grace. I am in charge of his well-being. How do you think it would affect him to see you treating so casually a woman that you do not plan to marry? You, who've already discussed not mixing too freely with the servants?"

"I would hardly flaunt my private life, Miss Shelby."

"From what I understand, you have no problem doing that very thing! Your mistresses are given generous gifts and money, and treated very well during the month you . . . require them. Then you release one woman—admittedly giving her a generous reward—and devote the next month to another woman. How could Stephen not notice this?"

A monthly rotation of mistresses? Richard thought in shock. However was he going to keep up the fiction that he was the duke, when he certainly would not *sleep* with his staff?

But maybe he could pretend to be indecisive. Maybe for once there were too many beautiful women for the duke to choose from. At least for a while.

"You need not worry, Miss Shelby," he said, rising to his feet and walking toward her. "I find I'm having a very difficult time choosing from among all the lovely maids."

"Then perhaps your conscience is trying to tell you that you should find a suitable woman—perhaps a widow—elsewhere."

Her skin took on a rosy blush the closer he got to her.

And inside him a little devil started whispering about how easy it was to tease Meriel. He felt like Cecil more and more, but he couldn't stop himself.

He wanted to touch her. She was breathing rapidly as he closed the distance between them. He could see the rise and fall of her breasts, and the way a little pulse beat at the hollow of her throat. He wanted to know the taste of her moist lips, to finally satisfy his curiosity about her passionate nature. He slowly lifted his hand, just meaning to touch her cheek with his fingers . . .

But that was something his father would do—what Cecil would do.

And Richard couldn't allow himself to go that far, to be what they were.

"I'll take your words under advisement, Miss Shelby," he said, bothered by how hoarse his voice sounded. "Go enjoy the rest of your evening."

She escaped from him so quickly that he was sickened by his own behavior. Had he frightened her? Did she feel that she would have no choice but to please him however he wanted?

Not Meriel Shelby, not that strong woman who confronted a duke about his misdeeds rather than risk harming her pupil. She would keep her distance and keep herself safe from him.

But he could still smell the scent of her skin after she'd gone.

"Your Grace?" said a voice from the doorway.

He shook himself out of his musings, and found Hargraves and Mrs. Theobald. They waited calmly, but he sensed an underlying tension.

"Come in," he said, going to fix himself a brandy.

"Allow me to do that, young sir," Mrs. Theobald said, hurrying toward him.

He froze with a decanter lifted in the air. That's what she'd called him his whole life. What she'd called Richard, not Cecil.

He stared at her, but she wouldn't meet his eyes as she poured him a brandy. When she held out the glass to him, she lifted her gaze, and he searched it. Hargraves, seeming embarrassed, went back and closed the door.

"How long have you known?" Richard asked softly.

Mrs. Theobald sighed. "Not at first, young—Your Grace. You were very convincing, even with the reasons for your sudden concern about young Lord Ramsgate. But though the maids flung themselves across your path, you didn't care. And then . . . fishing? The duke was too concerned with his clothing even as a child to allow himself to get that close to dirt."

"Yes, you're right," Richard mused. "But I had to get Stephen alone, to confirm my suspicions. He already knew the truth."

"He's a perceptive lad," Hargraves said. "But what we need to know is why?" He lowered his voice. "And where is the duke?"

"Then you don't think I'm here for nefarious reasons?" Richard asked dryly.

"Mr. O'Neill, I could never believe such a thing!" Mrs. Theobald said with outrage.

"It's strange to hear my own name again, but thank you. Cecil is still very ill. His doctors prescribed complete rest and silence for recovery. Our cousin Charles is pushing Cecil to be named Stephen's guardian, and Cecil was worried that if he looked too ill, Charles would try to exert even more control. He is the next in line for the dukedom after Stephen."

"Has he made threats?" Hargraves asked.

Mrs. Theobald wrung her hands with worry.

"No, not yet. But at the assembly the other night, someone spread a rumor that the duke cheated at cards. I can't imagine Cecil would stoop so low."

"Of course not!" Mrs. Theobald said, aghast. "You think Sir Charles could gain something by doing such a thing?"

"He wants control of Stephen—and Stephen's inheritance," Richard said grimly. "What better way than by making the duke look incompetent? Already, the finances are in a shaky state, and I can't tell yet if it's Cecil's ignorance or something more sinister."

Mrs. Theobald put her hand on his arm. "It is good of you to help your brother."

Richard covered her hand with his own. "I could not abandon him. I've done a decent job so far as the duke, but Miss Shelby just told me about Cecil's mistresses."

"Miss Shelby told you such a thing?" Hargraves asked in shock.

Mrs. Theobald shrugged her shoulders. "*I* told her. The other maids are quite jealous of her, so I finally had to tell her the truth."

Richard smiled. "She's worried that my unsavory life could harm Stephen. I was even asked at the assembly if I'd chosen a mistress. But I simply cannot do such a thing."

Mrs. Theobald looked at him with sympathetic kindness. "Of course not, young sir."

"I've decided to pretend to be indecisive. Mrs. Theobald, maybe you can explain to the maids that they're all so beautiful, I can't make up my mind."

"You'll have to tease them a bit, sir," Hargraves said awkwardly. "They won't understand if you continue to ignore them. They know the duke's usual habits, of course."

Mrs. Theobald hesitated. "Miss Shelby already thinks you pay too much attention to her."

"I know. And I'll have to continue it, I suppose." He wasn't truly reluctant, not with Meriel. He enjoyed her reactions too much. It was a dangerous game he played with her, because he sensed she was capable of making him forget his mission, forget his masquerade, forget everything but how she made him feel.

Richard looked between the two servants, people he'd known his whole life. "I'm glad you both know. It's been hell trying to keep it from you. But please, we must never talk about this, not unless we're certain we're alone. And even then, we should do so infrequently."

"Of course, Your Grace," Mrs. Theobald said, taking a step back. "Is there anything else you need before I retire for the evening?"

"No, go off to bed, both of you. Thank you for your help—and your friendship."

When he was alone, he gave careful thought to how best to flirt with the maids, without leading any to think she'd been chosen. He would do his best not to be alone with any of them; group flirting would suit his purposes.

He told himself that Meriel would always be with Stephen, who could act as a buffer between them. But deep inside, Richard knew that if he wasn't careful, he would find a way to be very alone with the governess.

Meriel hardly slept that night, and she awoke with a headache the next morning. Every time she dozed off, she saw the duke again, standing too close to her. He had lifted his hand, and in her dreams, he finally did touch her. Each time, her traitorous body awoke her, feeling all hot and trembling and . . . strange.

As she washed and dressed, she tried to tell herself that some women were always attracted to men they couldn't have. Maybe that was her problem. It was as if her brain just . . . turned off when he was near.

She had to content herself with the knowledge

that she'd done all she could on Stephen's behalf. She could not dictate the duke's behavior, but perhaps she'd helped improve his discretion.

At midmorning, Meriel left Stephen in his nurse's care so that she could walk into the post office in Ramsgate. She went back to her room for her bonnet, and was heading down through the house when she passed the red drawing room. She heard the distant sound of giggling. She peered in and saw no one, but the doors to the conservatory were thrown open.

Though it was none of her business, she crept to the inner doors, then stepped behind a giant fern in the conservatory. The voices were more recognizable. It was clearly the duke, but who were the women? Because there were several. She ducked behind a palm tree, then a clump of bushes, getting close enough so that she could peer at the duke through the foliage. He had his back to her. He was dressed in his riding clothing, with boots up to his knees, and a shorter frock coat. He looked so elegant, so above her. He tapped his top hat against his thigh as he laughed.

Three maids gathered in front of him. Meriel wondered sourly if they had followed him, or if he'd found them working and had begun to weave his magic. The women were giving one another nasty looks.

He had told her he was having a difficult time choosing a mistress—foolishly, she'd thought that meant Stephen was safe from such sights for a while. The duke had not bothered to mention that he would be hosting auditions for the role!

As Meriel came close enough to hear what was going on, one of the maid's—Joan? Meriel thought—stepped forward to catch the duke's eye. She had the saucy look of a barmaid rather than a downstairs maid, but surely the duke recruited his staff even from unsavory places.

"Your Grace, you look fine in those ridin' clothes. I never been ridin' because I'm always worried I'd fall off. But if I rode with you, your firm thighs'd keep me up."

Meriel covered her face in shock and peeked between her spread fingers.

"Ladies, I'm afraid I don't have time to teach anyone to ride today," the duke said. "Have a pleasant morning."

Meriel's indignation faded as she finally saw his face. He looked relieved to be escaping.

Didn't he enjoy watching future mistresses fight for his attention?

•

Chapter 11

As Meriel walked down the dirt lane lined with hedgerows, she knew her pace was far too brisk for such a warm summer day. But she didn't care. Her bonnet shielded her face, and perspiration dampened the edges and trickled down her temple, and still she marched along, fuming at those three women throwing themselves at the duke. What if Stephen had seen that bawdy performance?

Meriel had a good mind to tell Mrs. Theobald—

But the duke's beautiful maids, personally hired, were behaving exactly as he wished.

Meriel wondered why she kept hoping that he was different. Why had she thought he'd take her warning under advisement, maybe even act on it?

She heard the steady beat of an approaching horse, and moved to the side of the road without looking back. Instead of riding past her, the horse slowed at her side. She knew who it was before she even looked up, past the man's long legs, up that broad chest to that smiling, knowing, too-handsome face.

He touched his hat with two fingers in a jaunty salute. Gritting her teeth, she looked back down at the road.

"Not even a hello?" he said.

"Hello, Your Grace."

"I sense such pent-up anger, Miss Shelby. Perhaps I should be the angry one, since you were spying on me in the conservatory."

She closed her eyes in mortification, then stumbled over a rock.

"Now, now, don't turn an ankle," he said, "or I'll be forced to minister to you."

She glanced up at him, trying to appear as coolly detached as she wished she felt. "I came upon you accidentally. The maids were giggling rather loudly, after all. It's a good thing your son was not with me."

He continued to ride at her side, his horse firmly under his command at such a slow pace.

"Ah, so that's why you're so angry," he said. "I assure you, I did not seek those women out."

"They wouldn't seek *you* out if they didn't think they might be rewarded."

"Ah, but they do offer me opportunities to narrow down my options."

"But you promised—"

"Promised?" he interrupted. "I said I hadn't chosen. That was all."

Had she only hoped there'd been a promise buried in his words somewhere? She couldn't walk any faster, but she could ignore him.

"Can I give you a ride into town, Miss Shelby? After all, my thighs are firm enough."

She sent him an indignant look, but she saw that he was enjoying her reaction.

"Is that a 'no'?" he asked.

"You can leave, Your Grace," she said, then realized she'd ordered a duke about like a servant.

But he only touched his hat again, grinned, and veered off the road between two hedgerows and across a pasture. She watched him ride and hated that she appreciated the sight.

That evening, after taking Stephen up to his bed, Meriel was coming down the grand staircase when she saw the duke confronted by the maid Joan outside his study. The woman boldly tried to press up against him, but he managed to step aside without looking like he was deliberately fleeing.

But that was the impression Meriel received anyway. Hanging back on the stairs, she watched the maid flounce away in disappointment. The duke retreated into his study, and Meriel stared at the closed door.

She could not understand him. Before her arrival, he'd been a man who seduced his servants and ignored his son and his duties, if the whispers she'd heard about his finances were true. Since her arrival, he'd befriended his son, taking him fishing and training the wolfhounds. He was avoiding the women he'd picked as his conquests, avoiding the parties he so loved, though the invitations arrived every day, and he seemed fully recovered. And then there was that first day he'd ridden up alone and started toward the servants' entrance instead of the main portico. And now people were accusing him of cheating at cards?

What was going on?

She sat down on the stairs in contemplation, watching the coming night creep up over the windows to darken the corridor.

Maybe she'd been thinking about this all wrong. The duke was young yet—twenty-five, or so she'd heard. Perhaps he was just finally maturing. Today alone there had been several chances to take advantage of a number of women, and he'd looked as if he couldn't get away fast enough.

The thrill of taking meaningless mistresses must have run its course.

Now she had to prove it.

She found herself knocking on his study door before she could think of a plan and its consequences. When he called for her to enter, she went in as if she owned Thanet Court.

The duke wasn't sitting behind his desk, far enough away from her. He was near the door, studying a county map framed on the wall not five feet away from her.

She closed the door, leaned against it, and just looked at him. There was no smile on his face now, just an odd intensity that seemed to warn her. She wouldn't believe it. He might smile and flirt, but she had logically figured him out. He would not try to press his advantage over her. She refused to consider that her deductions might be wrong.

But between them sprang up a crackling tension she hadn't anticipated, and had created no defense against. There was an ache deep inside her that she'd never felt before, a need she had no answer to. He stepped closer and she couldn't think, didn't want to escape, although the door was at her back.

She kept telling herself that he'd changed, that she couldn't be wrong about him, even as his face was above her, his body too near. His hands came down on either side of her shoulders, and she was trapped within the confines of his arms.

He still didn't touch her; she knew she was taunting him with her silence and her acquiescence. But he wasn't the same man anymore; he'd changed—

And she kept thinking that as he leaned near, and the warmth of his breath spilled over her. She looked up at him, her heartbeat so loud in her ears, she barely heard him say, "Stop me."

"I don't need to," she whispered, trusting that he would control himself.

She suddenly realized that he didn't take her words as she'd meant them, and then it was too late.

His mouth touched hers with a brief, exquisite sweetness that caught her by surprise, that made her forget every logical plan she'd woven to protect herself. Then he pressed harder, his lips moving across hers, tasting, seeking entrance, she knew.

Somewhere inside her a logical voice cried out that she'd kissed before, that because she knew what to expect she should be in total control. But she wasn't. She was left with a drenching of passion that made her will not her own anymore.

She put her hands on his chest to steady herself, but that was a mistake. He was warm and solid, and she could feel his heart beating quickly in time to hers. His groan vibrated through her hands. His arms came around her, crushing her to him, and she gave no thought to escape. She only opened her mouth and surrendered what he demanded, what she, too, wanted. His tongue swept into her mouth, and she boldly met it with her own. He surrounded her, filled her, excited her beyond reason. His hands swept down and cupped her backside, pressing even more of her against him. Through her clothing she felt the strength and heat of his body, and she wanted nothing in between them.

And it was that thought that finally doused her with logic, and her control came screaming back in horror to overcome what she'd lost.

She twisted her head away and broke the kiss with a gasp, pressing her hands hard against the chest she'd just struggled to be near. He let her go immediately, and she was once again flat against the door, wide eyes staring at him, her spectacles crooked, wanting to deny what she'd just experienced.

She'd been wrong again, so terribly, completely wrong, it had cost her her self-respect, her governess position, and her chance to help Stephen grow into the man he could be. What had she been thinking, that this man, this *duke*, could be other than the powerful, selfish nobleman he'd been raised to be? He hadn't changed at all, and neither had she. She still could not trust herself.

"Meriel."

His voice saying her Christian name so intimately broke the frozen spell that held her in place.

"Let me go," she whispered, straightening her spectacles.

"I'm not touching you."

"Then back away!"

He took two steps back. "Meriel—"

After flinging open the door, she ran up the stairs, thankful it was late enough that no one would be wandering about to see the tears of defeat and humiliation that dampened her cheeks.

How had such a serious misjudgment happened again? The last time she'd trusted her emotions, not only had she discovered that her parents had lied to her about their finances, but her father had committed the ultimate act of cowardice by killing himself, leaving his wife and daughters to face the ruin of his finances alone. And Meriel hadn't seen it coming, hadn't understood his desperation. After that, she'd given up trusting her emotions, feeling betrayed by her own nature.

With the duke, she'd told herself to use only logic. Hadn't she read the signs in his personality? She could have sworn that no emotion played a part in her judgment that he'd matured.

But the duke hadn't changed—he'd just made

his choice in mistress, and it was *she*. No wonder he'd avoided the other maids.

She ran into the nursery suite, careful to remain quiet even though her chest heaved with silent sobs. She would have to leave first thing in the morning. The prospect of abandoning Stephen made her cry harder, but she had to begin packing. Reaching the schoolroom first, she opened cupboard doors and started pulling her books and papers out onto the desk. Something toppled backward, deeper into the shelf, and she cursed silently. After wiping her wet face with both hands, she drew a chair over to stand on. She swept her hand inside—

And hit something hard and wooden. It felt like a storage crate, but she had to be certain it wasn't something of hers that she'd forgotten about. Reaching for a candleholder on the desk, she brought it up to set on the edge of the cupboard. She could see books within the slats of the crate. The name Richard was written on the outside in a childish scrawl.

Gooseflesh broke out along her arms. She found herself pulling the crate out, balancing it against her chest, then turning to set it on the desk. After hopping to the floor, she looked inside. Besides books, a blank slate, chalk, and papers were stacked haphazardly, some of the writing still legible though faded. "Richard

O'Neill" was scrawled across several, and the date of 1822. Each book had his name inside the cover, with dates ranging from 1820 to 1830, and as the years increased, the difficulty of the books did, too.

The duke would have been in the schoolroom at the same time, and since he was too young for the first few dates, it had to be someone older. With an Irish name like O'Neill, she couldn't imagine it would be a cousin. A ward of the old duke's?

She shouldn't care; she had to pack and leave this place before she embarrassed herself further.

But it was a mystery that called to her. She couldn't just let it go, even if it was only a distraction from the turmoil of her thoughts.

Watching to make sure she wasn't seen, she ran to the library, carrying a candle that shook with her hurried steps. Once inside, she closed the door behind her and went to the massive Bible on display on its own podium. At the beginning, she located the births and deaths of the family, and was amazed to see that this Bible was almost a hundred and fifty years old.

Above Stephen's name, there was only one child listed, his father, Cecil Irving, now the Duke of Thanet.

She couldn't control her nervous anxiety; something wasn't right. She kept scanning the page, looking for something else—and she found it, written in a child's uneven printing at the bottom of the page, almost hidden by the decorative border. Someone had written the name Richard, born in 1814. His parents were listed as Fiona O'Neill . . . and Roger Irving, Duke of Thanet.

Though there was no proof, this indicated that Richard O'Neill was an illegitimate son, brother to the current duke, older by five years. Richard himself could have written it as a child—or perhaps it was the work of young Cecil, wishing that a servant's son was his brother.

Meriel slumped into a chair and put her face in her hands, chilled although the evening was warm. These were crazy thoughts. Perhaps the duke *did* have an illegitimate brother. What did that matter?

But there was something wrong about the duke—she had known that from the first moment she'd seen his return to the estate. The reasons she'd earlier given herself for proof that the duke had "matured" now seemed like proof that he wasn't the same man.

Since Richard had been educated in the schoolroom, he must have grown up here, at least part of the time. He would know all the servants, all the neighbors; he would know the current duke's personality and behavior.

She wanted to laugh at her own stupidity. What

were the odds that two brothers not identical twins could look that much alike?

She hurried back to the schoolroom and put all the books back in the cupboard, including her own. She couldn't leave Thanet Court until she knew the truth, until she could be certain that Stephen was safe. Let the duke—or whoever he might be—think what he wanted about their kiss, but Meriel would not be able to rest until she was certain Stephen's own father was taking care of him, instead of an impostor with a hidden agenda.

She needed some kind of proof, or she'd begin to fear that the real duke was dead.

Chapter 12

Alone in his room, Richard collapsed in a chair and let his head fall back.

What had he done? He was supposed to flirt with the maids and avoid Meriel all together. Instead, she'd come into his study, and he'd forced himself on her the moment they were alone.

Hell, he'd asked her to stop him, and she hadn't. But she was an innocent young woman, and he was a man who knew where such things led. She had morals and principles; sleeping with an employer was something she would never do.

Richard knew that it would be better for him were she gone. There would be no danger of losing control as he flirted with the maids, unlike with Meriel, who set his mind dwelling on provocative thoughts rather than his real mission at Thanet Court.

And Meriel was too intelligent not to eventually discover the truth about his masquerade.

But how could he punish her by relieving her of her governess duties after only a few months? He could not take away her only source of livelihood when it was his fault that she was in this predicament. What if her sister's husband refused to have her in his household?

Richard would just have to apologize and hope she accepted. He would promise to stay far away from her.

But the real duke wouldn't apologize, nor would he leave her alone. What was Richard supposed to do?

The next morning, Meriel used her free time to search out Mrs. Theobald, who was overseeing the kitchen maids as they made preserves.

When they were finally alone in the housekeeper's sitting room, Mrs. Theobald stood with her hands on her hips. "Miss Shelby, I don't mean to be rude, but I'm very busy. Can we not talk later?"

"I'm sorry, Mrs. Theobald, but this is my only free time until dinner, when I'm certain you shall be far too busy to talk to me." She took a deep breath. "I was reorganizing the schoolroom and came across some books and papers with the name Richard O'Neill on them. Do you know who he is?"

Meriel thought that Mrs. Theobald's face paled, but it was hard to tell since they'd just left the hot kitchen.

"The duke's half brother, miss," the housekeeper said, lowering her voice.

So there *was* a brother. This changed everything.

"It's been over ten years since he lived here," Mrs. Theobald continued. "It's an awkward situation, with Mr. O'Neill being illegitimate and all. The duke asked the staff not to discuss his brother with his son, so you won't need to cover Mr. O'Neill in your ancestry lessons. Now if you'll excuse me."

Meriel had no choice but to let the housekeeper leave. She had a feeling she wasn't going to get any more from Mrs. Theobald—or the rest of the staff—about such a sensitive subject. And if she blurted out her suspicions about the duke being replaced by his brother, everyone would think she was crazy. After all, Richard O'Neill could be a balding, portly man.

Who else could she talk to?

Renee Barome had been a friend of the duke's

since childhood. Miss Barome had asked her to tea, but Meriel had been unable to go before leaving for London. Meriel would just have to rudely invite herself over. She ran back up to her room, wrote and sealed a note, and found a groom willing to deliver the letter.

But she still had to face dinner with the duke—or whoever he was. She could only imagine the knowing smirk he'd give her after the way she'd kissed him. Would he think she stayed because she was *encouraging* his advances?

Her impending confrontation with him affected everything she did. Stephen complained when they did all their lessons in the schoolroom instead of venturing outside. Meriel did not want to risk running into the duke.

She watched the little boy with pity heavy in her heart, worried about the effect on him should the duke be an impostor. Stephen finally felt like he had a father to cherish.

What was she supposed to do if she found out that her suspicions were fact? She could tell the senior staff and let them deal with it. Or she could confront the impostor or go to the police.

Her mind was awhirl with disjointed thoughts and conflicting theories. The day passed much too quickly, and then it was time to bring Stephen to the dining room.

She tried to downplay her features, pulling her

hair back tight enough that her eyes felt stretched apart. Since she hadn't slept much last night, her face was surely lined with fatigue. Her heart pounded so loudly that she could swear her bodice vibrated.

The duke—she could think of him no other way, not yet—was already sipping wine when they arrived. She deliberately looked anywhere but into his face as she sat down beside Stephen. The boy chattered on about the latest training session with the wolfhounds. Her throat ached with suppressed tears as she listened to his happy words.

When Stephen stopped talking long enough to take a bite of his pigeon pie, the duke said, "Miss Shelby, I thought I would hear about new plans of yours today."

She was caught off guard and looked at him without thinking. He watched her as directly as always, but he looked neither apologetic nor smug. Simply curious.

"Your Grace, you're not asking me to consult you about Lord Ramsgate's lesson plans, are you?"

"Of course not. But when I didn't see you and Stephen today, I thought something new must have happened to distract you. I'm glad to see I was wrong."

She knew exactly why he was curious—he was

wondering if she was leaving his employ. Did he expect her to? Or did he assume she would not dare to? She wished she knew the truth, so she could decide how to think of him. As it was, she felt confused and worried and still too attracted to him.

Whoever he was.

God, what did that say about her judgment? she thought bitterly. Either he was a lecherous duke or a criminal impostor. And she *still* wanted to experience his kiss again. There had been something magical, something soul shattering between them, and she worried that she would never experience its like again.

She wondered how she could lock her door to keep *herself* in at night.

For two days, Meriel kept an entire house between herself and the "duke" except for dinner, where she spoke very little. She assumed the duke thought she was still angry about the kiss—which she was, of course, but she was more upset that he might be an impostor. She felt terribly, terribly confused.

On Sunday afternoon after church, she requested the use of a horse to ride to Miss Barome's. After receiving directions from Mrs. Theobald, she rode through the countryside, smelling the sea, which was out of sight behind the rising hills. Miss Barome's home was not a mansion like Thanet Court, but it was old and elegant, as befit the station of her widower father, who was a local landowner and justice of the peace. Meriel assumed that Miss Barome took care of him. Certainly she could have been married if she'd wanted to.

Miss Barome showed her to the garden, and they sat outside amid the roses and had tea at a little white marble table with matching benches. For several minutes they talked about their education and their pastimes. They even had a friend in common. Meriel was enjoying herself so much that she almost hated to begin steering the conversation toward her true goal for the day.

Miss Barome smiled as she poured Meriel another cup of tea. "So how was your sister's wedding?"

"Lovely, thank you," Meriel said, accepting her cup and saucer. "Victoria does not know her husband well, but he seems like a decent man. I hope they'll be happy. I'm anxiously awaiting her next letter."

"If she's anything like you, I'm sure she'll succeed admirably."

Meriel eyed her. "Miss Barome, that is such a gracious compliment, but how can you assume that about me?"

"You've had to make your way in the world as

a governess," Miss Barome said, offering a plate of tiny sandwiches. "I often wonder if I could be so brave were my circumstances reduced."

"Of course you would be. Just look how you stand up to the duke." Now they were into the subject Meriel really wanted to discuss.

"But that's easy. It's just Cecil, after all. To me, he'll always be the boy who pushed me into streams and brought me frogs."

"Ah, so there was no one to curb his boyish enthusiasm?"

"There was his brother, Richard, of course," Miss Barome said matter-of-factly.

Meriel found herself sitting on the edge of her seat, tea forgotten.

"Cecil worshipped him," Miss Barome continued, "but not enough to follow his example. You see, Richard was a serious, quietly ambitious boy."

"I'm surprised there is not a painting of the duke's brother in the portrait gallery," Meriel said.

Miss Barome lowered her voice. "Well, that is the sad part. Richard is illegitimate."

"Oh my." Meriel felt like a fraud, but how could she confess that she'd already come by this information by snooping?

"Before the old duke married, Richard was practically treated as the heir. But once the duchess arrived, and then Cecil was born, she made sure that Richard knew his place."

Meriel felt a twinge of sympathy, but she quickly banished it. After all, Richard O'Neill could be taking out his anger on the family right now.

"So was he sent away?"

Miss Barome sighed. "Are you sure you don't mind hearing all these old tales? I don't wish to bore you."

Meriel tried to smile normally, though she was tense with the need for the truth. "It's important to know these things. He is my pupil's uncle, after all. So how long did he live at Thanet Court?"

"Until he was twelve, when he went away to school like so many other boys his age."

"Then he was treated decently by the duke, fed and housed and educated."

"Oh yes, and he would be the first one to tell you that."

"You've seen him recently?"

"No, he hasn't been home for many years. There probably are not that many good memories for him. But he used his chance at education well. Last I heard, he'd graduated from Cambridge, and was quite the successful investor and businessman in Manchester."

"Did he and the duke remain close?"

"I can't say for certain, since even the duke and

I don't see each other enough anymore. My father has been ill, so I don't get up to London as often as I used to. But from what Cecil has led me to believe, he still sees his brother several times a year."

"That's surprising. I didn't think the duke liked being out of London—except for Thanet Court, of course."

"Richard occasionally comes to London on business. When the two of them are in the same city, I imagine the sightings begin again." Miss Barome smiled, her eyes full of fond memories.

"The sightings?" Meriel asked in confusion.

"That's what we used to call it when someone would mistake one brother for the other."

Meriel simply blinked at her hostess, while inside her, panic and fear bounced off each other. "So they looked alike?" Her voice squeaked, and she had to clear her throat.

Miss Barome laughed. "We noticed it most when Richard would come home from school for holidays. By then, Cecil was getting old enough that the brothers were more alike in height. Cecil used to enjoy teasing his mother, but I know Richard didn't care for the masquerade, because of the duchess's furious reaction. Richard had a hard time saying no to Cecil. During those years, wherever one would go, he would often be mistaken for the other. Cecil used to tell us, 'I had another sighting today,' and make us laugh with how he would lead the poor person on as a joke. When it happened to Richard, he was always very careful to correct the person immediately. He never wanted to be accused of taking the place of a future duke."

"But he had to know that the dukedom could have been his, but for the circumstances of birth."

Miss Barome sighed and sat back, looking out over her garden. "He never talked about it. In fact, I thought he rather disapproved of the way his father and Cecil behaved as peers."

So would Richard scheme to prove that he could do it better? Meriel would have enjoyed discussing it with Miss Barome, who probably could have provided more answers. But she didn't want to entangle the woman in what could be a dangerous plot.

On the ride back to Thanet Court, Meriel considered every motive that Richard O'Neill could have for assuming the dukedom. Had he hidden his lust for power all these years, plotted and planned until he could make it happen? Maybe he had even come up with the scheme as a young man, when everyone was constantly mistaking him for the duke. Or perhaps his investments had gone bad, forcing him to find another way to support himself.

But killing his brother? It just didn't seem like the serious, studious boy Miss Barome described. Nor could she imagine that this man, who seemed to enjoy spending time with Stephen, could kill the boy's father.

The duke was rumored to have been seriously ill. Could he have died, and Mr. O'Neill simply have taken over his life?

Or perhaps the real duke was only being held somewhere while Mr. O'Neill got something he wanted. But what? He seemed in no hurry. He spent his days as Cecil did, although he socialized less. Meriel had even overheard that the tenants had never seen so much of the duke before.

Perhaps he really was righting wrongs, being the duke and the father that his brother should have been. But then did he plan on leaving the country when Cecil came back? Or even going to jail as a martyr to a cause?

Meriel didn't know what to think, or especially what to do. There was no physical proof for her suspicions. Perhaps she should tell Mrs. Theobald, and let *her* decide.

Meriel knew she was letting her own feelings intrude, and she could not trust herself to make the right decision. She'd been lied to by her own parents, and hadn't realized it until it was too late. She'd trusted with her heart and her emotions, not her intellect.

Now with the Impostor Duke, she'd once again submerged the little suspicions she'd had along the way. She'd let her improper feelings for him sway her.

A small part of her considered just putting this behind her, getting out before the impostor was aware of her dangerous knowledge. She knew she could stay temporarily with her married sister.

But Meriel couldn't be that cowardly. Stephen was going to be crushed when he discovered the truth. And if his father was dead—

She couldn't imagine how the boy would recover from such a thing. He needed her now—he needed her to find a way to the truth. If she tried to bring in the police, no one would believe her, and she'd be removed from the household, leaving Stephen vulnerable.

She would have to discover Mr. O'Neill's motives, and what he hoped to accomplish. She needed proof, so that she'd be taken seriously. It would help to have accomplices, and she'd gradually see if Mrs. Theobald or even Miss Barome might believe her.

But until then, she would have to work on her own. And she could never leave Stephen alone with his father again. For after all, Mr. O'Neill had been showing too much interest in his nephew, the future duke. What reason could he have for that? Her first thought was that he needed to win the boy over, in case Stephen might have suspicions about his real identity.

But maybe Stephen himself was somehow part of Mr. O'Neill's purpose. The boy could be in terrible danger.

Chapter 13

The next day, Meriel took Stephen for a long walk in the garden. It was good to get away from the tension of the house, where any moment she might run into Mr. O'Neill, the Impostor Duke. He had not attempted to repeat his seduction, and she was glad of it. She was worried that she would not be able to keep her suspicions to herself if he cornered her.

Stephen walked at her side, occasionally looking up at her. As they followed an ornamental stream running through the grounds, she heard him sigh.

"Is something wrong, Lord Ramsgate?" she asked.

"Miss Shelby, you're too quiet today. Aren't you going to talk about things?"

It was her turn to sigh. "Sometimes our thoughts are so chaotic, it's hard to turn them off. When I was growing up and needed to sit and think, there was a corner of our garden in London, surrounded by trees and shrubs on three sides, and a high wall on the fourth. We called it Willow Pond, because there was a pond beneath a giant overhanging willow tree. It was rather overgrown, so my sisters and I always felt like it was our secret place, where we told each other things no one else should know."

"You were lucky to have sisters," Stephen said. "I always wanted a brother, but Father says he's not getting married again anytime soon. Do you want me to show you my secret place?"

She smiled down at him. "That would be wonderful, my lord."

Stephen's secret place involved crawling beneath the edge of a vine arbor, but in the end, it was worth a dirty skirt. The sun peeked through vines overhead, and the ground was covered in the softest moss. She was too tall to stand, but she could sit, and Stephen was there with her, safe from his uncle.

Did she dare question him?

"So you always wanted a brother," she repeated, as he showed her the unusual rocks he'd collected.

He nodded. "I'm only six. There's still time. Father knows lots of pretty women."

She pressed her lips together to hide a smile. "You'd think he'd understand your concerns, since he had a brother."

Stephen glanced at her. "You know about my uncle?"

"I've heard a little about him," she said slowly, hating to lie. "Have you met him?"

He bit his lip. "Yes."

"Then you're lucky. My aunts and uncles lived far in the north, near Scotland, so I never got the chance to know them."

"My uncle lives in the north, too, in Man—Manch—"

"Manchester."

"Yes!"

"Maybe we can study that city. I hear your uncle is a successful businessman there."

"He owns trains and ships and other things."

Meriel nodded. The success of Mr. O'Neill's business interests was something she might be able to find out, although she wouldn't make the mistake of questioning the household staff just yet. She would try the gardeners and the grooms first. If Mr. O'Neill was still wealthy, then money could not be his motive—unless he craved even more of it.

She couldn't think of a subtle way to continue a conversation about Stephen's uncle, so she said, "Well, my lord, I suggest we head back to Thanet Court. We have music to study today. Nurse tells me you've been practicing your piano."

She crawled beneath the arbor behind Stephen and smiled as he cautiously looked both ways before emerging onto the gravel path.

When she was standing beside him, he said, "After my music lesson, I'm going down to the huntsman with my father and the hounds. Is that all right?"

She wished she could refuse him permission. "Of course, my lord. Could I join you and watch? I've been doing some reading on dogs that might interest you."

He grinned and nodded.

Richard was looking forward to seeing Stephen alone. It seemed as if Meriel followed the boy everywhere. Even though he was beginning to think that Stephen would be able to keep his secret, Richard could never quite relax around the governess, mostly because of his masquerade.

But it was also because of the way she made him feel, full of desire mixed with uneasiness and suspicion and longing. The more he saw her, the more he wished she knew who he really was—a man who didn't flirt with the maids or recklessly go through his inheritance. A couple of weeks into his masquerade, and he was already sick of playing Cecil.

Stephen came running to the conservatory, where they'd agreed to meet.

"Father, we have to wait for Miss Shelby. She's coming, too! She just had to talk to Nurse Weston first."

Richard tensed. "Did you invite her, Stephen?"

"She invited herself."

"She doesn't usually come to the huntsman with us," Richard said, frowning.

"She said she's been reading about dogs."

"We'll go now, and she can join us when she's able to. She won't mind." He hoped Meriel forgot the way there. Every time he saw her face, he remembered the taste of her kiss and the way she had fit tight against him, from the thrust of her breasts to the sweet curve of her hips. It was distracting and unnerving and . . . frustrating, because nothing could come of it. She would certainly never let him touch her again.

As they walked down through the garden, Stephen swung his arms merrily. "I showed Miss Shelby my secret place."

"And where's that?" Richard asked, smiling.

"I can't tell you. It wouldn't be a secret!"

"You told Miss Shelby."

"I know, but—oh, she asked about you."

Richard's spirits plunged. "Me, your father?" he said in a lower voice.

"No, you, my uncle," Stephen whispered back.

Richard casually looked around, but they were alone. "What does she know about me?"

"I told her you were from Man—Manch—"

"Manchester."

"She already knew you worked there. I told her you owned lots of things."

"And that's all?"

"Of course . . . Father," Stephen said, giving him a sideways smile.

Whyever would Meriel bring up Richard O'Neill?

"Hello, I'm coming!" called a voice behind them.

He looked over his shoulder to find the governess practically running after them, her skirts high enough to show her ankles. Richard would have enjoyed the sight if he wasn't so concerned.

Why was he feeling uneasy? Meriel had been telling Stephen about his ancestors. Surely in her research, someone might have mentioned Richard's name.

She caught up to them, breathing a little heavily, strands of blond hair coming loose from her chignon. Her spectacles glinted in the sunlight as she looked between them.

"Father didn't want to wait for you," Stephen said.

Richard inwardly winced. "I knew you'd have no problem finding us, Miss Shelby."

"Of course not, Your Grace," she said, her voice cool and unperturbed.

Every time she spoke, he sensed her hidden disapproval of him. How could he blame her after how he'd kissed her? He kept telling himself he was only playing Cecil, but that was a convenient lie. He hadn't felt driven to kiss anyone else, only Meriel.

And now she was beginning to ask questions. Perhaps he needed to do something else Cecil would do, another way to stop Meriel from having a reason to discuss him.

Perhaps he should have a dinner party. Surely when he was surrounded by people, all of whom didn't suspect his masquerade, Meriel would be forced to back down.

When they reached the kennel, she sat on a bench nearby, leaving Richard with the distinct impression that she didn't want Stephen to be alone with him. Another reason to convince her that he was the duke.

A dinner party would give him another chance to find out if Cecil's suspicions of their cousin were right. Richard would invite Charles Irving, the man Cecil seemed to fear. If Charles had started the cheating rumor, or if he had any designs on controlling Stephen, perhaps he would betray himself among company.

But either way, Richard had to do something bold. He needed to evaluate the enemy, to see if Cecil was just imagining things or not. Richard would station some men in the house as a precaution, and of course Meriel would never let the boy out of her sight.

As the huntsman showed Stephen the new tricks the wolfhounds had learned, Richard strolled to the governess and sat down beside her. She tensed as if he'd touched her.

"So you decided to visit the hounds with us today, Miss Shelby."

He looked down at her, and she kept her gaze fixed on Stephen. But her breathing seemed a little rapid.

He had to stop looking at her breasts.

"Lord Ramsgate tells me how improved their behavior is," she said, "so I had to see for myself."

"You could have seen them up at the house."

She hesitated, and he wondered if she was going to back down.

"Perhaps, but I was so curious, especially since your son says the dogs finally like you, Your Grace. So it took time to win them over?"

Her hints made him uneasy, so he decided to keep her off balance. He leaned back, hands flat behind him on the bench to brace himself. It put his fingers quite near her skirts, and she straightened even more, as if she could sense what he did.

"My best rapport seems to be with women rather than dogs, I guess," he said.

He watched the blush steal across her cheeks.

"I've decided to have a dinner party and invite some of the fairer sex."

"Then perhaps your staff will feel safe for a while," she said between clenched teeth.

"You don't feel safe around me, Miss Shelby?"

Stephen waved at them, and they both waved back.

"You have made sure that I cannot, Your Grace."

"Have no fear. I have never forced myself on a woman."

"Your position ensures that you never need to."

Maybe this was where all her hostility came from, a woman feeling threatened rather than suspicious.

"Are you saying that you would give in to whatever I suggested, regardless of your feelings, Miss Shelby? Because I would like to point out that you certainly did not kiss like a woman who didn't want to be kissed."

Her cheeks were bright red now, and she bit her lip. He wished she'd stop doing that, he thought, needing to adjust himself.

"I forgot my circumstances, Your Grace."

She practically hissed the words, and he remembered that she had only recently been one of the beauties at London parties. He did not think she'd welcome his sympathy.

"Ah, your circumstances," he said. "Are you saying that were you not my governess, you would choose to kiss me?"

"No!"

She spoke too loudly, and Stephen looked up from where he rolled around on the ground beneath one of the massive dogs.

"I'm all right, Miss Shelby!" the boy called. "Albert won't hurt me."

"Oh, very well," Meriel called with a bright voice that was patently false.

Richard slid his hand a little closer, until the fabric of her skirt just brushed his fingertips. He was teasing her—and tormenting himself. "So kissing me was something you willingly did, then later realized was a mistake."

"Oh, could you please stop bringing it up," she said with a heavy sigh.

He should have listened to her; he should have stopped right there, gone to Stephen and ended this.

Instead, an unfamiliar devil inside him made him lean a little nearer. "That kiss is not easily forgotten."

"But you must, Your Grace. I will not be your next mistress. I do not approve of your immorality, especially around your son."

She did not hesitate when she called Stephen his son, so Richard forced himself to relax. She couldn't know anything about his other life; she was just concerned about her own threatened innocence.

"You should find a wife," Meriel continued. "Use your dinner party as an opportunity."

"A wife who wants to kiss me."

She spoke so softly that he almost didn't hear her. "If you can find one."

"Ah, that's a challenge if I ever heard one, Miss Shelby."

She gave a little moan and covered her eyes with one hand. "Your Grace, please don't think that I—"

"Miss Shelby, come pet the dogs!" Stephen called.

"Here I come!" she answered quickly and shot to her feet.

Richard let her go—for now.

Chapter 14

Meriel managed to avoid the Impostor Duke for the three days leading up to his dinner party. She had a few scattered conversations about the duke's brother with several stable hands and grooms, but most were too young to remember. A boy suggested that the head coachman knew Mr. O'Neill, but Meriel had not been able to find time to interview him. Stephen's welfare was more important than her investigating. She always had to make sure that the boy wasn't alone with the Impostor Duke.

The day before the dinner party, Nurse Weston took Stephen so that Meriel could go for a walk.

Meriel headed straight for the stables. She had brought tarts from the kitchen on the pretext that Mrs. Theobald had sent them. Luckily, she found the coachman alone in his coach house office, and she gave him his tart. He was an older gentleman, still trim, his livery clean and pressed.

After putting aside the harness buckles he was polishing, he grinned and ate half the tart in one bite.

Meriel smiled at him and began to nibble on her own. "Mrs. Theobald can be very thoughtful," she said.

He nodded and took another bite.

"You deserve it, after you've helped look after Stephen when he wanders the estate."

He shrugged. "I don't mind."

"Were you here when the duke was young?"

He nodded and reached for another tart.

"It must have been even more work for you, what with two curious boys."

"They weren't bad, though the duke himself could be a regular mischief maker."

Meriel smiled. "I hear he liked to pretend to be his brother."

"He was good at it, too. Not so much the other way around. Master Richard didn't like to tease people."

"Have you seen him lately?"

"In London, on occasion, when the brothers

meet." He sat back and closed his eyes in thought. "Master Richard had the newest carriage when I saw him six months ago. Four horses that put ours to shame, they did. It's good to see him doing well for himself."

Meriel gave her excuse of passing out the rest of the tarts and took her leave of the coachman.

So Mr. O'Neill was still wealthy, at least a few months ago. It would be hard to imagine a man losing so much in the brief time since the coachman had seen him. Meriel's own father had tried to correct his financial fate for years, until it had all fallen apart.

Money didn't seem to be a strong enough reason for Mr. O'Neill's masquerade. Another reason could be the power of the dukedom, but if it were that, Mr. O'Neill must be biding his time, for he hadn't exercised much power. What made more sense was that he thought he was a better duke than his brother was, and needed to prove it.

But where was the real duke? Did every second's delay put him in greater danger?

The next day, the dinner guests started to arrive early in the evening. Richard moved between the small chatting groups in the drawing room, feeling more and more at ease when no one seemed uneasy or overly curious. The women wanted to be teased, and he was more than capable of doing that. The men wanted to laugh, so he had prepared some fictitious London stories guaranteed to make everyone believe he spent much of his time there.

His cousin Sir Charles Irving was the last to arrive. Richard studied him from the far side of the room, only slightly paying attention to the mama discussing the merits of her marriageable daughter. Charles was six years older than Richard, but he had kept himself in trim form. His favorite amusement was hunting, Richard remembered, whether it was fox or grouse. He rode endless hours in the saddle to keep himself well prepared. Whenever they'd been together as children, competition was something Charles relished, and winning was the only goal. His dark hair was gray at the temples, but that didn't stop other mamas from seeking him out. Richard wondered why he'd never married. Maybe he didn't want to spend his wealth on anyone but himself. Richard delayed their reacquaintance just enough to annoy Charles. When he finally approached his cousin, he thought Charles's eyes were narrowed in poorly concealed anger.

"A good evening to you, cousin," Richard said, oozing too much charm in Cecil's teasing manner. "I'm glad you could attend my reentry into hospitable society."

Charles smiled. "Your illness seems to be a thing of the past, Cecil."

"I am still a bit fatigued, but I'm resting well at Thanet Court."

"I'm glad to hear of it. And how is my young cousin, Stephen?"

Was that a deliberate taunt or an innocent inquiry?

"Doing well, thank you. He'll come down to greet everyone after dinner."

"I was hoping to see how much he'd grown since I last saw him."

As if Charles cared about children, Richard thought, remembering the special pleasure his cousin used to take in making other children cry.

Hargraves alerted him that dinner was ready, so Richard led his guests into the dining room. He had seated Charles far enough down the table so that he wouldn't have to speak to him during the meal.

After dinner, the women waited in the blue drawing room, and Richard made sure the men joined them after only one drink. He was anxious to finish this evening, to see Charles's reaction to Stephen and be done with it. After a game of charades, he sent for Meriel and Stephen.

The women oohed and aahed over the boy. Richard remained alone near a wall and watched

Charles. His cousin barely noticed the boy at all, which was surprising. Charles's gaze was fixed on Meriel, who had retreated to a window seat.

Charles approached her, and she rose to her feet. At first Richard couldn't hear what they said. He moved closer, standing just out of their line of sight, in time to hear Charles say, "For only six years old, Stephen is quite accomplished."

"You are being too kind, Sir Charles," Meriel said. "I have only been in charge of Lord Ramsgate's education for two months. But he is a bright, inquisitive boy, and he learns quickly."

How could it help Charles to put Stephen's governess at ease?

Unless he wanted easy access to the boy.

A governess would have no influence on whether Charles was named Stephen's legal guardian, should something happen to Cecil.

But of course, something had already happened to Cecil, and Stephen was vulnerable.

"So you are the duke's cousin," Meriel said, a bit too conversationally for a governess.

What was she up to?

Charles nodded. "I see you recognized my name."

"I've studied Lord Ramsgate's family, so that I can help him understand how everyone is related. Do you have any stories I can share with him about his father and his uncle?"

Richard was too surprised to interfere immediately.

Charles only laughed. "They were both younger than I, so we did not see much of each other. Our parents were not close. I'll be candid and admit that that was mostly my own mother's fault. Jealousy was not something she easily overcame."

"I wonder if that's a natural feeling between siblings," Meriel said.

"I wouldn't know."

If Meriel was fishing for information, it seemed Charles was not going to take the bait.

Richard approached them. "Charles, I see you've met my governess."

Meriel looked up at him with blank eyes, and he gave her a wide, innocent smile.

Charles saw it and looked between the two of them, but said nothing. Let him think what he would about Meriel and the duke—it was Stephen who was important.

"As usual, Cecil," Charles said, "you choose the loveliest of women."

Meriel took a deep breath, but said nothing, though her subtle anger was palpable.

"She was well qualified for the position," Richard said.

A mistake, for Charles's eyebrows rose. "I was not suggesting otherwise," he said.

Richard decided to change the subject. "I assume your estate is flourishing, as usual."

Meriel excused herself to return to her window seat.

"Do you remember that property I'd bought from Richard eight years ago?" Charles asked.

Richard nodded politely, but inside he tried to imagine every reason that Charles could be mentioning such a random thing.

"Of course you remember it, Cecil," Charles continued. "You were the one who forced Richard to sell his inheritance."

"You can't believe everything my brother says," Richard said dismissively.

"When you took his inheritance money, what else could he do but sell the land to begin investing?"

"Richard and I have gotten past that misunderstanding, Charles. You don't need to bring it up."

"You asked me how my estate was doing. That property I purchased from Richard has become a profitable farm since then. My tenants' harvest has succeeded my expectations year after year."

Richard smiled. "You always had a way with money."

"And you don't," Charles said bluntly. "You could use my help."

"To what are you referring?"

"You haven't made the wisest investments, Cecil. Good heavens, your clothing expenditures alone would feed a nation."

Richard laughed and clinked his glass with Charles's. "You can stop worrying about me, cousin. I've gone to my brother for advice."

Charles looked surprised. "Have you, Cecil?"

"I will admit I still have much to learn. That's why I'm here, taking control of my estates. We all grow up eventually."

"Ah, but not as far as your female servants are concerned, dear Cecil," Charles said. "Still choosing them all for their beauty—though I now realize that you don't want to say so in front of them. I regret the error with your governess. Have you chosen your latest mistress yet?"

Richard resisted the urge to sigh. He had thought flirting and debating his choice might work, but of course people outside the household wouldn't see that. They'd only see that the duke was not choosing a mistress.

"Charles, there are so many lovely women to choose from."

"I know. You even hired one away from me a few months ago," Charles said, shaking his head in a rueful manner. "You can be quite devious."

"But I offer them so much, Charles." Richard shrugged and donned an innocent smile. "They just can't help themselves. Now if you'll excuse me, Miss Barome obviously needs my assistance."

Meriel sat very quietly, withdrawn within her window seat, and watched with worry as the Impostor Duke left Sir Charles. She could see Miss Barome waving at Mr. O'Neill from across the room as she searched through sheet music at the piano.

Stephen was happily occupied with the wolfhounds, who were behaving themselves for the guests and performing their tricks on Stephen's command.

Meriel could see Sir Charles's profile. He still watched the man he thought was the duke, and though his face held no expression, the glacial coldness of his eyes chilled even her.

What was she to make of everything she'd overheard? Her own questions to Sir Charles had yielded nothing, but it was obvious that there was rancor between Sir Charles and—both the duke and his brother? It was difficult to tell, for Mr. O'Neill was a superb actor.

Sir Charles knew about the mistresses—maybe every man knew, and in the way of men, thought nothing of it. Meriel considered Mr. O'Neill's reaction, and she wondered how *he* felt, being forced to choose a mistress. Maybe his claim of indecision was actual . . . reluctance?

She didn't want to think well of him, and of

course there could be many reasons he did not choose a maid to seduce. He probably just didn't have the time, what with keeping his dark secret.

What was most shocking to her was that the real duke had cheated Mr. O'Neill out of some of his inheritance. That was a strong motive for Mr. O'Neill to seek revenge, or even to take the money back. But if it was only money, he could have obtained that easily by now, with his access to the accounts.

Sir Charles had hinted that the duke had financial problems. Maybe there wasn't enough actual currency for Mr. O'Neill to take. If his inheritance was what he wanted, then perhaps he found himself overseeing the dukedom to correct its finances. After all, maybe it was true that the real duke had come to his brother for help—and gotten himself kidnapped for his effort.

All the while she was thinking, Meriel kept a close eye on Stephen. The Impostor Duke had previously sent word that Stephen was not to wander the house alone while they had guests. Did that mean he thought she would lose the boy, and embarrass the duke? Or was this for Stephen's safety? If only she knew what Mr. O'Neill had in mind for his nephew.

She looked around for Sir Charles and found him conversing in a corner with several gentlemen, local landowners all. He was the closest family member Stephen had. Should she confide her worries to him?

But Sir Charles had come between the brothers. He'd deliberately bought property from the illegitimate son, and made sure to throw it back in the face of the duke, even years later.

No, she couldn't trust him, either. In his zeal against the duke—maybe he was jealous, just like his mother—he might go directly to the police. The element of surprise would be lost.

No, she was still in this alone.

When the dinner party was over, and the last guest—Renee—had gone home, Richard was approached by Hargraves, who wished to speak with him alone.

In Richard's study with the door closed, the butler's usual remote expression gave way to worry. "Your Grace, you wanted to know if Sir Charles did anything suspicious during the evening."

"Did he?"

"Yes. While you were occupied singing with Miss Barome, Sir Charles left the drawing room."

Richard sat back in his chair and swore. "Where did he go?"

"Since I had servants stationed all over the house, no one ever lost sight of him. I did have to tell everyone that you were worried about a thief, of course."

"Yes, yes," Richard said impatiently. "But what did Sir Charles do?"

"Nothing, Your Grace. He simply walked from room to room and . . . looked."

"Looked?"

"He studied portraits and sculptures, almost as if he'd never seen them before."

"As if he was cataloguing what was still here," Richard said softly. "He might believe that Cecil was selling things off to support his vices."

Hargraves could only shrug.

"And he was in sight of someone for the entire evening?"

"Yes, Your Grace."

"Very well. Thank you, Hargraves."

When the butler had gone, Richard stared unseeingly at his desk. What was Charles up to?

After a sleepless night revising his plans, Richard sent for Mrs. Theobald.

When she arrived in his room, looking concerned by such an unusual summons, Richard put a finger to his lips and closed the door, summoning her near the window.

"Mrs. Theobald, I need your help," he said in a soft voice. "My plan to flirt with the maids is not working."

"I know, young sir," she said, glancing worriedly at the door. "They're beginning to fight over you, keeping the servants' wing in an uproar with their arguing. And I hear from the head coachman that the grooms are grumbling over their betting."

Richard closed his eyes for a moment. "I'm sorry. This is not fair to you."

"You learned nothing from Sir Charles last night?"

"Nothing much. He is a cunning man. But when even *he* asked me about my mistress, I knew something had to change. I've decided to choose one."

Her eyes widened as she searched his face. "You'll . . . do such a thing, young sir?"

"Not really, of course, but I can pretend. And the only one who'll fight me is Miss Shelby."

"Oh, sir, she'll be terribly angry. She insisted I inform you she'll never be your—the duke's—mistress."

"Then that's perfect, isn't it? I don't want a real mistress. She can refuse me all she wants, and it will look like for the first time a woman has said no. And of course I won't give up my pursuit."

"A woman did say no once, young sir, and the duke respected her wishes. Miss Shelby knows this."

"Ah, but I'm smitten this time, Mrs. Theobald.

I'll continue to pursue Miss Shelby, in hopes that I'll be rewarded."

She frowned.

"I mean that's what the duke would hope," Richard quickly said. "I personally know she's too proud to ever give in."

"But won't it seem like you would eventually give up, as you did the last time?"

Now it was his turn to frown. "Hopefully it won't come to that. But I have no choice. I have to stop the maids from fighting, and I have to *be* the duke. So today I need you to prepare a picnic lunch. I'm going to begin wooing the object of my affections."

Chapter 15

Meriel and Stephen were studying a globe in the library when the Impostor Duke made a grand entrance. She looked up to see him flinging back the doors, carrying a large basket.

"Stephen, you must be hungry," Mr. O'Neill said.

Meriel frowned at him in suspicion. "It is almost time for our luncheon, Your Grace. I'm certain Mrs. Theobald will send our meal up to the nursery, as she always does."

"Not today. I've told her you'll be dining with me. Stephen, shall we have a picnic?"

The little boy was beside himself with eagerness. "Can we take Victoria and Albert, too?"

"Of course we can."

Meriel would have done anything to remain at home—except put Stephen at risk. And by the slyly amused expression Mr. O'Neill wore, he guessed her feelings. But that didn't stop him from languidly sweeping his gaze over her behind Stephen's back. His amusement faded, and the smoldering look that replaced it made an answering heat blossom inside her. She wouldn't let this happen—but that didn't stop her body from responding.

The dogs were already out in the corridor, and they followed their master and Stephen adoringly, leaving Meriel to bring up the rear. She refused to look at the man as he walked, for that wouldn't help her physical reaction to subside.

As they walked down the spacious corridor, she noticed the servants peeking out from various rooms to watch. Then to her mortification, Mr. O'Neill suddenly decided to wait for her and took her arm to pull her along between them—right in front of Beatrice and Clover. Meriel had to turn away from their angry, disappointed faces.

Her arm was tense linked with his, and she subtly tried to pull away, but he refused to relinquish his grasp. His arm was warm and very hard, and the curve of muscle made her feel flustered.

On her other side, Stephen was skipping to keep up with them, and when he put his hand in hers, she softened and stopping fighting his uncle.

"You must continue Stephen's lesson on the walk," Mr. O'Neill said. "When we're outside, you can tell us the names of all the flowers we pass."

The sun seemed to burst upon them as they stepped outdoors. It was a rare, warm summer so far, and she didn't even regret her lack of a bonnet. She finally was able to disentangle herself from Mr. O'Neill, so that she could point out the various flowers and plants. She didn't know how much of it Stephen actually absorbed in his excitement, but she felt calmer being able to talk. The dogs cavorted beside them, and after one word from their "master," they stayed out of the flower beds.

They were only a hundred yards past the stables in a small clearing when Mr. O'Neill said, "Let's spread our blanket right here."

"In full view of the outdoor staff?" Meriel asked suspiciously.

"I have a meeting early in the afternoon, so I can't be too far from the house. Stephen, take the blanket and find us the perfect spot."

The little boy did as he was asked, and though Meriel attempted to follow him, once again

Mr. O'Neill took her arm and slowed her down. She could feel every groom and stable lad gawking at them.

"You're doing this deliberately," she said in a low voice.

"Doing what?" he asked, full of innocence.

"Touching me while in a public place. What other purpose could there be?"

"A father needs no other reason than being with his son for a picnic."

"You'll get your garments stained. Surely you can't want that."

"Stop fighting, Meriel, or I'll hold your hand next."

She pulled away and glared at him. They both heard the hoots of laughter from the outdoor staff.

"I did not give you permission to use my Christian name, Your Grace—and you would not dare touch my hand in front of your son."

He sighed. "No, I would not dare. But what he can't see—"

She groaned and stomped away from him to help Stephen, who was struggling to lay out the large blanket. The dogs kept lying on it.

Meriel understood that Mr. O'Neill was deliberately wooing her in front of the servants to prove himself the duke. But at least he was being very public about it, rather than cornering her alone, where her strength to resist would be so much harder to maintain.

When she and Stephen had the blanket laid flat, she was startled when something brushed her skirts. It was the Impostor Duke as he moved past her to lay himself out on the blanket, hands behind his head.

She put her fists on her hips. "Yes, it was a terribly long walk from the house, Your Grace. You must be exhausted."

Stephen laughed. "That's sarcasm, Father! Miss Shelby taught me what the word means."

"Sarcasm?" Mr. O'Neill echoed. "And it's so unnecessary, Stephen. Miss Shelby doesn't understand how tiring it is to host a successful dinner party."

"Especially when you have servants to do all the work," she said.

"She's doing it again!" Stephen said gleefully.

Meriel couldn't help smiling at the little boy as she ruffled his unruly hair. "Why don't you see what's in the picnic basket, my lord?"

She knelt on the far side of the blanket from Mr. O'Neill and watched as Stephen unearthed cold chicken and fruit and cheese, along with stoppered bottles of lemonade. The dogs sat beside him and attempted to look pathetic and hungry. Stephen wanted to serve the adults, and she bit back a smile as he carefully set out plates and napkins.

"There aren't any forks," Stephen said, burying his face in the basket to look.

"We don't need them." Mr. O'Neill came up on his elbow. "Chicken tastes better when you eat with your fingers."

Stephen giggled and dug in. Meriel stayed focused on her pupil and her food, but when she was licking her fingers, she glanced up and realized that Mr. O'Neill was watching her, his smile fading. She froze with one finger in her mouth. Something unnameable flashed between them. It was awkward and riveting and . . . exhilarating. She looked away and quickly found a napkin. The sun was suddenly overly hot, and she wished for a bonnet to hide behind.

"Father, have you ever boxed?" Stephen asked.

She sighed with relief when Mr. O'Neill's attention left her.

"Yes, I have," he said. "Many gentlemen box for recreational purposes."

"What does that mean?"

"We box for fun."

Meriel glanced at Mr. O'Neill witheringly. "Hurting other men is fun?"

He grinned. "The object is not to get hit, Miss Shelby. Stephen, how have you heard of boxing?"

"The grooms box, but they were worried I'd get hurt."

She nodded solemnly. "You are far too young for such things, my lord."

"Father, can you teach me?"

"Lord Ramsgate," she began, "I still think—"

"I can teach you a little," Mr. O'Neill interrupted, "but it is not a sport you should attempt without me."

That mollified her somewhat, and she held her tongue when Stephen pulled his uncle to his feet. To her shock, Mr. O'Neill began to disrobe. He flung his coat down where he'd been lying, and his waistcoat followed. Even his cravat and stock were dropped to the ground, and she finally looked up past his long legs to find him grinning down at her as he rolled up his shirtsleeves and unbuttoned several shirt buttons. She was relieved when he finally joined Stephen, instead of looming over her, inspiring dangerous thoughts.

Off toward the house, she could see the stable boys sitting along fences, waiting for the show. And Mr. O'Neill provided it. He taught Stephen how to hold up his fists to protect his face, and how to throw a punch. He was light on his feet as he moved around the little boy. Meriel hated that she noticed how his damp shirt clung to his back, outlining the width of muscle, and the narrowness of his hips where the shirt disappeared into his trousers. She was glad that she could pretend it was the heat that made her fan herself.

She was more than relieved when they moved on to the next sport, archery. She was skilled at it, but she did not mention it. Sitting and drinking her lemonade was all she wanted to do, as a groom brought bows and arrows, and a target was set up against a bundle of hay. Stephen's arrows all missed their target, and one even sailed into the lower branches of a tree.

The exercise and the sun were finally affecting Stephen, because he pouted at the thought of losing one of the arrows. Mr. O'Neill lifted him to reach it, but his fingertips were still a foot away.

Stephen came running toward her as she was packing up the basket. "I can't reach it, Miss Shelby," he said, sniffing back tears. "But you can."

"I'm certainly not tall enough, my lord."

"But if my father lifts you, you'll be just right. Come on!"

"Lord Ramsgate, I cannot possibly allow your father to lift me into a tree!" she protested, hearing her voice rise unprofessionally.

But he was pulling on her hands, and for the first time since her initial week here, she thought he might disintegrate into tears. He took his embarrassment seriously, and the last time he'd cried in front of servants, he hadn't wanted to leave the nursery for days. How would he feel crying in front of his father? And wouldn't

Mr. O'Neill insist on her help anyway, just to annoy her?

She found herself on her feet, Stephen dragging her forward. Mr. O'Neill was leaning against the base of the tree, his white shirt bright in the shade, his dark eyes showing nothing but amusement.

With every step closer, a voice inside her rose ever higher, telling her that this was a bad idea. She stumbled to a halt in front of him.

"Use her, Father," Stephen said, giving her a push.

Mr. O'Neill caught her arm, and she shivered at even that contact.

"Turn around."

Was his voice rougher than normal? She couldn't decide, even as she obeyed.

And then his hands were on her waist. Oh, there were plenty of layers between their skin, but just the strength of him took her breath away. He lifted her, and she felt the pressure on her rib cage, in her back. She went higher and higher, her feet dangling.

"Reach for the arrow!" he said.

She was shocked to feel the movement of his jaw against her backside as he spoke. Her trembling fingertips brushed the arrow.

"Higher!" she cried.

He groaned, but soon she had the arrow in her

hand. She looked over her shoulder to see Stephen on his knees in the dirt across the meadow, not even paying attention anymore.

And then Mr. O'Neill was letting her down, but so slowly as to make her want to scream with frustration. He was deliberately brushing against her. Her backside slid down the length of his chest, and even lower, across his hips. She was not a naive girl, unaware of a man's hidden form, so she understood the protrusion just above his thighs. It should disgust her.

But when her feet touched the ground, she could not move for a moment. She was overcome by a wave of longing and desire so fierce that it shocked her. Everything she knew about him didn't matter in that moment when they were still touching. She wanted his attention; she wanted to be with him in ways she could hardly imagine.

"Stop it," she whispered, not daring to look over her shoulder at him.

"I can't. I won't."

She felt his lips against her head. His hand moved, sliding forward around her stomach—

Tossing an angry look at him, she pulled herself away and strode to Stephen. Every stable boy and groom on the estate had witnessed the duke's crude assault. He could have shouted his lascivious intentions from the windows and reached fewer people.

He'd *chosen* her.

She was trapped.

At dinner that night, there were enough flowers to begin another conservatory. Stephen giggled at this new game. When she retired to her room for the evening, she found several new carpets and pillows, even a more comfortable chair by the hearth.

She collapsed into her new chair and put her face into her hands. What was she supposed to do? She still had no clue what the Impostor Duke's intentions were—except for attempting to ruin her reputation.

And poor Stephen, who was so enjoying his father's attention—he would never be the same when he discovered he was being tricked.

She picked up the letter she'd received in today's post. It was from her new brother by marriage. He had sent her a generous allowance, which he hadn't needed to do. It was enough for her to leave, to anticipate beginning a new life.

But she couldn't.

Childishly, she pounded one foot on the floor.

After a second, someone pounded back.

Oh God, she'd forgotten that the master suite was right below the nursery. The man who haunted her days and nights was but a staircase away.

She tucked her feet beneath her and tried to concentrate on the other letter she'd received, from her sister Victoria, the new bride. More and more, Victoria's optimism was proving well founded. She and her husband were slowly becoming happier with each other.

Meriel was relieved for Victoria—and selfishly sad for herself, trapped in a mystery she had to unravel for the sake of a little boy, drawn to the criminal himself.

But the next afternoon was no better. Meriel was forced to go along in a rowboat across a pond. Again, she was treated to the Impostor Duke coatless, cravatless, and damp from splashing water. Stephen sat in the bow so he could see where they were going, leaving Meriel in the back, an umbrella over her head, facing Mr. O'Neill as he rowed.

He didn't bother to hide his interest. And he wasn't looking at her face. He smiled and let his gaze roam down her body as if she were a piece of art he owned. And everywhere he looked, her skin sizzled. She'd worn the plainest gown with the highest collar, and still it wasn't enough. Would she have to start binding her breasts just to keep them better hidden?

She deliberately dipped the umbrella so that her face was blocked from him. But still his feet were on either side of hers in the tiny rowboat, just under the hemline of her skirt, she realized with dismay. Then he lifted his toes, and her skirt rose a few inches, revealing her black shoes. She gave him a murderous glare from beneath her umbrella, then drove her booted heel onto his foot. He winced silently, grinned, and wobbled his eyebrows.

She had to wipe the smugness off his face somehow, and she recklessly didn't care if she endangered herself to do it. "Your Grace, Stephen tells me he has an uncle. Why did you not have a portrait painted with your brother?"

His smile faded a bit, and he put more effort into his rowing. Now that she had the upper hand, she let herself admire how the damp shirt stretched across his muscled arms.

"The duke and duchess wouldn't allow such a painting," he said, in a voice as smooth as ever.

Was he truly so unruffled? "Why not?"

"Forgive the crudeness, Miss Shelby, but my brother was born on the wrong side of the blanket."

If it still hurt him, he didn't show it. He'd made a success of his life. He had nothing left to prove. So why was he here, pretending to be a duke?

"Father, stop so I can see the school of fish!" Stephen called, pointing into the water.

Mr. O'Neill put up his oars, then casually grabbed hold of the boy's shirt as he leaned over the edge. The perfect father.

Yet he never took his eyes off Meriel.

"Your brother's birthright was surely not his fault," she said.

"No. And he never let it come between us."

If only she could figure out the truth from the lies.

"Stephen tells me that his uncle grew up here with you. He was older, yes?"

"Five years."

"A vast distance when you're young."

"Not so vast."

"Did his mother live here, too?"

He rested one hand on the bench behind him and crossed his feet, his toes tangling in her skirt once more. She didn't look down this time, knowing he wanted to distract her.

"No, my father gave her a house of her own, right here on the estate. That was more generous than most men would have been."

"You admired your father?"

"Of course."

"But how generous could he really have been, when he wouldn't allow her son to live with her?"

She had to admire him, how perfectly normal he kept his expression, polite and amused. She realized she might be hurting him and found herself again sympathetic. It was the woman in her, when she should remain the detective.

"My father was generous enough to house and educate Richard," he said about himself. "Fiona

O'Neill knew it was for the best. The duke gave her son what he could, including an inheritance."

She lowered her voice, glad that Stephen was so distracted. "But I heard Sir Charles say that you cheated him of it."

He laughed. "And you believe that envious man?"

"Why would he be envious? He's wealthy, isn't he?"

"But he's not the duke. I am."

You're not, she thought. Did Mr. O'Neill deliberately taunt her, suspecting she knew the truth?

He leaned toward her, and his eyes drifted down her bodice and back up again. "Are you accusing a duke of a crime, Meriel?"

She stiffened. "I have not given you permission—"

"Are you accusing me of a crime?"

"I heard you tell Sir Charles that it was a misunderstanding."

"My brother would say the same thing."

"Would he?"

Even she did not know which brother they were talking about now.

From the bow, Stephen asked plaintively, "Why are you fighting?"

Chapter 16

Richard heard the pain in the little boy's voice. He'd almost forgotten that Stephen was with them in the boat. All that had mattered was Meriel Shelby, and her suspicions and her many temptations.

Stephen was all that *should* matter.

He saw the wide, dismayed look in Meriel's eyes, even as he turned to drag the boy into his lap. It was the first time he'd allowed himself to hold his nephew. Stephen squirmed and giggled.

"Now, young man," Richard said in a deep voice, "you're throwing accusations at us. We weren't fighting, we were having a spirited discussion. Should I toss you overboard?"

He dangled one of Stephen's feet over the edge, and the boy laughed aloud.

"Father! You're teasing me!"

Meriel leaned toward them and looked Stephen in the eye. "My lord, I'm sorry we upset you. We were being too serious and forgot this was supposed to be an afternoon of fun."

"Then keep rowing," Stephen said. "We need to reach the far side!"

Richard obliged his nephew, rowing even harder, so the little boy laughed with glee. Meriel put a hand on the boat to steady herself, but otherwise she kept the umbrella over her head and stared out across the water, away from Richard.

And he looked his fill. His muscles ached, he was sweating, but that only made him think of other ways he wanted to ache. They involved a bed—and Meriel.

He could still feel her delicate waist when he'd lifted her to reach the arrow; he hadn't wanted to let her go, but the process of doing so was a pleasurable torture, with her sliding down against him. Now his feet were beneath her skirts, where the rest of him wanted to be.

He was fast forgetting that this could be only a pretend seduction. Her every response—reluctant, innocent, yet obviously aroused—inflamed him more every hour of each day.

Her room was above his; she slept so close. He imagined using that private staircase to reach her. Who would know?

But although she might desire him, she was taunting him, too. She had very deliberately brought up his own life story to distract him. Was that because Charles's careless comments about the inheritance had intrigued her? Or was she truly suspicious of the "duke"?

He didn't know how much longer he could continue his attempts to seduce her, not without driving her away. And then he'd have to choose another maid. He told himself that they were very willing—it was he who balked at the thought of sex with his female staff, especially when he was lying about his identity.

How much longer would Cecil be away? And was his illness getting worse? Cecil had refused to allow Richard to contact him. Only if there was a true emergency could Richard send a letter to Cecil's solicitor in London, and it would be forwarded. And who knew how long that would take.

But Charles had done nothing overly suspicious at the dinner party, beyond asking about Stephen and trying to ingratiate himself with the governess. Maybe Cecil was imagining plots where there weren't any.

* * *

When Meriel went to bed, she found a tiny box on her pillow. She knew who it was from, and she opened it angrily. A diamond pendant winked at her by candlelight, and she gaped at it.

He wasn't going to stop, she realized. He was going to push and push until he forced her to leave Stephen. She couldn't let that happen. Somehow she had to make him understand that it was cruel to take advantage of servants—or to do so merely to prove one was really the duke.

Beyond thinking rationally, she threw on her dressing gown, clutched the diamond bribe in her fist, and walked down the corridor to the private staircase leading to the master suite below.

She hurried down the stairs and knocked firmly before she could change her mind. When she heard nothing, she knocked again, then leaned her ear against the wooden door. She heard a faint call to come in.

She flung open the door, and it cracked against the wall, making her jump. She didn't see the Impostor Duke anywhere.

"Where are you?" she demanded, walking into the room. It was elegant, with massive old furniture and a carved ceiling. Were naked sculptures of women holding up the mantel?

She stalked past an open door, then came to a

halt when candlelight caught her eye. Mr. O'Neill was lying in a sunken tub, water up to his neck. She was too far away to see anything beneath the water. Moisture glistened on his face, and through his slicked-back hair. Surely she must be gaping at the erotic, sensual image he formed.

"Care to join me?" he asked. "There's plenty of room."

She gasped and stepped out of the doorway, putting her back against the wall and struggling to remember what she had even meant to say. Luckily, she still had the box clutched in her hand. "We need to talk. Come out of there at once."

"Very well."

She heard a lot of splashing and closed her eyes. It didn't stop her imagination from racing away with her.

"But I must warn you," he continued. "I have no clothes in here."

"Stop!" she cried. Frantically, she looked around the room. "Where are your clothes—I'll toss them to you."

"I already have a towel. It'll be enough for now."

"No!"

She ran past the washroom, headed for the staircase. This had been a terrible idea. She should have confronted him in the morning. Just as she reached the stairs, she heard him advancing behind her. He grabbed a handful of her dressing gown, stopping her on the first step.

"So why did you come to see me?" he asked.

"Release me!" she said without turning around.

"Not until you tell me what prompted your unexpected but well-timed visit."

She tossed a tiny box over her shoulder. It hit something—his naked chest?—and bounced to the ground. She thought he retrieved it, but he kept his hold on her.

"Ah, you came to tell me how much you appreciated my gift."

"Appreciated—" she began in an appalled voice.

She slapped at his hand. He released her, and she spun to face him, keeping her gaze on his face. Moisture spiked eyelashes that framed black, indecipherable eyes. He looked down her body, and she knew he realized she was wearing her nightclothes. She should be frightened, but she was too angry for that.

"You gave me diamonds!" she cried.

His mouth turned up in a grin. "Lovely, aren't they?"

"You gave your *governess* a diamond necklace! Do you know how that looks?"

"Exactly how I mean it to look."

He fully intended to keep up this seduction!

"You are insufferable!" She pointed a finger at him. "I don't want your diamonds, or your carpets and chairs. I don't want boat rides where I have to fend off your rude advances in front of a child. I want to do my work without any interference from you!"

"That won't happen," he said, his voice low and rough. He picked up a curl of her hair and rubbed it between his fingers. "I can't help myself. You are far too lovely to resist."

"Choose a willing woman, for I shall never be one. And while you're at it, stop giving diamonds that aren't yours!"

Momentarily shocked and dismayed by what she'd revealed, she realized that it was too late to take back the words. Squaring her shoulders, she glared at him.

"Not mine?" he said softly. "Why would you say that?"

"They must be for your future wife." She knew she was a terrible liar, and she couldn't meet his skeptical gaze. But that left her staring at his chest, still wet from the bath. Scattered hair could not conceal the lean, well-defined muscles. His abdomen rippled downward, and she followed the path laid out for her with a feeling of fate she didn't bother to fight. The towel was tucked around his waist, and she thought it might reveal more than it hid. His bare feet seemed like the last indecent straw.

How could she think about his nearly naked body, when she'd just clearly told him that she knew the truth! She tried to escape up the stairs again, but he caught her arm and pulled her inside the room, firmly shutting the door. The double doors on the far side of the room might as well have been on the far side of the mansion.

"Don't bother trying to run," he said, "because I can reach them first. Why don't you say what you've been keeping inside?"

"Why don't you?" she countered, pulling away from him and crossing her arms over her chest.

"This is not a game of dare, Meriel."

"You're the one who's treating this like a game! How could you do this to Stephen?"

"You mean my son?" he said quietly.

"He's your nephew!"

The silence between them stretched taut as they stared at each other.

He came toward her, his stride still elegant, still so graceful. How had she not seen from the beginning that he wasn't the duke? That he wasn't that silly, arrogant, childish man? Richard O'Neill was an adult—dangerous and unknown.

"Why do you say that?" he asked.

"Oh, please, do you need me to explain everything to you? You are Richard O'Neill. What have you done with your brother?"

There, it was out in the open, and the relief of not trying to couch her words was great. But she'd unmasked him; how desperate was he? And what would he do to keep her silent?

To her surprise, he turned away from her and ran his hands through his wet hair, then rested one hand on the back of his desk chair. In a low, tired voice, he said, "Cecil is fine . . . I think."

She stilled. "What do you mean, 'you think'?"

"He was in recovery from consumption when he demanded I submit to this insane masquerade."

She was still closer to the door—she could make it into the corridor before he could catch her. But what would that do for her? She'd just have to leave Thanet Court and never return, making Stephen even more vulnerable. And now her curiosity was far too great not to want the whole story.

"The duke asked you to portray him?" She took a step closer so that she could keep her voice soft.

He glanced up at her, his expression resigned, even sad. She had never seen him look like a real person instead of an arrogant duke. She kept telling herself that he was a criminal, but she wanted to hear his reasons.

"Cecil didn't want anyone to know how serious

his illness was, how slowly he was recovering. He thought it made him look weak."

"Then he should have just retired to the country where his London friends couldn't see him."

"You don't know my brother," he said heavily. "His vanity is everything to him. And he knew if he didn't get away, he wouldn't be able to resist being out among society."

"It seems a weak reason for a successful man like you to leave his own life behind."

He arched an eyebrow, but that slight amusement was gone. Was it only the duke's?

"So you know about me?" he asked.

"I know a bit, especially after I became suspicious and made some discreet inquiries."

"Discreet? I would not call our conversation about me this afternoon as discreet."

"Well, no, but . . . you were provoking me."

"And you were trying to distract me."

He looked down her body again, and she wished for the layers of clothing to protect her.

"Did it work?" she asked, feeling a little breathless and hating herself for it.

"A little."

"But *I'm* not distracted, Mr. O'Neill. Why would you go along with such an insane request from your brother? Especially when he was the one who pretended to be you when you were children, not vice versa."

He smiled and shook his head. Even his smile seemed different to her, more guarded.

"You have sisters, Meriel. What wouldn't you do for them?"

She felt a chill of recognition. She and her sisters had made a pact to hide the truth of their father's suicide.

"It's a fine line to cross when your family is asking for help," he continued. "Cecil . . . Cecil is my brother. He wanted me to remain a part of his family, even when our father kept himself distant, even when our mothers objected. That portrait you looked at?"

There was a note of bitterness in his voice now.

"Cecil wanted the two of us together in it, and his mother refused. He said because we looked alike, it would be ours to share, our secret. I know that he's become a foolish man, who does thoughtless, stupid things, considers no one but himself. But when he was a little boy, he still wanted to include me, and didn't want me to be hurt. When he asked for this favor, I couldn't refuse him."

She didn't want to empathize with him. She had been so blessed to have two sisters she adored, whom she could count on for anything.

But she had no idea if a man who could pretend to be another so easily was capable of spinning an even greater web of lies. He seemed truthful about his relationship to the duke. But . . .

"Mr. O'Neill, I would find it easier to believe you if it weren't so obvious that you *like* being the duke."

His jaw clenched, and his eyes narrowed, but she still wasn't afraid.

"Meriel, you'll never know how hard it was to become something that I despise. My father wasn't a nice man, and I fear that Cecil is becoming more and more like him every day. You aren't as knowledgeable as you think, if you imagine that a man raised as I was could *enjoy* this way of life."

"I think you protest too easily," she said, giving her voice a coolness she didn't necessarily feel. Then she used the lie she'd prepared to protect herself in case this situation ever happened. "I've already spoken to Mrs. Theobald about my suspicions, since I don't trust you. If I don't appear tomorrow, she'll know what happened."

He started to laugh, and even his laughter was deeper, harder, different. He sank into a chair and crossed his legs before her. The edge of the towel slid down one thigh, but she didn't dare look away.

"She already knows everything," he said.

Meriel just stared at him, knowing that he'd given her a way to judge the truth. Or the truth he wanted her to know.

"I couldn't hide from her—Hargraves, either," Mr. O'Neill said. "I'll make sure to tell her she can speak freely with you. But if you risk my position here, risk Cecil's reputation, risk Stephen's heart—"

"You'll what, Mr. O'Neill? Kill me?"

"That is an ugly thing to say to a man doing a favor for his brother."

"You're living your brother's life—I'm supposed to trust that you're doing him a *favor*?"

"Meriel," he said, his voice full of warning.

"And did you just dare to talk to me about risking Stephen's heart? You, who've led him to believe that his father has grown to love him?"

For the first time, he looked away. "Cecil loves him. He just never learned how to show it."

"But you did, and you were raised together."

"But raised very differently, Meriel. If you lived in a peer's household, you'd know that."

"Your excuse is a poor one, *Your Grace*," she said with sarcasm. "That boy's disappointment will be a terrible thing."

He leaned his head back in the chair, looking exhausted again. "That is what I most worry about. But I can't change it now."

"Then be more like his real father! And find the duke, for heaven's sake. End this!"

"I can't, to any of your requests. I owe Cecil.

And I need to be with Stephen, the nephew I never was able to know."

"Because the duke kept you apart."

He didn't answer.

"And you claim you're doing all this on that man's whim? I can only hope you hurt fewer people than you think you will."

She walked toward the door to the private staircase.

"Meriel, you can't talk about this with anyone other than Mrs. Theobald and Hargraves. Promise me."

Of all the nerve! She would make her own decision about going to the police, but she wasn't going to discuss that with him. She stalked back and stood over him in anger. "Then you promise me you'll stop this attempt at seduction."

He shook his head. "I can't. I have to be Cecil, and he chooses a mistress every month. He's a fool, but I can't change him now."

"Then pick someone else!" she cried.

He came to his feet, and suddenly there was too much bare skin before her, drawing her gaze.

"Meriel," he murmured, "you're the only one I can trust to resist me."

She tossed her head and scoffed. "You think you're that irresistible?"

He pointed to the double doors. "To those

women I am. They expect to be in my bed, and I could never—"

He broke off, and she wondered what emotion he didn't want her to see.

"You're developing scruples now?" she asked bitterly.

"I'll do some things for my brother, but not that. So expect to be pursued, Meriel, and you do your best to resist me."

She was outraged now. "You sound like you think I won't be able to!"

He came closer and she stood her ground, expecting to feel repulsed now that she knew the truth—or some of the truth.

But her anger was threatened with a sinful feeling of desire that licked at her insides like a small flame, threatening to turn into an inferno. She'd felt this since she'd first met him, the Impostor Duke, a man whose very body called to hers. But she wouldn't back down, wouldn't let him know that he had any kind of control over her.

His head was above hers, his chest so very near that if she inhaled too deeply, her breasts would touch him.

"Resist me, Meriel," he said softly.

His breath disturbed the curls near her forehead; his eyes looked deep into hers.

Again, he said, "Resist me, Meriel, because God

help me, I don't want to resist what you make me feel."

She put her hand on his chest to push the threat of him away, but her palm felt scalded, and her will was suddenly not her own. Her logic had flown, and she was swamped by reckless emotion, a woman who'd spent her life fighting this loss of control.

His hand cupped her face, and he leaned into her. She remembered the sinfully wonderful touch and taste of his mouth. Every kiss she'd ever experienced seemed like a childish peck on the cheek compared to the hot, overwhelming way he made her feel.

And he was admitting that he shared her emotions.

Or was he just trying to control her, to keep her from revealing his secret?

She pushed hard and stumbled back just before their lips met. "Your seduction won't work. I know who you are. You're a liar, and I'll never trust the word of a liar again."

She turned her back and ran up the stairs to the nursery, barely remembering to lighten her step as she walked down the corridor past Stephen's room. When she was in her own room, she collapsed on the bed and hugged a pillow to her chest, desperate to find a way to ease the ache that never went away inside her.

That man knew her weakness for him, and he would try to find a way to exploit it. He was already exploiting her fondness for Stephen, trusting that she wouldn't want to hurt the child any more than necessary.

But Stephen would find out eventually. If Meriel went to the police now, she could end his suffering before it grew worse.

But she was still stuck in the same frozen position—no proof, no means to prove her case. All she could do was talk to Mrs. Theobald and gauge her opinion. If the housekeeper was being forced to keep quiet, if the woman's instincts also said this was a dangerous situation, then together they could go to the police.

Meriel didn't trust anything Richard O'Neill said. He was a man who would use his body to convince her to keep silent. That kind of man could be up to anything.

Chapter 17

After Meriel had gone, Richard dressed quickly, silently, in case she decided to eavesdrop. He went through the silent house in the dark, knowing his way since childhood to the servants' wing. He slipped into Mrs. Theobald's sitting room unannounced, but knocked quietly on her bedroom door. She opened it after a few minutes and stared up at him in surprise.

"Your Grace, is something wrong?" she asked, tying the sash of her dressing gown.

"Meriel knows who I am."

"Oh dear," the housekeeper said, walking past

him to take a seat on the sofa in her sitting room. "Is she going to the police?"

"I don't think so," he said, sitting down opposite her. "After all, what proof does she have? But she doesn't trust my reasons, and of course I don't blame her, because I didn't tell her everything. That's why I'm here. I know she'll come to you for confirmation in the morning."

"Then tell me what you said, young sir. I'll be very convincing."

He smiled with relief. "I know you will. The only excuse I gave her was that Cecil didn't want people to know how ill he is. I didn't tell her anything about Charles. I'm worried that if she sensed a threat to the boy, she'd go out of her way alone to investigate Charles."

"She obviously considers herself a detective of sorts," Mrs. Theobald said thoughtfully, "since she was able to discover your identity, and she a newcomer to the household."

"Exactly." He rested his elbows on his knees as he leaned forward. "I'm antagonizing her with this flirting, but I told her I couldn't stop."

Mrs. Theobald raised an eyebrow.

He quickly said, "Because I need to look like Cecil. You know that."

"Of course, sir."

Richard felt foolish and transparent. Mrs. Theobald must see how easy it was for him to pursue Meriel. He rose to his feet. "I'm going to tell Hargraves what I've told you. But I'm certain she'll come to you first."

Mrs. Theobald saw him to the door. "Have no fear, Your Grace. I can handle myself with the intelligent Miss Shelby."

After having a talk with the butler, Richard finally climbed into bed, feeling so exhausted, he thought he'd fall immediately to sleep.

Instead he stared at the ceiling—and wondered where Meriel's bed was above him. He tossed and turned, haunted by her wild mane of golden curls that had hung to her waist. Without her corset and petticoats, she was smaller, more delicate, but still rounded with femininity.

And she was a threat, a danger to his—and Cecil's—plans. He had to remember that, to treat her with caution so that she didn't believe she could solve all their problems. He wondered who had lied to her, to make her so wary of his motives.

On her morning break, Meriel visited Mrs. Theobald in her sitting room and was not surprised when the woman confirmed Mr. O'Neill's story.

Meriel gritted her teeth and walked away from the housekeeper to stare blankly out the window. "And you have no problem with this deception, Mrs. Theobald?"

The housekeeper came to her side. "Of course I do. But I was not consulted. Mr. Hargraves and myself discovered it on our own, as you did. What would you have me do? Mr. O'Neill is doing a favor for his brother the duke. Am I supposed to go against that?"

"Are you certain that's what he's doing?" Meriel demanded, facing the housekeeper.

Mrs. Theobald met her stare calmly. "Above all of the family, Mr. O'Neill is the one I would trust the most. He had the worst situation here as a child, and he handled it with more equanimity than most adults could have. He was kind to the servants, even respectful to the duchess, who went out of her way to make him out in a poor light, so the duke would throw him out. Mr. O'Neill never responded to her behavior."

"Maybe not then, but don't you think a childhood like that can eat away at a person? Maybe his bitterness built and built, and now he has an opportunity for some kind of . . . redemption, a way to prove that he was the one who deserved the title most of all."

Mrs. Theobald put her hand on Meriel's arm. "I understand why you could think that, but you wouldn't if you knew him. He's made a success of himself—isn't that the best revenge?"

Meriel sighed and closed her eyes. "But Mrs. Theobald, Stephen will be so hurt! Even if he never discovers the lie, the duke will return and ignore him once again. He'll think it's all his fault!"

"I trust the duke and his brother to make things right with the boy."

But Mrs. Theobald couldn't meet her eyes as she defended them.

Meriel had gone to the housekeeper hoping to feel relieved, and left feeling more disturbed than before. For some reason, she knew that a part of the puzzle still eluded her. Someone wasn't being truthful. She had no one to trust, including herself.

Early in the afternoon, Stephen went off to play with his nurse, leaving Meriel to plan out the next day's lessons. She was having a hard time concentrating, when her mind was still sorting through all the evidence about Mr. O'Neill that she'd uncovered.

And then she heard a pounding down the corridor, and Stephen came running in, his face wet with tears. Nurse Weston was right behind him, looking resigned.

"Miss Shelby," Stephen said, "do you know where my father is?"

She tensed, suddenly uncertain about whom the boy actually meant. Before she could even think up an appropriate response, Stephen hurried on.

"We were supposed to have a boxing lesson, and he never came!"

Nurse Weston shook her head. "I tried to explain to his little lordship that sometimes the duke is too busy to make time for him."

Meriel took the boy's hands. "My lord—"

He pulled away. "No, you're wrong! He promised me, and he hasn't broken a promise since he returned."

It dawned on Meriel that Stephen was right. Mr. O'Neill seemed to have devoted himself to spending time with his nephew, and for him to not even send word of a change of plans seemed unusual.

Meriel stood up. "My lord, I'll go find him for you. Someone in the house will know where he is. He can make another appointment to be with you, and this time I know he won't forget."

Stephen stomped his foot. "We already did that! He's not in the house, and he's not anywhere in the park. We talked to Mr. Tearle the steward, and Hargraves and Mrs. Theobald. No one knows where he is. What if he's hurt?"

Nurse Weston scoffed at that, saying, "My lord, he simply forgot. People make mistakes, and you must learn to accept it and forgive. I'm certain he'll have a good excuse when he returns. Now let's go wash your face. And then perhaps a nap for the afternoon. You don't mind, do you, Miss Shelby?"

"Of course not. Lord Ramsgate, I'll see you when you wake up."

Stephen ran down the hall.

Nurse Weston lowered her voice. "I didn't have the heart to tell the poor lad that his father is probably in the arms of a woman as we speak."

Meriel tried not to blush. "So he's chosen his new mistress."

"I didn't think so, but maybe that's what he's doing right now. Of course, we all thought it was going to be you," she added with a shrug. Then she raised her voice. "Here I come, my lord."

Meriel had a bad feeling, a feeling she was learning not to ignore. She did not believe that Mr. O'Neill would sneak off with a woman and tell no one where he was. Especially when he'd seemed so convincing about choosing no one but Meriel.

But could everything he'd said have been a lie? Did Mrs. Theobald really know him after all these years?

Meriel tried to go back to her lessons, but she couldn't do it. She found herself wandering the house, until she finally had to admit to herself that she was looking for Mr. O'Neill.

Whenever anyone questioned her, she said she

needed to discuss his son with him, but some people still looked at her with embarrassed sympathy. Everyone must think he'd abandoned his seduction of her.

Why did she almost want to defend herself? Finally, she found someone who'd seen him that morning. One of the gardener's staff, a boy who usually pulled weeds all day, said he'd seen the duke walking into the woods. He pointed into the distance, past the orchard, where Meriel could see the beginning of a wooded copse she'd never explored before.

She considered and abandoned the thought of asking for help. What could she say that wouldn't sound ridiculous?

And what if Mr. O'Neill truly had gone off on an assignation with a servant? Meriel needed to know if nothing he said could be trusted. So she set off through the park, past the orchard, and down the gravel lane that slowly gave way to bare dirt. The gray sky overhead released a light shower, and she quickened her pace to enter the woods.

At first she walked briskly, for the trees were spaced far enough apart to let in the light. But soon everything grew closer together, and she began to wonder if perhaps this wasn't a wise decision. The path hardly looked well traveled, so she couldn't imagine it being a profitable place for a thief to work.

She was just about to turn around and head back in defeat, when she thought she heard something. She froze and looked about her, but all she saw were endless trees and the occasional bird flittering from branch to branch.

Her skin suddenly crawled with gooseflesh, as worry coalesced into fear for her own safety.

And then she heard a muffled groan.

"Hello?" she called tentatively.

She cocked her head to her right, where she thought the sound had come from. She heard twigs breaking, dead leaves scattering.

"Is someone there?" she demanded.

There was another groan, louder this time, and she took several steps off the path and peered around a large ash tree. Richard O'Neill was crumpled in a heap facedown on the ground.

She gasped and dropped to her knees beside him. "Your Grace? Your Grace? Can you hear me?"

He got one hand under him and tried to roll onto his back. She pushed his shoulder, and together they moved him until she could see his face. His eyes remained closed, shadowed by lines of pain, and blood trickled across his cheek, coming from his hair.

"Good heavens, what happened?" she asked, not at all certain what to do.

She tried to lift his head into her lap, but he

groaned, so she stopped, feeling helpless and afraid and suddenly very vulnerable in the dense woods.

Mr. O'Neill's eyelids fluttered, then finally opened, and he winced. "Have to go . . . have to protect him . . . Meriel?"

She leaned over him, her hand on his chest, feeling relieved at the steady beat of his heart. "I'm here. Shall I go for help?"

"Oh God, Stephen!" He gasped out the words, then came up on his elbows. He looked wide-eyed and frightened and not himself.

She put her arm beneath his shoulder, not sure if she was trying to comfort him or hold him. "Stephen's fine, I left him with Nurse Weston."

He shook his head back and forth. "But Charles . . . got to keep him from Charles . . ." His head lolled back against her shoulder.

She didn't understand what he was talking about; what had put him in this condition? Running her hand across his scalp, she found the large bump almost immediately. Her fingers came away sticky with blood.

Shocked, she stared about, wondering if he'd fallen. She didn't see a rock, or any mark on a nearby tree. But she did see a thick branch lying in the leaves about five feet away, one end covered in blood.

As if someone had hit Mr. O'Neill as he was walking by.

Could there be thieves in these woods, so close to the ducal estate? But surely if someone had meant to rob him, he would have done it already.

Unless she'd scared the thief away, and he was only waiting for a vulnerable moment . . .

"Your Grace, we have to get you back to Thanet Court. Can you stand?"

He tried to push away from her, but he was so weak, she could easily hold on to him.

"No," he murmured, "He can't know . . . his plan . . . worked."

"Who can't know?"

But he only shook his head, and she wondered if he was talking about his cousin, Sir Charles Irving. Mr. O'Neill had just said he needed to protect Stephen from him. She felt a chill of uncertainty and wished desperately that she knew what was going on. She'd had a premonition that he was keeping something from her. Did it really have to do with Stephen?

"Your Grace—"

He took several deep breaths, and she could see the calmness return to his eyes—or at least cover up his panic.

"There's—there's an old hunting lodge . . . another hundred yards down this path." He squinted and groaned and put a hand to his head. "Take me there."

"I don't know—"

Mr. O'Neill grasped her hand, and his eyes blazed darkly into hers. "He can't know he succeeded!"

Every instinct in her said that something was terribly wrong, that he'd lied to her about his purpose in masquerading as the duke. But she looked into his face, so full of desperation and worry, and could only help him. She'd question her own motives later.

"All right, can you stand up?" she asked.

Between the two of them, he was soon on his feet, shaky, leaning on her heavily, but seeming in no danger of falling down. With his arm around her shoulders, his body pressed tight to the length of hers, she felt almost shy and flustered, two things no other man had ever made her feel.

"Are you certain you can walk that far?" she asked.

He nodded and began to put one foot in front of the other. She led him out onto the path, and he tripped over a root, threatening to send them both sprawling.

"Your Grace—"

"I can do it," he said heavily.

The farther they walked, the more he leaned on her. The weight of him bent her spine and made her shoulders ache. Even her legs began to burn with pain.

The path curved, and there was the hunting lodge.

The front door hung ajar, and the shutters over the windows were broken in places. The roof was thatched, but a corner of that had somehow been stripped off to reveal the bare wooden slats of the ceiling. It looked like no one had hunted or lodged there in years.

"Your Grace, are you certain it's safe?"

He nodded. "Spent my . . . childhood here."

She glanced up at him curiously. He had his own secret place, just like her Willow Pond.

She helped him inside, and though the place smelled musty and damp, it was cozy enough. There was a small bare cot, a crooked wooden table, and two chairs that looked as if they might hold a child's weight. Mr. O'Neill leaned heavily on the table, then lowered himself into a chair. She winced, but it held him.

And then she saw the blood trickling down his neck from the gash in his head.

"You're still bleeding," she whispered. She put aside her feeling of helplessness and went to the battered cupboard in the corner. "Do you have supplies in here?"

He closed his eyes and shrugged. "We used to."

She found a bucket, a half-burned candle, flint and steel, a knife, and a couple of rags. She held a rag up with two fingers and grimaced.

"What did you use these for?"

He opened one eye. "Cleaning rabbit carcasses?"

"Ugh." She dropped it back in the cupboard.

"I'm just teasing. I can't remember. But there's a stream out back for washing."

She had no choice. She washed out the rags as best she could, filled the bucket with water, and came back inside. Mr. O'Neill was sitting up straighter, and his face was regaining some color.

She set to work, parting his hair until she could find the wound and cleaning it out as best she could. There were bits of tree bark to remove, but the blood flow itself had almost stopped.

"So you didn't see who hit you?" she said.

"No, he came from behind. Probably just a thief."

She straightened to see his face. "That's not what you implied."

"My head had just been dented. I'm sure I wasn't making sense." He gave her a lazy grin.

"Do not try to be Cecil with me. I will no longer be so gullible."

"I'm not trying—"

"You think by distracting me that I won't

remember what you said, how frightened you were for Stephen's safety? And you said it all had to do with your cousin Charles."

"I'm sure I didn't mean—"

"Richard!"

She used his Christian name in a forceful, angry tone.

He blinked up at her, so close, yet so far away.

"You're still lying to me," she said. "I knew it wasn't only Cecil's vanity at stake. That rationale just didn't make sense!"

But he was stubborn, remaining silent until she was finished cleaning the wound.

"Meriel," he said in a soft voice, "forget about this."

"I won't. I can't. If Stephen is in danger, I need to know."

"It's none of your business."

She glared at him. "Everything to do with Stephen is my business."

"I can take care of everything. This is just a misunderstanding."

She saw it now—his stubborn insistence on protecting her, as he was protecting Stephen. He was a liar and a cad . . . but maybe for the right reasons.

She didn't like how her feelings toward him were undergoing a rapid change. When he was just humoring his brother, playing tricks on all his staff and friends, she could despise him for the easy way he lied. And she hated liars.

But now that she knew he had deeper reasons for what he did—honorable reasons—her heart was melting, along with her resistance.

She needed to know the truth, and if her femininity would help, then she'd follow Richard's lead and do what she had to. She approached where he sat and stood between his legs, her skirts touching him. He suspiciously looked up at her, and she did what she'd wanted to do for so long. Putting her hands on his face, she looked into his eyes. He flinched but didn't draw away. His skin was warm, slightly damp, with the faintest rasp of whiskers along one side of his jaw where his new valet had missed a spot when shaving this morning.

Then he put his hands on her waist and pulled her even closer, so that her breasts were just below his face. She inhaled swiftly, but didn't struggle.

"Is this what you want?" he asked.

"I want the truth, Richard. You must tell me."

She looked into his eyes and willed the words to come out, but all he did was reach up and remove her spectacles, laying them behind him on the table. She found that she was trapped in his gaze, in the way he studied her face like a man who might never see again.

He kept her tight against him, even as he began to pull the pins from her hair. She should protest, she should pull away, but she stayed there, his arm around her, his thighs on each side of her.

Locks of her hair started cascading down around her shoulders, even falling forward to touch his cheek where her head was above him. He caught that curl between his fingers, smelling it with his eyes closed, then looked at her knowingly while he wrapped the hair about his finger, pulling her face closer and closer.

"Richard, tell me," she said, her mouth almost against his, their very breath mingling.

"I like how you say my name."

He tugged once more, and their lips met. The kiss was passionate and desperate and full of a temptation she'd never felt before meeting him. Inside her head a war began, with part of her saying, *Who would ever know?* and the other part insisting that she'd be going against everything she'd been taught to believe in.

But his mouth lured her; his tongue seduced her and made her forget everything but the two of them alone in the woods.

Where a villain had struck Richard down.

She broke the kiss. "The man who hit you could still be here."

"I doubt it." He cupped one side of her face,

and his thumb brushed her lips. "You taste . . . like the sweetest candy."

His touch, his words, made her knees suddenly weak. She was leaning heavily against him, and with one simple move, he swung her off her feet and across his lap. Now he was above her, cradling her.

"Richard, we can't do this. Stephen will be looking for me—for us. He's the one who knew you were missing. He was waiting to box with you."

He frowned and glanced at the open doorway. "You're right. When you drape yourself across me, it's difficult to think."

Aghast, she cried, "Drape myself—"

"Ah, Meriel, you are so easy to tease. Up you go."

He set her on her feet, then stood up beside her. He swayed once, and she caught his waist.

"No, no, I can't kiss you again," he said with a grin.

She ignored his teasing. "Will you be able to walk?"

"With you at my side, of course I can."

She put her hands in her hair, realizing her state. She surely looked like a woman who'd been well kissed by a man. How was she going to repair the damage?

Smiling, Richard held up his open palm and

showed her all the pins. "You didn't think I threw them on the floor, did you?"

"Your brother probably would have."

He arched a brow. "As you've already pointed out, I am not my brother."

And that was the frightening part. He was so much more appealing to her as a man rather than the duke. She turned her back on him and put up her hair as best she could. But it would be obvious to any woman that she'd done it herself, without the aid of a mirror.

Walking back through the woods, Richard leaned on her so much that she feared he would not make it. She had to keep one hand on his chest, just in case he pitched forward.

The closer they got to the open parkland, the more the rain showers dampened them. Just before they came into view of anyone on the grounds, Richard stepped away from her.

"Are you certain you can walk all the rest of the way alone?" she asked.

"I was able to conserve my strength with your help. I'll be fine." He cocked his head as he looked at her. "Your spectacles are rain-soaked and almost falling off your nose. Are you certain you can see like that?"

She found herself blushing. "I'll be fine."

He gave a slow grin. "You don't need them, do you?"

"Of course I do." That wasn't a lie. She'd needed to protect herself from employers like the duke—or his brother.

He shook his head. "It seems to me I'm not the only one wearing a disguise."

Chapter 18

Richard could not stop looking at Meriel, bedraggled from the rain, her hair lopsided, her spectacles useless. She looked . . . beautiful, stunning, and he could have gladly taken her back to the hunting lodge and—

And what? Seduced the virginal governess?

But he wasn't at Thanet Court to satisfy his own needs. He was here for Stephen, who now thought that his uncle had forgotten him—just as his father always had.

And he needed to see that Stephen was all right. How had he forgotten that?

"We'll talk about your spectacles another time," he said. "Let's get back to Stephen."

As they walked through the park, past the stables, through the gardens, he couldn't help noticing the attention they attracted. Everyone turned to stare at the duke and his governess, alone and wet and . . . disheveled. Heads came together in whispers, people knowingly nodded, and two grooms blatantly exchanged money.

Richard glanced down at Meriel. She couldn't have missed that they were the focus of everyone as they passed. But she only lifted her chin and kept walking, nodding and smiling at the people she knew. Only he could see the hot color in her cheeks. But she said nothing, made no protest.

He felt like a scoundrel, because he couldn't protest on her behalf. He was ruining the reputation of a good woman. Though he told himself it was for Stephen's benefit, his self-disgust wouldn't go away.

They entered Thanet Court through the conservatory, and once again it was as if the indoor staff had simply been waiting for their arrival. Some maids sighed and slunk away, while others—namely Beatrice and Clover—struggled to hide their anger and disappointment. Richard hoped they wouldn't take out their wrath on Meriel, because surely they knew that Cecil always grew bored with his latest conquest after one month.

But Richard would dare even Cecil to grow bored with Meriel.

The merest thought of his brother having power over her made him feel indignant.

But didn't the servants think that he himself used his power over Meriel?

Before he could sink any lower in his own estimation, he heard "Father!" coming from the grand staircase. Stephen came rushing toward them, Nurse Weston trailing behind, and skidded to a stop.

"You're all wet," Stephen said in a puzzled voice.

"It's raining outside," Richard said mildly. He put his hand on the boy's head. "Forgive me for missing our boxing lesson. Miss Shelby came to tell me what I'd done. I'll be happy to have our lesson right now—after I change, of course."

"It's all right, Father. We had a visitor while you were gone, but we both missed him!"

Richard frowned. "Who was it?"

"Our cousin Charles! But I was out playing with Nurse Weston, so I missed him, too."

Richard felt a stab of fear that turned into anger at his own gullibility. Someone had sent him a note to meet at the hunting lodge; it was unsigned, and promised information on Charles. Richard hadn't been able to ignore it.

Charles had succeeded in getting him out of the

house, just as easily as that. He felt Meriel's hand on his back, the weight of it meant to be a comfort. He took a deep breath and controlled his anger.

Had Charles meant to talk to Stephen, to begin to sway the boy's opinion of him?

Or had Charles meant to steal the boy away?

That couldn't be the case—what would he accomplish? Everyone would insist that Stephen be returned to his father.

But what if Charles suspected the truth about the masquerade?

Richard had to rethink all his plans, but right now Stephen was counting on him, and he found that he needed the comfort of knowing the boy was all right.

"Did Charles leave me a note?" he asked, looking toward Nurse Weston. Then he saw that Mrs. Theobald had come into the great hall as well. Though she wore her usual calm expression, there was something in her eyes that suggested she was as worried as he was.

"No, Your Grace," Mrs. Theobald said. "Sir Charles did not remain long, once he realized that both you and Lord Ramsgate were out of the house."

"It must not have been important," he said, smiling down at Stephen. "I'll change and meet you right here. Nurse Weston, can you wait with Stephen?"

"Of course, Your Grace."

"I'll send up your valet," Mrs. Theobald said, disappearing through the far doors.

Meriel excused herself as well. Richard wanted to talk to her, but it would have to wait. Stephen needed him.

At dinner that evening, Richard was the first to arrive. He did his usual Cecil impersonation by starting to eat without Stephen and Meriel. He had a forkful in his mouth when he caught sight of Meriel walking through the double doors.

And he froze there, not certain if he would remember how to chew.

Meriel wore her hair up in the latest London style, with several blond ringlets free to cascade to her shoulders—her very bare shoulders. Though no cleavage was even hinted at, he almost choked on his food, and took a sip of wine to get it all down.

Her gown was a brilliant, vivid red, with silk flowers sewn down her bodice and spreading out across her overskirt. Short puffed sleeves left her arms mostly bare except for her white gloves.

She looked like a princess—or a fallen woman.

Why did she allow everyone to think that she'd succumbed to his advances? It would have worked out fine if he only had to pursue her. He noticed that the footmen ogled her, barely able to fulfill their roles.

"Father, doesn't Miss Shelby look pretty?" Stephen asked, pointing to his governess.

"Stunning," Richard said, rising to his feet.

Instead of sitting on the other side of Stephen, Meriel came around and sat at Richard's right hand, like an honored guest.

The full understanding of her plan hit him, and his heart squeezed painfully. She was sacrificing herself, so that all would believe he was Cecil. Why had she changed her mind?

Stephen. Richard had given away his concerns about Charles this afternoon. Now Meriel was as deeply involved as he was.

After Meriel left to take Stephen to bed, Richard remained at the table, drinking a glass of brandy slowly, staring at the liquid as if it held an answer to the pain eating away inside him.

"Your Grace?"

It was Mrs. Theobald, but he didn't look up at her, just continued swirling the glass in his hand.

He heard the door shut, then the swish of her skirts as she walked toward him.

And suddenly the silence was too much.

"Did you see her?" he asked, speaking softly as if the words would hurt his throat.

"I did, Your Grace."

He closed his eyes. "She's letting everyone think that . . . that she's my mistress."

"That was your plan, was it not?"

He raised his startled gaze to find her watching him with concern. "It was not! You know that I only meant to *appear* to be pursuing her. She was supposed to resist, and keep her reputation intact. But then I accidentally told her that Stephen is in danger."

Mrs. Theobald sighed and sat down on his left. "Accidentally?"

"My brain was scrambled from a blow to the head."

She gasped aloud, her hand going to her throat.

"I'm fine. Meriel found me. But I wasn't making sense, I know, and my fears for Stephen were what I spoke about first. I must have been lured out there so that Charles could meet with Stephen alone."

"Thank goodness that didn't happen," Mrs. Theobald said with relief. "So you told Miss Shelby about the plan to pretend to seduce her?"

"And she took it further." He slammed his hand down on the table, and the housekeeper twitched. "I didn't want this to happen!" He spoke more forcefully than he'd intended to.

Mrs. Theobald's eyes were filled with sympathy.

"But it was her choice, Your Grace. You cannot fault yourself."

"This has happened to her before, Mrs. Theobald. You can tell by the way she tries to hide within those plain garments. I'm using her, and she's willing to be used, and it makes me feel—"

He broke off, hating himself in that moment. And still Mrs. Theobald waited, and the words came out though he tried to hold them back.

"I feel like I'm seducing the governess, like my brother would have done." He clenched his jaw. "Though it started out as an illusion, it doesn't feel that way anymore. Is being the duke changing me so much? Am I turning into my father?"

Mrs. Theobald touched his arm gently. "You could never be that, young sir."

"But today I almost forgot about Stephen because I could only think about her!"

"You were hit on the head," she said firmly. "And as for becoming your father, he would have had no guilt over using a woman any way he pleased. You should not feel guilty that Miss Shelby wants to help Stephen."

"There are other things concerning her that I can feel guilty about," he said darkly.

She hesitated, and he thought she might have blushed.

"Are you . . . coercing her into something she does not want?"

"No." The kiss they'd shared had been equally passionate. He was shocked by how much her willingness made their relationship seem all right.

"Then all you can do is talk to her, young sir. Keep everything open between you."

"My motives wouldn't be pure. I know I should tell her so that she can understand the danger and minimize the risk to herself, but a selfish part of me wants her to know the full truth about me, so that she doesn't think I'm like my brother. What does that say about my motives?"

"That's something only you can answer, young sir. Be as honest with her as you can be." She smiled. "Although it sounds to me like you have far too many things to think about where Miss Shelby is concerned."

He grimaced.

"But if she wants to help you protect Stephen . . . how can you refuse?"

Richard waited until midnight, then he climbed the private staircase to the nursery. He remembered where the governess's bedroom was, and he knocked softly on the door.

Meriel opened it a crack and stared up at him. "May I help you, Your Grace?"

He rolled his eyes. "You know why I'm here."

She let him in, then closed the door. She was

wearing the same dressing gown again, buttoned up to her throat, belted at her waist, falling in smooth lines over each curve of her body. By candlelight, her hair shone in its loose braid, and her spectacles were nowhere in sight, letting him see the glistening blue of her eyes.

She waited patiently for him to begin.

"Meriel, almost every servant saw you in that red dress, and those who didn't surely heard about it from someone else."

She inclined her head as regally as a queen. "I saw the way everyone looked at us when we came out of the woods. I simply took it a step further."

She was a proud woman; this could not sit easily on her. Why didn't she yell at him?

"But Meriel, flirting would have been enough. They were all betting on whether I'd win."

"Or how long I'd resist," she said. "And how long do you think that charade would have contented everyone who knew the duke? I could not have delayed my answer to you beyond a few days. Will this masquerade be over by then?"

He had no answer for her.

"I thought not. I've solved your problem. As long as Mrs. Theobald and Hargraves know the truth of our relationship, I'm content to let the other members of the staff think what they will. The duke has captured his newest prize."

A feeling of tenderness washed over him, startling him, leaving him speechless for a moment. She was so strong, so courageous. Finally he cleared his throat. "But Meriel—"

"And in return, I demand answers," she said, advancing toward him.

He found himself backing up a step toward her bed.

"Meriel—" he repeated, this time with a warning in his voice.

"No, you are not keeping me in the dark a moment longer. Stephen is with me more of each day than he's with anyone else. I will not go on in ignorance, now that I know he could be in danger. You think you're protecting me, but you're wrong. Only the truth can help us now. So what is Sir Charles up to?"

He sighed and sat down on the edge of her bed. Her eyebrows shot up, but she remained silent, only crossing her arms over her chest.

"Cecil did ask me to take his place so that he wouldn't look weak, but it's because of our cousin Charles. He's next in line to the dukedom after Stephen. Cecil owes him money, and is repaying it on time, but Charles used this to press his advantage on the subject of Stephen's guardianship. He wants to be named the legal guardian should something happen to Cecil."

"Is there one already appointed?"

"No. But Cecil is thinking about naming me, and he knows that won't sit well with the part of the family that is offended by the circumstances of my birth."

Meriel tried to distance herself from her sympathy toward him. She could not allow her thoughts to be muddled by mere emotion. Only her intellect and logic would help Richard.

"You would make a good guardian," she said evenly.

One corner of his mouth lifted. "High praise indeed."

"Better than Sir Charles, at least."

He put a hand to his chest. "You wound me, my lady."

"I am not your lady. Kindly remember that, and go on."

He smiled. "It's simple. I'm here to protect Stephen, should Charles nurture any ideas about controlling the dukedom through the boy."

"But the duke is alive."

Richard nodded, but she saw the grim look in his eyes. "But he didn't look well. He's frightened, Meriel, and that succeeded in swaying me more than anything else. There is a chance that he is holding something back from me." He went on after a sigh. "But I have no way to know. I can only take things as they happen. So far, I would have thought Charles was content to hover out there and take a chance for control if he saw it. I haven't given him that chance—in fact, I've consolidated a bit and eased Cecil's financial problems, at least temporarily. But after today . . . I just don't know."

She remembered her fright when she'd seen Richard crumpled unconscious in the woods. The thought of him dead, of never seeing his smile, of never again being the recipient of his attention—she couldn't imagine it.

"I knew it wasn't thieves," she said with subtle sarcasm.

"My head was a bit muddled when I came up with that," he admitted. "But . . . I didn't want to involve you any more than you already were."

"I'm very much involved, Richard. Obviously it can't be a coincidence that Charles arrived at Thanet Court when you were unconscious in the woods." She felt a shock. "Or do you think he meant to kill the duke, not knowing it was you?"

"No. Whoever it was could have done that easily. Charles had succeeded in making me believe he was just sniffing around for any weakness, and so I let my guard down. But now I know he's making his own gambit, and it involves Stephen foremost."

"Charles asked for *you* when he came to the door," she reminded him.

"Just covering for himself. He wanted to see Stephen."

"Do you think he would have taken the boy?" She hugged herself against a chill, moving even closer to Richard as if he offered a warmth she no longer could feel on her own.

He reached for her hand, and she found she couldn't draw away. It felt natural to touch him.

"Taking Stephen would have exposed his plot to harm me," he said. "No, I think he just wants Stephen to get to know him should there come a time he's able to exert guardianship."

"But then why render you unconscious? Why not just lure you away, so you wouldn't suspect him?"

He grinned at her and rubbed her fingers with his. "Ah, Meriel, you're far too good at this. Yes, that would have been the smart thing. And I have received many invitations of late from friends I have in common with Charles. I've refused them all, which perhaps foiled his plan to get me away from the house. But it's hard to believe he was desperate enough to resort to something so obvious . . . unless he doesn't care that I know."

She opened her mouth in shock, but could think of no response.

"You see," Richard continued, "Charles might believe he has the upper hand."

"He thinks he's controlling the duke monetarily," she said slowly.

He nodded.

"And that the duke couldn't go against him."

"But I'm not the duke."

His voice was low and dangerous, promising a strong response to Charles's threats. Meriel looked at him and couldn't control a shiver. Without the mask of the duke's arrogant amusement, Richard looked like a man who succeeded at whatever he wanted to do.

She hadn't thought it possible, but she was even more drawn to him now, as if the truth had wiped away the chasm that had once gaped between them. He was looking at her, and she was looking back. She tried to school her features, but wasn't certain she succeeded. The candlelight was low and bathed him in a warmth that made everything intimate. They were alone. No wonder young ladies were always with a chaperone.

She had to distract them both.

"So what do you plan to do next?"

He turned her hand over and stared at her palm.

"Do you see the future there?" she asked, hoping levity would lighten the intensity between them.

But he looked at her from beneath dark brows, and only said, "My future or yours?"

Oh good heavens, why didn't she think before speaking?

"Richard, you know what I meant."

Again, his mouth turned up at one corner, and she began to associate that little half smile with Richard, not the false grin he used to represent his brother.

"I spent this afternoon sending word to men who work for me in Manchester. We need more guards at Thanet Court, and I don't mean gardeners and grooms. I don't want Charles getting through the front gate again without advance warning. I have been content to wait here and see what Charles is up to, but no more. If he can keep an eye on us, we'll keep an eye on him."

Throughout his speech, he let their linked hands drop to his thigh, where he continued to absently massage her fingers. His thigh felt rock hard and warm and far too intimate a thing for her to be touching.

"The police probably can't help us," she said, wincing at how breathless she sounded.

He smiled. "So you've considered them recently?"

"I was forced to," she said primly. "When I had my first suspicions about you, I was worried that you'd killed the duke and taken his place."

"But you believe me now?"

She could only nod and stare at him.

"You're right about the police," he said.

All the while he spoke, she had the sensation that he was watching her mouth.

In a husky voice, he continued, "Charles has done nothing suspicious, and after all, I'm the only one guilty of a crime in the eyes of the law."

For several moments, they just looked at each other in silence, feeling an intimacy that even Meriel couldn't deny. She tried to tell herself that she felt this way only because of the secrets they shared, because they were now working together.

But that would be a lie. She could no longer regard him dispassionately. She saw a man who'd raised himself above a shameful birth and made a success of his life all on his own, though his family had tried to hinder him. He had a brother who used him and called that love. Yet Richard risked everything he'd built to help a nephew he'd never met before. And now he was risking his life.

How could she fight the appeal of that?

She reminded herself that every time she thought she knew the truth, another lie was revealed. The lies of her parents had scarred her, had made her doubt everything about herself.

He tugged on her hand and she moved closer to him, closer to the bed he perched on.

But she wanted to trust him, to put her faith in something again. She didn't remember how to do that anymore.

He pulled her closer by her upper arms until

the bed pressed hard against her stomach. She was between his legs, and she didn't know what to do with her hands as he leaned over her. She ended up with them flat on his thighs as he lifted her up against him, so that her toes only brushed the floor.

Each kiss was as wondrous as the first, even more so now that she knew his true identity. His lips moved over hers with ever-increasing urgency, and she found herself caught up in it, all her cares disappearing under the intensity of these raw, rare feelings. She was the one who opened her mouth to explore his. His groan made her feel powerful, aware of what they had between them. With her tongue, she tasted his lips, his mouth, so intent on her exploration, her body pressed willingly to his, that only distantly did she feel his hand slide from her waist to her ribs, then up to cover her breast.

Now it was her turn to moan, to writhe against him as the new, incredible sensation swept through her. There were only two thin garments between their skin, and it might as well have been nothing at all, so much did she feel the imprint of his hand. He kneaded and caressed her, then plucked at her nipple gently until it pressed in a hard point against his hand. The shot of pleasure moved down through her body into an ache between her thighs. There was something more waiting for her, and she wanted to reach for it, to explore everything he could make her feel.

He lifted her up and set her on his lap. She found herself straddling his thighs, her nightdress riding up her legs. Their arms were about each other, and she couldn't get enough of his kisses. She kissed his forehead and into his hair as he moved his lips in a hot line down her neck. She arched backward, letting him tug at her neckline with his teeth. She felt the clasp of her dressing gown come loose under his deft ministrations, and the garment spread wide until only thin silk separated her from his kiss. Open-mouthed, he skimmed downward, then met her gaze for a heart-stopping moment as his lips hovered over her breast. Her anticipation built and built until she moaned his name with eagerness and longing. Then his mouth covered her breast, wetting the silk, bringing her nipple between his lips to suckle.

She almost cried out, so intense was her building need, but some distant part of her retained enough will to choke back the sound. She hung in his arms, letting him taste her through her nightdress, and he tugged her hips hard against him. He filled the open vulnerability between her thighs with the hard length of his penis, still trapped within his trousers. She pressed against him, rubbing, trying to find a way to ease her frantic need.

With every movement her breath came in gasps, her hips rocked harder and harder.

He suckled and licked one breast, and his fingers found the other to circle and tease. That was when she lost it, let her mind and body carry her away to a place of pleasure she'd never imagined existed. She shuddered in his arms for what seemed like an eternity, spasms rocking her, until she collapsed against his chest.

And in that moment, when her mind was coming back to herself, when she realized she didn't care that the man she'd willingly shared intimacy with was not her husband, she heard a child crying down the corridor.

Chapter 19

Richard was caught up in a need so profound he'd never felt its like before. To give Meriel pleasure had mattered more to him than his own. Now he was aching and unfulfilled, her hips cradling him, her warm depths still pulsating against the length of his erection.

He'd been amazed that she'd found her own pleasure, and it made him want to rip open her garments and give her more. Tasting warm, soft, bare skin—the imagined sensation screamed in his brain.

But Meriel had gone stiff in his arms.

"Did you hear that?" she asked in a low, tense voice.

He heard only his pounding heart, felt the throbbing in his groin as he began to move against her.

She sat up, pushing herself back along his thighs, trying to keep his arms from drawing her back.

"Meriel," he whispered her name.

"Richard, I think I hear Stephen in the corridor!"

He straightened and forced himself to think beyond his own lust. There was a soft cry from somewhere within the suite.

Richard's mind snapped back into awareness as a rush of worry moved through him. Was someone trying to get to Stephen?

"Oh heavens, Stephen can't find us together," she whispered, sliding to the floor. She pulled her dressing gown over the wet silk of her nightdress.

He rushed to the door, pressing his ear to it. Meriel joined him.

Stephen still cried, and he seemed to be wandering the corridor. Was he alone? Or was he running from someone? Richard couldn't afford to wait; he needed the element of surprise. As he went for the door handle, Nurse Weston's soothing voice joined Stephen's, and they could hear her leading him away.

Meriel slumped as she heaved a sigh.

Richard was glad he had said nothing to alarm her about the possibility of Stephen being in danger. He let his worry slumber again as he put his hands on her shoulders.

"So tense," he murmured into her hair. "I would have thought you totally relaxed by now."

She blushed and turned her face away. "I can't believe that I—I behaved like that."

He caught her face in his hands so she would look at him. "It was a true honor to have you enjoy yourself in my arms, to know that you trusted me that much."

"Did you think that was trust?" she whispered uncertainly.

"Oh yes."

"It didn't feel like that to me. I felt . . . overcome, as if I couldn't control myself."

He was beginning to realize how much she needed her control. "Meriel, don't—"

"You need to go now, Richard. I have to—to think about all this, about everything."

She still didn't want to meet his eyes. He knew she'd never experienced true passion, and that she was shocked by it. But was overanalyzing it the right thing to do? He doubted it, but he had to accede to her wishes.

As he stepped away from her, she gaped at his trousers.

"How will we hide *that*?" she demanded, her voice still soft but higher.

He hadn't had to worry about this problem in years, but he obligingly looked down and realized that the front of his trousers, still tented outward, were wet from her pleasure.

Her wide eyes met his, and he grinned.

"Did you bring a coat?" she asked frantically.

He shook his head. "It will dry."

"So you know that from experience?"

He shook his head. "I didn't mean—oh hell. Good night, Meriel. I'll be dreaming about you."

She bit her lip and nodded, and he went out into the dark corridor.

Back in the master suite, Richard found himself pacing. He'd experienced sexual frustration before after being drawn to women he'd resisted.

But that wasn't what concerned him. He had to be honest with himself. He didn't want to keep this affair for the public eye only. He wanted her in his bed. The nights stretched out endlessly without her. Before Meriel, the women in his life had always seemed too needy. So attracted to his money, they wanted only to be taken care of. But Meriel was a woman who stood on her own. Perhaps *he* was the needy one in this strange relationship.

That thought went against everything he believed about himself. He'd never needed anyone, for there was no one he could ever depend on. Surely these intense feelings for Meriel were only because of the isolation of his masquerade.

Meriel lay in bed and still experienced the tiny little tremors fading away inside her body. She felt new and different, now that she was truly aware of the powerful pleasure men and women gave each other. She was not foolish enough to think that Richard had experienced what she had.

But she was not going to feel guilty, not when he had known what to expect, and she had not.

Once again, she was giving in to feelings that were growing more powerful than her intellect. She barely remembered trying to resist the pull of desire. She'd been held hostage by her body, and it had taken over, using Richard's body for satisfaction.

With a groan, she pulled her pillow over her face. She'd just . . . rubbed against him mindlessly. And it had felt so good, so right.

How was she supposed to recover herself, to distance herself after this? Would Richard expect even more the next time they were alone—and would she give in and allow it? Was there nothing left of her common sense?

The questions hovered in her mind all the next morning, and she was glad when the post arrived with a letter for her. It was from her sister Louisa, who was working as a companion to an elderly lady. Meriel was so grateful for the diversion. She didn't want to think about her own problems anymore. And she so enjoyed Louisa's stories of helping the shy granddaughter of her employer prepare for her Season. Louisa had a true gift for understanding and compassion.

But Meriel's smile gradually faded the longer she read. Louisa was back in London, living with their sister Victoria. She'd had to resign her position because the male relatives of the old woman had pressed their attentions too forcefully, and the females of the household had blamed Louisa.

Meriel put her face in her hands and shuddered. Impoverished ladies were so often treated shamefully. What would Louisa say if she knew that Meriel was willingly portraying a mistress, and that the previous night it had almost become a fact? She'd begun this charade only to help Stephen, and instead she'd lost all sense of control.

Meriel tried to tell herself that Louisa would recover from her experiences, that she'd be happy again in London society, where she'd always had such success. But there was an undercurrent of sadness in the letter that Louisa had obviously been trying to hide. Meriel resolved to write her a funny, cheerful letter. She would not burden Louisa with her own problems.

* * *

That afternoon Richard's men began to arrive, and Meriel was glad his attention was diverted from her. For the benefit of the servants, he managed to make it seem that he was concerned about security after a nobleman's recent kidnapping.

When Stephen wasn't working on his lessons with her, she allowed him to tag after his "father." She knew that she was encouraging this as a diversion. She felt too raw, too uncertain to be alone with Richard. But at dinner she wore another of her beautiful London gowns, and afterward, when Stephen went up to bed, she allowed Richard to persuade her to join him in the drawing room.

The doors were open to the corridor, servants came in and out, and Meriel still felt too publicly alone with Richard. She burned with the memory of how brazen she'd been, what pleasure she'd taken in his touch. As she paced, he just smiled and watched her, pleasure in his eyes, reminding her of the pleasure she'd taken from him.

She hastily retreated to the piano and began to play. He came over and used his body to make room for himself beside her on the bench. Closing her eyes, she did her best to concentrate on the music. How did people ever behave normally toward each other after they'd shared such intimacy?

Finally, she glanced at him and whispered, "Isn't this too public for a man's affair with his mistress?"

He grinned and leaned close to speak in a low voice. "Normally I'd agree with you, but I consulted Mrs. Theobald, and she claims that once chosen, a mistress did little work, and enjoyed a life of leisure—which included keeping the duke company wherever and whenever he wished."

Her breathing was far too rapid with his nearness, and she took refuge in her practical governess voice. "Make sure you tell your brother that he should find a wife to perform that function, so that his son doesn't grow up as he did."

"You mean as *we* did, he and I?"

She looked for signs of distress, but he showed none. "Didn't it . . . bother you, knowing what your father had done to your mother?"

She thought of her own family and what her father had done, the suicide that had been even more of a betrayal than the secret of their faltering finances. But she would not let self-pity distract her.

He looked down at his brandy for a moment. "I never could find a way to ask my mother if she had been willing or . . . forced."

"Oh, Richard," she murmured, feeling the sting of tears.

"When I was young, I chose to think she had

wanted the duke's attention, her own house, and never having to work again. I thought she was proud that her son was raised in the duke's household."

"I'm sure she was."

"No. As I grew older, I began to think that she resented me." He laughed without humor. "God, that sounds selfish, as if it were all about me."

She stopped playing and put her hand on his arm, reminding herself of his masquerade. "No, Your Grace. But why would you think that about your mother?"

"I believe the allure of her own home blinded her for a while to how isolated she truly was from everyone she knew. The duke had several new mistresses before I was even born." His face darkened. "The duchess did her best to make my mother miserable. Then Mother took to drinking, and it ruined her health. She was dead before she even saw me enter Cambridge."

"You can't think she resented you, Your Grace. You were an innocent in the decisions made by adults. Maybe she was disappointed in the choices she'd made as a young woman."

"I'll try to think of it that way," he said, giving her that little half smile. "Because of course I turned all my resentment on my father. He'd used her for a momentary pleasure, and left her to suffer the consequences."

"But he did support her, and you. Maybe he even loved her in his own way," she suggested, hoping to ease his pain.

"If so, it was a brief love. That's what this place"—he waved an arm to encompass the room—"this vaunted position in life does to people. Even I, who should know better, occasionally enjoy the power of dozens of servants at my beck and call."

"But you're a wealthy man, aren't you? Don't you have your own servants in Manchester?"

"A few. But trust me, it is not the same. I guess I never realized it," he added with a sigh. "I keep telling myself that I wouldn't have been like Cecil, like my father, if I were in their shoes."

"I'm sure you wouldn't have."

He laughed with little apparent amusement. "Humoring me, are you? That's what one does to a duke."

She nudged him with her elbow. "You know that's not what I'm doing."

"Hmmm."

She went back to the music, and it made her feel safe, removed from the frightening emotions he so easily inspired in her. In her mind, she kept hearing her own words of comfort to him, that he was an innocent in decisions made by adults. She was good at giving out advice, but not at accepting it. She, too, had been an innocent in her parents' blunders—logically, she knew that. But she could not escape her own deduction that she should have seen it coming, should have been prepared. She was no child, as Richard had been when tragedy had happened to him.

"So tell me about the spectacles," he said.

Meriel looked down at the keyboard. "They're spectacles."

"But they're made of simple glass."

"Very well, yes, they are."

"So they *are* a disguise."

She smiled and shook her head. "No, they're protection."

"That, you're going to have to explain," he said dubiously.

"I had one other position as governess before I came here. After that, I decided it was best to . . . downplay my features."

He put his hand on her thigh and spoke in a low, controlled voice. "Did your employer try to hurt you?"

"Heavens, no. You were far worse than he was."

He blinked. "Oh. Well then. What happened?"

"His wife could not overcome her jealousy toward me. She was convinced that her husband hired me for inappropriate reasons—"

"Like my brother did," he said softly.

"Exactly. The husband could not accept her

constant need to keep track of me—and to keep track of him. Finally, he had to let me go. After that, I resolved to . . . alter my appearance a bit. He gave me wonderful references though," she added brightly.

He leaned closer. "And I'm sure Cecil was very concerned about those."

She lifted her nose in the air. "He was. We discussed Stephen's education extensively. He wanted only the best for his son."

"I'm glad to hear it."

If he was smiling, he hid it behind his glass.

"Stephen often comments on how pretty you are," Richard said. "He tries to be very casual about it, but I think he's matchmaking."

She softened at the thought. "What a sweet boy. Surely someone on the staff must have told him that a duke could not possibly marry a governess."

"Of course he knows that, but—" Richard suddenly cleared his throat.

Meriel got a strange feeling, and she stopped playing to face him. "If he knows that, then why would he—" She broke off and stared aghast at Richard. "He knows!"

"Meriel—"

Her voice dropped to a shocked whisper, and she glanced at the open drawing room door. They were still alone. "He knows who you are!"

"I didn't tell him," he said tiredly. "He's just too smart to believe that his father might have changed so easily toward him. I first found out that Stephen knew the truth when he was correcting my food preferences. He's been very helpful ever since."

She stared at Richard as if she didn't know him. "You used that boy as a—a coconspirator! You let a six-year-old lie for you?"

He shrugged. "What else was I supposed to do? I couldn't leave. I told Stephen the truth, that his father is still sick and doesn't want to appear weak before the world. That made perfect sense to him."

"But—"

He took her hand and she let him, but only so that no one would see her struggling in anger.

"Meriel, he's been invaluable to me in my disguise. He wanted to help; how could I refuse him?"

She sighed, knowing he was right. "This just isn't natural. What if this somehow . . . hurts him?"

"He could be hurt far worse, if we're not careful. He's been very good, never calls me anything but Father. Even you were fooled, and you spend most of the day with him."

"Your Grace, I—" Meriel broke off as Beatrice entered.

The maid's expression was respectful, even toward Meriel, as she asked if His Grace needed anything else. When she'd gone, Meriel used the awkward pause to rise to her feet.

"I'll wish you a good night, Your Grace."

He stood and took her hand between both of his. He lifted it to his mouth and kissed her a bit too long. His lips were warm and soft and made her feel almost faint with longing. She admitted to herself that she wanted to be close to him.

And she'd just discovered another of his lies! Well, an omission, anyway.

"Your Grace," she murmured. "Please do not come to me tonight."

He studied her, betraying neither anger nor disappointment. "Are you well, Meriel?"

She nodded. "I just . . . It's all so new to me that . . . Oh, heavens."

"Go to your solitary bed then." One corner of his mouth teased her with a smile. "Dream of me."

Her eyes widened, and she fled the drawing room. Did he already know he'd invaded her dreams?

Chapter 20

The next afternoon, Meriel was listening to Stephen's Sunday catechism when she received word from Clover that Miss Renee Barome had come to see her. Nurse Weston took over with Stephen, and Meriel went downstairs to the drawing room. She came up short in the doorway and kept her pleasant smile, even though her visitor was not alone. Sir Charles Irving stood talking to Richard and Miss Barome.

Richard gave her a nod as one would to a governess, and went back to his conversation. Miss Barome stepped away from the gentlemen to meet Meriel.

They curtsied to each other, then Miss Barome took her arm and led her to a window seat.

"I just happened to be traveling here at the same time as Sir Charles," Miss Barome said, spreading her skirts as she sat down. "It was enjoyable to have companionship on the road. Although I must say, Cecil's new gatekeepers were almost rude. They had to consult with Cecil before even allowing us in!"

"He has increased his security after the most recent London kidnapping," Meriel said sympathetically. She glanced at Richard and wondered how he'd felt admitting Sir Charles. At least he'd gotten a few minutes' warning! She looked back at Miss Barome. "Did you come to visit His Grace?"

"No, I came to see you, since you did not send word that you were visiting me. I hope you do not mind."

"No, of course not," Meriel said, not looking at Richard and Sir Charles, though it proved very difficult. "Forgive me for not writing—this has been a very busy week."

Miss Barome studied her for a moment, betraying a seriousness that made Meriel uneasy.

"Of course I understand," the woman said. "You'll have to tell me all about it."

Meriel hoped she wasn't blushing, and was relieved when Beatrice pushed a cart with refreshments into the room. They joined the gentlemen, and Meriel poured everyone tea and passed out cakes.

When the topics of the weather and horse breeding had been exhausted, Miss Barome said brightly, "Cecil, do tell us when you plan to host the Thanet masquerade."

"Ah yes," Sir Charles said. "The locals are all atwitter over it." He turned and gazed directly at Richard. "It will be hard to top last year, don't you agree?"

Meriel sipped her tea and was glad she was not in Richard's place. Since he had not been home in many years, he would know nothing about the masquerade.

"I top myself every year," Richard said, sharing a grin with Miss Barome.

Meriel tried to let her breath out slowly, before her lungs could burst.

Sir Charles smiled. "Ah, but that fountain full of performers—surely that will remain the most memorable. Don't you agree?"

There was a pause as Richard finished chewing a bite of cake. The cake might as well have been ash in Meriel's mouth as she waited.

"Charles, it must not be too memorable to you," Miss Barome said, laughing. "Surely you remember that the fountain was the year before."

Sir Charles shook his head, all self-deprecation. "Of course, how foolish of me."

Richard lounged back in his chair, eyes half hooded with amusement. "Charles, last year was the performance of lit fairies in the park at midnight. I was chasing a fairy until dawn."

The men laughed, and Miss Barome smiled indulgently at Richard, as if whatever the duke did, no matter how crass, couldn't be bad.

"Cecil," Sir Charles said, setting down his teacup, "I'd like to see that new horse you bought this year. Care to give me a tour of the stables?"

When the men had gone, Miss Barome rose from her chair and came to sit beside Meriel on the sofa.

"How is young Lord Ramsgate?" Miss Barome asked.

"He is doing well, but then he's an intelligent boy, just like his father."

"Yes, just like his father." Miss Barome frowned down into her teacup. With a sigh, she looked up and said, "Speaking of Cecil, well . . . I hadn't meant to bring this up but . . . I don't mean to presume upon our acquaintance, yet—"

"Miss Barome, I've never heard you speak with such hesitancy. Please feel free to tell me anything."

To Meriel's surprise, the woman's face reddened.

"Then I shall be frank and hope for the best,"

Miss Barome said. "Rumors have reached my servants, and consequently me."

It was Meriel's turn to experience a hot blush, but she remained silent.

"I understand that Cecil has chosen you as his next mistress." Miss Barome covered her face. "Oh dear, that sounds awful. I wouldn't blame you if you simply wished me a good day and sent me home. I was just so worried that he'd somehow . . . forced you—"

Meriel reached for her hand and clasped it tightly. "Miss Barome, please do not upset yourself. The fact that you cared enough to bring me your concerns moves me deeply. I feel that I have found a friend."

"You have, my dear, you have. But Cecil—in the way of many a peer, he believes that what he wants . . . he can have. I sometimes wish I could hate him. It would make things so much easier."

There was a wistfulness in Miss Barome's eyes and voice that startled Meriel. Had the woman harbored feelings for the duke for all these years? Even a smart woman like Miss Barome—like Meriel—could lose herself because of the charm of the men in this family.

How must Miss Barome feel about this succession of mistresses?

"You don't need to hate him," Meriel said

quietly. "He is not a man to use force with a woman, but his charm is more than adequate." She leaned toward Miss Barome. "I will be honest with you. My family's financial position is poor at best. The money the duke is offering me cannot be underestimated. And all I have to endure is his kindness and generosity."

"Oh, I knew it—he *is* using force, in his own way!"

"No, that is not how I see it, Miss Barome," Meriel said firmly. "I had a choice, and I made it. I would understand if you think less of me."

To her surprise, Miss Barome hugged her and practically upset both of their teacups.

"Oh good gracious, look what I almost did," the woman said, pulling away and offering an embarrassed smile. "Please, don't ever think I would presume to judge you. A woman alone is very vulnerable."

Meriel felt a threat of tears. "Thank you, Miss Barome."

"Please, will you not call me Renee? And I shall call you Meriel, and I promise I'll be a good friend to you. Now tell me, do you paint?"

Meriel laughed and nodded. "I attempt watercolors, but I fear a horse would be better at it than I am. But a certain six-year-old seems impressed."

* * *

Richard walked silently beside Charles and decided to let him begin the conversation. They passed through the gardens and down to the stables. Richard gave the order to have Cecil's new gelding put through its paces, and he led Charles over to a fence to watch. They both leaned their elbows on it and waited.

Richard was waiting for more than the horse. What could Charles want? Surely he knew that Richard suspected him, after being knocked unconscious in the woods the other day—or maybe not. Maybe it would not occur to him that there was anything to suspect him of.

The gelding was led out, and Charles nodded his appreciation. "Are you going to train him for the hunt?"

"Perhaps. I would naturally consult you for your opinion, as I know you are an expert at hunting."

"How good of you."

Charles turned to look at him, and there was an anticipation in his eyes that Richard knew had nothing to do with hunting.

"Although I'm not sure you'll want much to do with me," Charles said gravely, "after I give you some sad news."

Though tense, Richard kept his smile pleasant. "Ah, Charles, you know I never let sad news worry me for long."

"But this is not the same, I fear." Charles shook his head. "I regret to inform you that Cecil has passed on to a better place."

Richard stared at him, the smile wiped from his face. "You're not making sense, Charles."

"But of course I am . . . Richard. Please don't think me a fool and deny your identity. I've known from the beginning."

Richard knew he should be plotting, strategizing his next move—but the pang of loss he felt at the thought of Cecil's death was almost overwhelming.

Yet Charles exuded a secret delight behind his solemn expression, and suddenly Richard wanted to put his hands around his throat and strangle him.

"I assure you that I'm not lying about your brother," Charles continued amiably.

He reached into his coat pocket, and Richard tensed, but all he pulled out was a ring. The ducal ring.

"Ah, I see you recognize it," Charles said. "The poor man—he was very ill."

"You could have had that ring stolen from him," Richard said, abandoning any attempt to deny his identity. "He seldom wore it, and didn't even think I needed it. But you covet it."

"The ring? Heavens, no. I want the power it stands for. Right now it's merely a piece of jewelry.

But if you'd like more proof than my word about your poor brother, I've brought along his valet, who of course would never be parted from his master—unless there was no more work to be done. See, I've even instructed my carriage to be brought around."

Both men turned to look back at the house, where a carriage was just passing. It pulled up within yards of Richard. At a signal from Charles, the coachman got down and opened the door, and Cecil's valet stepped out. The valet held the door for support, but otherwise looked unhurt.

"Evans," Richard said, "is it true about your master?"

Evans pulled a handkerchief from his pocket and blew his nose. "Yes, sir. His Grace is dead."

"That's enough, Evans," Charles said. "When we're done here, my coachman will take you back to your master's body."

The valet disappeared into the carriage, and the coachman climbed up into his box to wait.

"You're not going to harm Evans," Richard said.

"Of course not, my good fellow. Besides, he only knows that the duke is dead, not the manner in which he died. And speaking of the duke, I'll hold on to the body for you until you have a chance for a proper burial."

Richard's heart gave another stabbing ache. If

Charles had killed Cecil, Charles would pay a terrible price for that betrayal.

"Do not forget that I stand between you and Stephen," Richard warned him in a soft voice.

"Oh I'm counting on that," Charles said with obvious delight. "What amusement would there be going up against a child? And by the way, you're welcome to go to the police with this little tale. But whom will they believe: a concerned cousin? Or the bastard who's masquerading as the duke, and who might have killed the poor man? Because believe me, I can make it look like you did."

"Why the open threats, Charles? If you're so powerful, why not spring your plan on us unaware?"

"But what challenge would that be, Cousin Richard? First you need to deduce what I'm after, don't you?"

"You've already told me it's the power."

"But there are so many ways to acquire that. Enjoy the little puzzle I've presented." Charles stepped up into his carriage, and the coachman drove away.

After the carriage had disappeared around the eastern wing of Thanet Court, Richard turned back to watch the groom riding the gelding, but didn't really see any of it. He could only think about his brother, dead.

Stephen was the new Duke of Thanet.

Chapter 21

Meriel couldn't discuss Charles's visit at dinner, and it took all her patience to wait until midnight to sneak down the private staircase to Richard's room. She remained fully clothed and vowed to guard against her unpredictable feelings.

She found Richard awake, still dressed, leaning against a window frame and staring at the night sky. She silently stepped beside him and looked out to see a sliver of moon. His face was pensive and sad, and she wanted to hold him, to comfort him. She settled for putting her hand on his arm.

"Are you all right?" she asked softly.

He only shrugged.

"What did Charles want?"

He heaved a sigh and looked down at her, his sad smile worrying her.

"He came to tell me that my brother is dead."

She gasped. "You mean he tried to tell you that *you* were dead?"

"Not me—Cecil."

After a long pause, she said, "Then he knows the truth about you? But how would he—surely you don't believe him!"

"He had Cecil's valet as proof. I don't see what lying about it would accomplish for him. If he wanted Cecil out of the way, killing him is the easiest way to do that."

"Oh, Richard," she whispered and leaned against him.

When he put his arm around her shoulders, she snuggled in against his body and held him.

"I cannot imagine how you must feel," she said. "If something were to happen to one of my sisters—"

"But this isn't the same," he said, still staring out the window. "Cecil and I were never exactly close, and adulthood further separated us. I maybe saw him twice a year. But . . . I never thought it would feel this way, to know that he was dead."

With her arm around his back, she felt a little spasm, as if he tried to control himself. When she looked up at him, she saw a tear slide down his cheek.

She whispered his name again and went completely into his arms, holding him tight, wishing with everything in her that she could ease his pain.

He held her for a moment, then gently pushed her away. Turning aside, he brushed at his face, and when he looked back, all his emotion was gone. He looked ruthless, determined—and deadly.

He told her about his conversation with Charles.

"So you don't know how long he's known about your masquerade?" she asked. "He certainly was trying to test you when he was talking about the entertainment at last year's ball."

He shook his head. "Thankfully Cecil always wrote me detailed letters bragging about the masquerade. No, today was all about Charles's love of the hunt. And we're supposed to figure out the target."

"Would that be you? Aren't you the one who stands between him and guardianship of Stephen?"

"That makes sense, of course, but somehow

that seems too easy. And we can't forget that Cecil was under his control, for however brief a time. Charles might have forced him to sign a guardianship document."

"But then you wouldn't be in his way, would you?"

His eyes softened. "Now I know why I keep you at my side."

"And here I thought it was for another reason."

She immediately regretted such playful banter, but Richard seemed to appreciate it. Some of the terrible tension went out of him.

He arched an eyebrow. "You mean as governess?"

She blushed. "I'm sorry I mentioned it. So the duke probably didn't name Charles as guardian."

"I don't think so. Perhaps Charles's plan is as simple as guardianship of Stephen, and I'm in his way. He's worried that a sympathetic court might side with me, considering that Cecil and I were raised as brothers. The duke housed and educated me—"

"And Stephen loves you."

He smiled. "I would like to think so. Though my illegitimacy might cost me some sympathy, Charles can't take that chance."

"So how far do you think he would go to eliminate the threat of you?"

Richard's mouth tightened. "If he killed Cecil . . . then he will dare anything."

"But Cecil was sick; you don't know for certain that Charles killed him."

"No. But if Charles only wanted to get me out of the way, all he has to do is announce my real identity. It will seem like I wanted the dukedom, and killed Cecil to get it. Maybe Charles is just biding his time, waiting to denounce me at the worst possible moment."

"But how do we protect Stephen from him? Heavens, that little boy is now the duke," she said, shaking her head in wonder.

"My first thought was to take Stephen out of England altogether, but it will only look like I'm kidnapping him for my own ends. Hiding him somewhere until this all plays out would mean I'd have to trust someone to protect him."

She studied him. "And trust doesn't come easily to you, I would assume."

He rubbed his hand across his brow. "No."

A part of her felt let down, and he didn't deserve that. She couldn't expect him to trust her unequivocally. She still didn't completely trust herself.

But why was his trust so important to her?

"So we keep Stephen here, and under watch at all times," he said. "The training we've done with the wolfhounds will come in handy now. They'll guard him well."

"Did you train them with this in mind?"

"Not at first, but when the dogs took to Stephen, I realized that they could be invaluable. They're sleeping in his room as we speak. I can't believe Charles will harm Stephen, because power is his goal, and he'll have it by controlling all the estates."

"How can we be certain of that, Richard?" she asked softly. "Just because he told you he wants power, doesn't mean it's true."

"You're right. I really can't assume anything about Charles's goals. But I won't let him harm Stephen."

"That puts you in the most danger," she whispered, startled again by how terrible that made her feel. Was this love—this worry, this want, this desperate need to be with him? She wanted to take all his pain away, to make him—to make both of them—forget for just one night that his own cousin wanted him dead. Her fear of her own emotions seemed meaningless now, with Richard standing before her hurting, but strong and capable and ready to take on a murderer to defend a family and a way of life that had treated him badly.

She didn't realize how long she'd been staring at him, or what expression she wore, until Richard betrayed a new tension by just the line of his body and the way his gaze grew hooded as it moved intently down her body. She remembered the bliss of his embrace, the feel of his mouth on her, and she wanted it all again.

"Meriel," he said, his voice husky, "if you wish to remain a virgin, I suggest you find your own bed."

She only shook her head. If she thought he'd been tense before, she didn't know the true meaning of the word. His body came alert, and a shock of passion seemed to jump between them.

He took a step closer. "You have to tell me, Meriel. Tell me what you want."

She closed the gap between them, and her corseted breasts brushed his coat. "Can't I show you?"

He closed his eyes and shuddered. "Will my heart be able to handle it?"

Her own heart gave an answering ache.

Any thoughts of embarrassment were long gone as she slipped her hands within his coat and placed them on his chest. She slid them up the warm, hard muscles, then pushed back his coat at the shoulders until, with a shrug, he let it fall to the floor. This time she wanted to see him, to know if he took the same wild pleasure in her touch as she did in his. The buttons of his waistcoat were tricky under her trembling fingers, but soon that garment was on the floor, too.

He was breathing heavily; his heart pounded

beneath her hands, and his brows were lowered over dark eyes that seemed to burn into her. She felt the tiny points of his nipples, and when she caressed them through his shirt, he caught his breath.

Suddenly impatient for more of him, she quickly untied his cravat and stock and tossed them to the floor. There were only a few buttons at his throat, and then she pushed his shirt up, and he obliged her by pulling it off over his head.

His chest startled her again with how very different it was from hers, all hard, rippling muscle.

"You didn't get this from investing," she whispered, then lifted her head to look at his face. "Boxing?"

"Keeps a man trim," he murmured.

His arms came around her, and he started unhooking her gown in the back. It came loose slowly, but even then she was still restricted beneath several layers of clothing. He pulled it down the front of her, revealing her corset over her chemise, and the several petticoats tied at her waist.

When the gown was on the floor, he said, "It's like opening a Christmas gift."

Her laugh sounded strange, all throaty and deep. "Do you need help?"

"I'll manage."

And he did. Her petticoats came off one by one, and then he was forced to turn her around so that he could unlace her corset. To her surprise, she faced a long mirror, and she could see herself all rosy-cheeked with excitement. He pulled the corset up over her head, and then made short work of the pins in her hair, scattering them everywhere. She watched her own blond curls fall about her breasts and shoulders and back.

From behind, he looked at her in the mirror, gathering her hair gently and drawing it to the back. The chemise she wore dipped into her cleavage, and was just translucent enough to reveal a hint of her nipples.

Richard groaned and buried his face in her hair. "I didn't know governesses wore such fine undergarments."

"Maybe they don't. I bought my chemises when I had no spending limit. I like pretty things."

"Thank God," he said hoarsely.

He knelt down behind her, and she gasped when she felt him lifting her hemline. Sliding his hands up her calves, he removed her shoes, garters, and stockings. All she had left beneath her chemise were her drawers. Richard didn't bother with those. He simply came to his feet, bringing the hemline with him, then drew her chemise over her head. For a moment, he stood still, looking through the mirror at her breasts.

She had once imagined she'd feel like covering her nakedness, but not now. Now she wanted to lean back against him and beg for his touch. She loved the look of admiration and desperation on his face as he watched her.

"There, we match," he breathed, turning her around and pressing her against him.

His skin was hot against hers, both on her chest and on her back, where his large hands held her to him. He leaned down and kissed her, and she put her arms around his neck to keep him with her. As their tongues mated, his hands slid up her sides and cupped the edges of her breasts. She groaned into his mouth. His thumbs moved between their bodies, rubbing her nipples in slow little circles that drove her mad.

"Please," she whispered against his mouth. "I want more."

She put her hands on his trousers and unbuttoned them, just as he unlaced her drawers. They each pushed garments down the other's hips, until their clothes pooled on the floor. She leaned against him, his penis hot against her stomach, caught between their bodies. It seemed to throb, as if it had a life of its own. She had rubbed herself against it the other day, taken her pleasure and denied him his.

Tonight they would revel in sharing their passion.

She tried to pull him toward the massive four-poster bed, but he stopped her.

"Boots," he said apologetically, even as his gaze continued to rove her body with hunger. "I should have thought this out better."

With only one hop, he was able to sit down in a chair. Meriel went to stand by the bed, leaning back against one of the posts to watch him. The bed curtains hung at her back, tickling her bare skin. She felt far too wicked, standing so brazenly before a naked man.

Then he was walking toward her, and she hungrily watched the way his muscles moved in beautiful motion. His penis hung heavily toward her, and she wanted to touch it, but didn't know how to ask.

He didn't give her a chance. He lifted her up and swung her onto the bed. As she reclined amid the half-dozen pillows, he stopped just to look at her again.

"Meriel, the sight of you there—" He swallowed. "Every night I've dreamed of this."

She reached for him. "You've been in my dreams—it's only fair that I've become part of yours."

As he crawled onto the bed, his long body took up so much room. He slid to her side, then pulled her back up against his front. He snuggled in behind her, his erection nestled by her buttocks.

She found herself arching back, and he groaned and rocked himself against her.

"Not yet, not yet," he murmured, letting his hand trail up her thigh.

She moaned and shivered as he drew her hair away and kissed the back of her neck and around beneath her ear. He moved his attentions back to her hip, his palm sweeping down over her stomach, his fingertips just brushing the curls between her thighs.

She caught her breath, then almost groaned her disappointment when he slid his hand back up her torso. He chuckled into her ear.

"I'm enjoying myself immensely," he whispered.

And she was enjoying everything he did to rouse her passion. He trailed the back of his hand up her stomach, then circled the lower curves of her breasts with his fingers. She wanted to grab his hand and move it where she wanted it, but that was only her sense of control trying to exert itself. There was freedom in allowing him to do whatever he wanted, in waiting expectantly for each shiver of pleasure.

And he didn't disappoint her. He finally cupped her breast, kneading it gently.

"Yes," she whispered. "Oh please."

His fingers found her nipple and began to tease, circling and rubbing and tweaking. He gave equal attention to both breasts, and soon she was shivering with the rising hunger that was taking over her mind, her very soul. She realized her hips seemed to be moving of their own accord, rocking, circling, and that he was enjoying it as much as she was.

Then he slid his hand back down her body and between her thighs, cupping her, pressing against her. She gasped and held her breath, the tense expectation making her rigid.

"Bend your knee," he said against her ear.

When she did so, he had even more access to the hot depths of her, and he rewarded her by sliding his fingers up and down her wet folds. She cried out, unable to control her panting gasps as the pleasure rolled over her, taking away her very thoughts. She existed in the world he created for her as he played her body.

He delved deeper, circling, plucking at the tiny nub that seemed like a switch turning on her body. Rising up over her shoulder, he pushed her torso flat to the bed. Then he started licking her, up the mound of her breast to the very peak, circling it, sucking it, licking it in long, flat strokes.

She was mindless now, so close to the summit of pleasure that all she could do was concentrate on it.

And then he took his hands away. Before she could even react, he moved over her body, sliding between her thighs. She lifted her knees, trying to fit herself against him, even as he held himself up so as not to crush her.

And then he pushed inside. The pain she'd heard whispers of was only a minor irritation, quickly forgotten in the pleasure of him so hard and deep. He withdrew and surged inside her again, and then she understood it. The pressure of his body against her very womanhood aroused her quickly once again. She held him and moved with the rhythm he taught without words.

And then the sharp stab of pleasure-pain engulfed her again, and she shook with the ever-decreasing tremors. Only then did she watch his face, see his concentration as he joined her in climax.

Richard barely kept himself from collapsing on top of Meriel. His mind was numb, his muscles trembled, but he was aware enough to know that never had he felt so joined to a woman before Meriel.

He didn't want to leave her body, didn't want to imagine the repercussions of this passion they'd shared. He knew he could not even think of losing her, of losing this rare closeness.

Coming up on his elbows, he smoothed the hair from her face. She was studying him, and he smiled.

"Ah, Meriel, you have to examine everything, don't you."

"No, I—" She shook her head, then shrugged. "I don't know what to think. I never thought I would . . . give in to this temptation."

He rocked against her gently, still feeling the tremors of completion. "Do you regret what we did?"

"No."

He was grateful that she didn't hesitate.

"Although I don't know what to think about it, either," she continued. "But no, never think I blame you, not when I wanted this."

"Don't you think I wanted this just as much?"

She smiled then, squeezing his hips with her thighs. "I can tell."

With a sigh, he slid off her to the side. He wanted to cuddle her close, but instead she sat up and tried to gather the blankets about her.

"I know this is foolish," she said, obviously embarrassed. "You've seen . . . all of me. But—"

"No, please, a woman's modesty is not a trivial thing. Shall I fetch your dressing gown from your room?"

"No, I can just slide my dress back on. I should go."

"Meriel."

He took one of her hands, while the other held

a blanket to her chest. "This was something we didn't plan. I don't expect more than you're ready to give to me."

She smiled and closed your eyes. "Your problem is that you're too good to me, Richard. It makes it hard to keep my distance."

"Then don't," he whispered, leaning in to kiss her cheek.

He could feel her hesitancy, yet she remained still beneath his gentle kiss, almost like a delicate bird caught between fleeing and staying.

"I must go." She met his gaze. "But what is our next move in regard to Charles?"

"We can't move against him, so we remain on guard and wait. He could be playing with me, hoping I might panic and do something foolish."

"What if he goes to the police about your brother's death?"

"That would be too awkward for him, even though I look like the criminal. And besides, he's getting a sick amusement out of his games. We'll give him a chance to make a mistake."

She looked into his eyes. "That's such a risk you're taking."

"I have more guards now. I'll keep Stephen safe. Are you worried about me?" he asked softly.

"Of course." She glanced away. "But right now I have to go. Stephen can't find me here."

"Would you stay otherwise?"

She smiled. "Probably not, even though I've become your mistress in fact now. I can't lie to myself about that."

"Meriel—"

She let the covers drop and went to pick up her garments.

"Let me help you," he said.

"No." She held up a hand. "I don't trust myself."

Richard pulled the blanket over his hips and just watched, unable to play the gentleman and turn away. Seeing that beautiful body covered was almost a crime.

When she had the gown on, it was obvious she usually had a maid's help with all the buttons. She hesitated, and he waited. Finally she walked to him and turned her back, saying nothing.

He grinned and buttoned her up. She gathered all her undergarments over her arm, and after giving him a small smile, she fled up the staircase.

He knew it would be a long time before he was able to sleep. He couldn't stop thinking about her last comment, that she couldn't trust herself. He knew she wasn't talking about his desirability. What had given a competent, intelligent woman such an opinion about herself?

She seemed to trust *him* more than herself, even though he'd lied to her. Did it have something to do with why a prosperous London family would be forced to send its daughters out for employment?

Unlike Meriel, he was a man who'd only ever had himself to rely on. He'd made his own way in the world, trusted no one *but* himself.

Masquerading as the duke, a position he once would have thought very solitary, had made him learn to depend on so many people: the silence of servants, the worship of his nephew, and the intelligence of Meriel Shelby. He had more help than he was used to, and he felt humbled by it.

Now he had to help his brother one last time. Richard would have justice, so that Cecil could rest in peace.

Chapter 22

Through the night, part of Meriel berated her weakness where Richard was concerned, while another part of her longed for his touch. The rest of the time, she was just confused.

She had breakfast with Stephen in the schoolroom as usual, and to her surprise, Mrs. Theobald herself came up to clear away the tray of dishes. Meriel stared at her, wondering if Richard had found the time yet to tell the duke's loyal servants that their master was dead. Something of her worry must have shown in her eyes, because after Stephen ran off to play with his nurse, Mrs. Theobald sat down beside her.

Meriel sighed, giving the older woman an assessing look. "You don't usually come to clean up the nursery, Mrs. Theobald."

The housekeeper only shrugged.

Meriel touched the woman's hand. "Please don't worry about me. I know what I'm doing. I'm helping Stephen."

"It is far too kind of you not to care about your reputation for the boy's sake."

Meriel felt a twinge of guilt—and though she knew she had to keep Richard's counsel about the duke's death, she could not lie to the housekeeper about anything else. "Mrs. Theobald, although you will think less of me, I must tell you that I'm no longer playacting the part of the mistress."

Mrs. Theobald nodded silently, and the condemnation that Meriel expected didn't happen. Meriel sighed as some of her tension seeped away.

Mrs. Theobald gave a small smile. "It is a relief to say such a thing?"

"To someone I trust, yes. And you know Richard, so perhaps you can understand why I . . . why I'm drawn to him."

"He is a good man."

"Yes, oh yes," she whispered, then her excitement grew as her thoughts coalesced. "I've spent so much time berating myself for those feelings that have been growing within me, but maybe for once I should have been listening to my own intuition."

"For once?" Mrs. Theobald echoed with obvious curiosity.

But Meriel didn't want to talk about her past. "Did you know who he was from the beginning?"

"No, although I knew *something* was wrong."

"And I did as well! Because I was so attracted to him, almost from the first. And I hadn't felt that way when I interviewed with the real duke. I should have trusted myself then; instead I was appalled by my poor judgment. But don't you see, I was right!"

Mrs. Theobald smiled indulgently, and Meriel blushed at how she must sound.

"He's not the duke," Meriel continued. "He's not an arrogant man who seduces the women of his household on a routine basis. Richard is nothing like his brother, Mrs. Theobald."

"You don't need to convince me of that, my dear."

"Of course, of course, but this is such a revelation to me. I was never attracted to the duke, but to Richard, not a nobleman, but a noble man who is trying to protect his nephew. Am I wrong to finally trust that my emotions can guide me down the right path?"

Mrs. Theobald rose to her feet and lifted the tray. "Miss Shelby, it sounds to me like you already know the answer to your own question. Why such a smart girl as yourself should ever doubt her own capabilities—well, it makes no sense to me."

Meriel knew she continued to grin foolishly long after the housekeeper had left the room.

As she did almost every day, Meriel allowed Stephen to choose which lesson they'd have outside. She enjoyed taking advantage of the rare string of beautiful weather, and she'd already had assurances from Richard that men were patrolling the grounds. And besides, even she needed to be distracted from the thought that Stephen's real father was probably dead. She wasn't sure that Richard should tell the boy if they weren't absolutely certain it was true.

Stephen chose his painting lesson, and together they carried out the watercolors and easel. They didn't go far from the house; she felt safe enough, being so near all the grooms and gardeners who worked about them. Victoria and Albert lounged in the shade nearby and snuffled in their sleep.

She was just speaking with Stephen about the various colors of green in the trees he'd chosen to paint, when she saw the boy's face light up at someone behind her.

Knowing who it had to be, she turned and watched Richard walk toward them. She felt uncomfortably warm and knew she was blushing; why was she so surprised by the same reaction she'd been having since the first moment they'd met?

Maybe because now she knew that he was just as drawn to her. She watched the way he looked at her, the way he tried to disguise his thoughts, but couldn't quite.

She inspired that in him, and the feeling was . . . wonderful. She felt special, not like a man's mistress, but something more, something she was afraid to hope for.

But how could she think about herself when there was a man out there who wanted to harm Richard?

Stephen rushed to Richard, who put a hand on his head fondly. The dogs joined the reunion with barking excitement. Only she saw the wince of sadness Richard didn't try to hide from her as he looked down on his nephew.

"Father, we're painting trees. Do you want to help?"

"That's what I came out here for. I'm excellent at giving my opinion."

"Not at painting?"

"Never had the talent, Stephen. You must get that from your mother."

The little boy brightened, and Meriel realized it wasn't often anyone brought up his mother. And at this age, he was beginning to realize that other children had one, but he didn't.

Meriel gazed at Richard, probably showing all her silly feelings right there in her eyes.

She was hopeless at romance. She'd never imagined herself a part of one, and once thought she'd be satisfied marrying a man who was only a friend.

A friend! Preposterous thought, now that she understood how Richard could make her feel.

She busied herself laying out paints for Stephen and tried not to be aware that Richard was watching her from where he sat on a bench. For a half hour, she instructed the boy as his watercolor took form.

"Father," Stephen finally called, "pretend it's hanging on a wall in the gallery. How does it look from back there?"

"Like perfect trees," Richard said.

Stephen rolled his eyes. "Miss Shelby, go stand next to him. You'll be honest, won't you?"

Meriel bit her lip to cover a smile as she walked back to the bench.

"Stephen, you don't trust me?" Richard said, pretending shock.

"Father, you love me too much to tell me the truth."

Meriel's throat felt tight, and she wanted to put her hand on Richard's shoulder in sympathy. What a difficult situation.

Stephen pointed with his paintbrush to one of the green blobs on his canvas. "Miss Shelby, can you tell which tree this is? I want to get them right."

Meriel deliberated on how to respond, and was granted a reprieve when Stephen accidentally dropped his brush. He bent down to retrieve it—and a gunshot rent the air. A bullet ripped through the canvas where Stephen had just been standing.

Meriel jumped, Richard came to his feet along with the dogs, and Stephen straightened in bewilderment.

"Father?"

Richard forced him to the ground, then grabbed Meriel by the arm, dragging her there, too. She collapsed on her stomach at Stephen's side and put her arm over him. Richard was on the other side, but he had his head lifted, scanning the direction the shot had come from.

"That couldn't have been aimed at me," he said in a low, furious voice.

Meriel understood: Stephen had become the target. Charles didn't just want to control the dukedom; he wanted it for himself.

"Father, it wasn't aimed at us," Stephen said,

trying to lift his head. Richard held him down as he squirmed. "There must have been hunters in the woods. They'll come to apologize."

Richard didn't answer, but Meriel could read his eyes: where were the men he had patrolling in the woods?

There were shouts from the gardeners and grooms and stable boys, all of whom seemed to be running this way and that. Meriel could see that some of the men were entering the woods to search, others were heading up to the house, probably to spread a warning.

Richard rose to his knees, and she wanted to yank him down. Her heart pounded loudly all the way into her throat, choking her. But there was no other gunshot. All they could hear was the servants' shouting.

Once on his feet, Richard looked down at them. "I'm going into the woods. Both of you stay on the ground, and don't get up until you see me wave that all's clear."

"Father, the hunters—"

"Stephen, that wasn't a hunter."

She could see Richard regretting the harsh tone of his voice already. But it was far too dangerous for Stephen not to know some of the truth. Even though the boy hadn't run off to hide recently, there was no guarantee he wouldn't—unless he was warned.

Stephen stared up at his uncle, wide eyes uncertain. But he remained silent and allowed Meriel to hold him as Richard strode away. When the dogs tried to follow him, Richard ordered them to stay behind. They sat down next to Stephen and whined softly, as if they were missing all the fun.

"Father's worried about us," Stephen whispered.

"He's the duke. It's his job to worry about everyone here."

How would Richard tell Stephen that *he* was the duke now?

Surely a half hour had to have gone by before Richard emerged from the woods and gave them a brief wave. The knot in her stomach lessened, but did not go away, not with the proof that the little boy in her arms, so young and innocent, was the target of a murderer. Slowly she sat up, drawing Stephen with her, holding him tightly. Nothing happened. She rose to her feet and kept him pressed to her skirts.

Some of his spirit returned. "Miss Shelby, let go!"

Richard heard Stephen's protest, but he left Meriel to deal with the little boy. He turned to watch six of his guards emerge from the woods, some looking stonily at the ground, others looking worried or sheepish.

Stephen's words kept ringing in Richard's head: *Father, you love me too much to tell me the truth*. Stephen had been talking to his Uncle Richard, not his father. And Richard had failed him.

The anger inside him raged out of control, and he heard himself speaking like Cecil—no, like his own father. Cecil had been too carefree to dress down the servants, but their father was a man who brooked no mistakes. And for once, Richard wanted to be seen as that kind of man.

"None of you has a good explanation for how this incursion happened," he said in a severe voice. "My son could have *died*. If something happens due to your incompetence, I'll hold you all responsible, and my retribution won't involve a prison sentence!"

He was shaking with rage, but even he recognized that this was no way to motivate men into working harder. What was wrong with him?

He wanted to apologize, but he couldn't—to them he was the duke. He tried to speak more calmly as they gathered around him. "The angle of the shot could only have been aimed at my son. We need to triple the patrols in these woods and along the cliffs, the most penetrable areas of the estate. But for now, our explanation for today's disaster is that someone was illegally hunting in the woods, and they escaped."

Richard found Meriel and Stephen in the

conservatory, telling Mrs. Theobald and Hargraves what had happened. Stephen slumped nearby on a bench, but he brightened when he saw Richard and came running. The dogs lifted their heads, but remained lounging on their sides.

Richard knelt down to hug the boy, keeping his arms around him so long that Stephen began to squirm.

"Father!" he said, laughing.

Did the boy think of Richard as his father now? He had to be told the truth. He had to understand why he was in danger. And he had to mourn his real father.

"Stephen, remain here on the bench for a moment, while I speak to the servants."

Stephen obeyed, kicking his legs and pulling a flower closer to study. Richard went to the huddle of three adults, all of whom looked at him anxiously.

"I'd like for the rest of the household to believe this was a hunting accident," Richard said quietly. "But I'm going to tell Stephen the truth."

"Are you certain that's wise?" Meriel asked. "He's so young."

"But we can't allow him to put himself at risk out of ignorance. And he has to know about his father. It explains why he's in danger."

"Have you heard from the duke?" Mrs.

Theobald whispered, looking around for eaves-droppers.

"According to Charles, he's dead," Richard said grimly.

Mrs. Theobald gasped, and Hargraves bowed his head.

"Charles had Cecil's terrified valet as proof," Richard continued. "I'm just not certain if he died from illness or if he was murdered. I'm going to assume the latter, because Charles is now shooting at Stephen, the only one who stands between him and the title." He looked at Meriel. "Stephen is no longer to go outside."

"Of course," she said quietly.

But she wouldn't meet his eyes, and he worried about what she might be thinking. She took on so much, and always held herself too accountable. He would insist on talking about it again when they were alone. But first, he had to speak with Stephen. He turned to look at the boy, now on his knees looking behind a fern. Only his backside showed.

Meriel must have seen something on his face, because she touched his arm. "Would you like me to be with you when you tell Stephen?"

"No, it should come from me." He put his hand on hers and smiled down at her. "But thank you."

He saw Mrs. Theobald look between them. He

would have to be more careful showing his feelings for Meriel—but did it matter? The entire household knew she was his mistress! His life was a public display.

He led Stephen and the dogs into his study and closed the door. He and Stephen sat down in big chairs before the bare hearth.

Stephen frowned. "Father, who tried to shoot you? Are you sure it wasn't hunters?"

"It wasn't a hunter, Stephen. Some very important things are happening right now. Since they involve you, I feel that you're old enough to know the truth." He tried to stare into the patient eyes of the little boy, but he found himself choking up. Instead, he looked at their joined hands, the little one so trusting in his. "Stephen, I've just found out that your father has died."

Taking a deep breath, he looked again into Stephen's face.

Solemnly, the boy said, "He was very sick, wasn't he?"

Richard couldn't tell him that his father might have been murdered, not without proof. "Yes, Stephen, he was more ill than he let on. I guess he didn't want us to worry."

"Where is he?"

That was far too perceptive a question, and one Richard couldn't answer. "We'll bring him home to be buried, I promise, but we can't just now."

Stephen gripped his hand even tighter. "Does that mean you're my father now?"

Good God. The little boy's eyes shone with tears. Richard imagined how Stephen was feeling, with no parents left to shield him from the harsh realities of life. Even Richard hadn't truly known how alone he himself had been at this age.

"I'll always be your uncle, Stephen, and if I'm allowed, you could live with me forever."

"But can't you do anything you want?"

"You're a duke now, son. The queen or the courts might have a say in who your guardian is."

"But—"

"But I want to be your guardian, Stephen," he said, pulling the boy onto his lap. "I'll fight in court to try to make it happen."

"What if I don't want to be the duke? Then can I live with you?"

"It's not that easy, Stephen." He hugged him tightly. "Right now we have a danger to worry about first."

"The person who shot at you?"

"Yes. We have to be very careful. Until we catch this bad man, you'll have to remain in the house and keep Victoria and Albert with you at all times."

"Does everyone else know my father is dead?"

"No. They still believe I'm the duke, and we have to keep it that way for a little while longer."

"Until we catch the bad man."

"Right. Stephen, I'm going to tell you who the bad man is, just so he can't try to take you away. He's my cousin, Sir Charles Irving."

"The one who tried to visit me when you were gone?"

"Yes."

"But if he's your cousin, why does he want to hurt us?"

Richard hesitated. "Because if something happened to you, Charles would be the next duke."

Stephen stared at him, a frown spreading across his face.

"But I'm not going to let him hurt you," Richard vowed.

"I know that, Uncle Richard. Can't I just let him be the duke?"

"You deserve the title, not him. He deserves to be in jail."

Richard looked into the innocent eyes of his nephew, and for a moment he debated going to the police with the whole story.

But if they didn't believe him, Stephen would immediately be placed in Charles's care. Richard couldn't let that happen.

For a moment, a dark thought made him pause. If Richard remained the duke, no one would challenge his right to protect Stephen. He could resurrect the pride of the title, be a better duke than Cecil ever was.

A chill went through him. Surely Cecil had once thought the same thing, that he could be a better duke than their father. But something had corrupted Cecil, as it corrupted everyone born into this power as they were treated like infallible gods. Even Richard, wielding power as a fraud, was not immune to it.

He had to finish this right now, capture Charles and end this masquerade. Or he, who'd always trusted himself, would lose faith in his own judgment.

Chapter 23

Meriel wanted to give Richard and Stephen more time alone, so she ate dinner with Mrs. Theobald in the housekeeper's private sitting room. Her conversation with Mrs. Theobald remained friendly and relaxed, and it was a relief not to think about dangerous plots. But later, Meriel's fears returned. She could still hear that gunshot, could still feel her terror when Richard had gone into the woods to face down a killer.

That night, Meriel stayed with Stephen until he fell asleep, with the dogs on either side of his bed. Nurse Weston gave her a curious look, but asked no questions. Meriel hoped she would just assume that the gunshot had rattled the boy.

At midnight, Meriel ran down the private staircase, and when she didn't see Richard immediately, she almost panicked.

"Your Grace?" she called, in case Richard's valet was still in attendance.

"I'm in here, Meriel," Richard called from the washroom.

She skidded to a halt, seeing him once again neck-deep in steaming water, the tub sunken beneath the level of the floor.

He studied her face. "I was going to come up and talk to you. I've devised a plan to rout Charles once and for all."

She didn't want to hear about plans and intrigue. He could have been killed today. She could have lost . . . everything she'd experienced with him, everything he made her feel. She'd gone through the day almost numb, unable to think about it without feeling terrified for him.

Now he had a plan, and it would surely be dangerous.

However their affair ended up, she couldn't waste a moment of it.

She loosened the sash of her dressing gown and let the garment slide to the floor. Richard stopped moving. His eyes were locked on her nakedness as she walked toward him.

She felt fluttery and nervous—and alive and full of passion for him. Could she be falling in love with him?

She stood at the edge of the tub, standing right next to him, her feet on the cool tile, on level with his face. He looked up her legs slowly, lingering at her hips, then up to her breasts—and stopped there.

Then he leaned forward and wrapped his arms around her thighs, lifting her off her feet. Gasping, she clutched at his head even as he put his face between her thighs. She was held against him, her lower legs dangling in the water, with no purchase to hold on to but him. She found herself arching back, spreading her legs as much as she was able to, and let him do as he willed.

She could feel his mouth against her now, parting her. She groaned and writhed as she realized the hot wetness was his tongue probing her, licking her, tasting her. She shuddered, gasping, already so aroused that it was nearly painful.

She gasped his name and desperately tried to lift one leg so he could reach her more fully. Her toes found the bottom of the tub, and then he lifted her leg high. He was free to explore her everywhere, and she even felt his tongue inside her. As he swept up again and sucked her inside his mouth, her body convulsed in an explosion that made her shudder and groan.

He pulled her down to straddle his lap, kissing her as he thrust up inside. She tasted herself on him, tasted his need and his lack of restraint, and she reveled in it. He arched her away from him, so that he could reach her breasts, even as he pushed into her over and over again. With his mouth and hands on her breasts, his penis inside her, she climaxed once more, and only then did he give himself over to her, falling back to the edge of the tub, arching up into her in a climactic shudder.

Then he sank under the surface of the water, and she laughed and gave his hair a pull. He came up sputtering and put his arms around her, nuzzling her neck, sighing into her ear.

"This was a lovely surprise," he murmured.

She kissed the side of his face and held him. "I've been so frightened for you all day."

"I shall have to be in danger more often if I'm going to get this kind of reaction from you."

She laughed softly, then sighed her disappointment as he drew out of her. But then he helped her turn around so that she was sitting between his legs, lying back against his chest. Closing her eyes, she let the warm water and his safe embrace relax her.

"How was Stephen when you left him?" he asked.

She tilted her head to look back at him.

"Subdued. Sad. But I get the impression he thinks he's *supposed* to be sad, more than he actually is. I stayed with him until he fell asleep."

Richard nodded. "He can hardly claim to know his father well. Maybe that will help him heal in the end."

After several minutes, he spoke with a hesitation she wasn't used to from him.

"Did you hear me when I was talking to the guards out in the garden?"

She shook her head. "I was too far away."

"I was so angry," he said in a low voice. "I had thought that they would be able to keep Stephen safe. When I yelled at them, it was like I heard my father coming out in my own voice—his disdain for the servants, the way he let a person know he was beneath a duke."

She glanced at him again, but he was staring away from her, his gaze unfocused, seeing other things. She squeezed his arms where they surrounded her. "Richard, you're *playing* the duke. And your nephew was almost killed. Anyone would react in that situation."

"I thought it would be more difficult to be like my father and brother. Sadly, it's not at all. I'm beginning to wonder if I . . . misjudged them all these years."

"What do you mean?"

"People treat me differently now, Meriel, just

like people treated them. It . . . corrupts a person, changes them. I watched it happen to Cecil, and I blamed him all these years, just like I blamed my father. But this morning, for just one moment, I thought remaining the duke would answer all my problems."

She held her breath in surprise.

"And then I realized I was becoming them."

"Richard—"

"No, hear me out. Yes, we all make our own choices, but Cecil was influenced by how he was raised, as was my father. How could they help but be little gods, when that's how they were treated?" He inhaled swiftly, then continued in a low voice. "There's a part of me that *likes* it, Meriel. And I realized today that I have resented them all these years, when I really should have forgiven them long ago. Maybe that's why my life has seemed so empty before now. But it's so difficult to let go of past hurt."

Tears blurred her eyes, and she lifted his hand to kiss his palm. "How, Richard, how can one forgive? I've never been able to. I'm still so angry at him."

Richard couldn't waste the opportunity she'd just presented him. He needed to know everything about her. "Since you can't mean Cecil, who are you still angry at?"

But she hesitated so long, he thought she was

going to ignore his question. He waited patiently, stroking her sides.

"My father killed himself," she said suddenly.

Stunned, he couldn't think of an immediate reply.

She let out a deep breath. "I can't believe I just told you that. I swore to my mother and sisters that I would never divulge that to anyone."

"So no one knows how he died?"

She shook her head. "We found him where he'd hanged himself in the stables behind our house."

"Meriel," he murmured against her neck, imagining her grief and fright—and the courage it took to do something about it.

"My mother was hysterical—she wanted him buried in the church graveyard. And she didn't want anyone to know what desperation had done to him. Me, I thought he was only motivated by cowardice." Bitterness etched her voice. "He was a banker, and he'd become rich from his investments, but somehow it had all gotten away from him. In the end, he killed himself rather than live penniless. He sentenced *us* to that."

"So that's why you were forced to seek employment."

She nodded. "We only had ten months until the return of the cousin who'd purchased the mortgage on our house. So Victoria stayed with Mama—"

"This is the sister who just married?"

"Yes. Louisa was a companion to a bedridden old woman, and me—"

"And you're a governess. That took much bravery to place yourself in an unfamiliar household."

"Many gentlewomen are forced to do it, Richard. And they fare far worse than I have. But it's Victoria who truly saved Mama. Me, I could have made things worse."

"What do you mean?"

She tried to sit up. "Richard, the water's getting cold. Perhaps we should—"

He pulled her back against him. "You are a brilliant woman. How could you have made things worse?"

"Because I failed," she said quietly, her body stiff against him.

"It seems like your father failed, not you."

"No, I should have seen it! I've always been the smart one, the one they all counted on—and I let my love for my parents cloud my judgment. They kept their financial problems from us, but there were clues, and I didn't follow up on them."

"Meriel, why would you think to do that? You trusted your father—you shouldn't have been expected to look for plots and secrets."

"But Richard—"

She gave a sob and turned in his embrace to hold on to him. He thought she was going to say something else, but instead she just shook her head and trembled.

Finally she wiped the last tear from her face and pushed herself up to sit beside him.

She gave a small, embarrassed laugh. "Sorry for practically using you as a handkerchief."

He smiled. "I didn't mind."

Her sudden shiver made her breasts tremble. He wanted to admire the sight a bit longer, but instead rose up and reached for two towels. He wrapped one around his waist, then gathered her into the other and scooped her into his arms.

"Richard!" she said, beginning to smile. "I think I can get out of the tub myself."

"And risk a fall? Never."

He set her down in the middle of his bedroom and dried her off as if she were the finest piece of china. Then he stepped back to look at her.

She blushed. "I'm not a statue, you know."

"Better than one. You've come to life."

She held up a hand as he advanced on her. "I'd better fetch my dressing gown. I want to hear all about this plan to rout Charles."

He groaned. "I was hoping you'd forgotten."

She darted around him back to the washroom, and when she emerged, she was safely covered from neck to ankles. He finished drying himself off, and liked that she watched him, her chin lifted defiantly.

"Should I stay like this?" he asked.

"If you'd like."

Nude, he went to sit down in a chair.

She covered her face. "Oh all right, put on your robe. You're terribly difficult to resist."

They tried to sit in opposite chairs to talk, but Richard couldn't bear to be separated from her. He drew her to the bed, fluffed pillows for them both, and encouraged her to sit beside him. She folded her legs beneath her and waited, her playfulness fading away.

He sighed. "Back to the world, I guess. With today's close call, I've realized we can no longer sit back and wait for Charles to make the next move. Knowing that my six-year-old nephew could have been killed changes everything. I'm going to host the annual Thanet masquerade ball this Saturday night."

"A ball? How will that help against Charles?"

"We'll invite him, and of course he won't be able to resist coming. He'll wonder what we have planned. He's arrogant enough to think he can master us whatever the situation. Hopefully this will keep him from another attempt on Stephen's life during the week."

"But what about Stephen during the ball?"

"We'll have him taken to the old hunting lodge, close enough but out of the way. There will be guards with him. I don't want him anywhere near Charles. All of the surrounding gentry will attend—including the constables."

She started to smile. "So you're going to give yourself up?"

"I haven't quite figured out how that will work yet," he admitted. "The most important thing is to eliminate the threat to Stephen. Charles, as usual, will not be able to resist gloating when he's alone with me. I'll get him talking, while you keep the constable within earshot of us. I'm sure you can manage to lure him anywhere you wish."

"I met several constables in town," Meriel began suspiciously. "Aren't they married, and therefore resistant to my allure?"

He grinned. "Two of them are, but not the third. Maybe you can target him."

"And here I was, the mistress of the duke, about to offer myself to the married ones. After all, I'll certainly need another 'protector' in three weeks or so."

"So cynical." Richard shook his head. "But you won't be the mistress of a duke much longer."

She tilted her head quizzically.

"Because I won't be the duke much longer."

"I see," she said with a nod.

She continued to study him, and there was a very awkward pause, as they each considered life after this masquerade was over.

Richard wondered if she'd stay with him. Would she want to be married to the illegitimate son of a duke? Maybe if she loved him, none of that would matter. Could he make her fall in love with him? Or was she still too afraid to trust herself?

"We only have five days, Richard," she said, getting out of bed and walking to his writing desk. She found paper and a pencil and came back. "Are you certain everyone will come with such short notice?"

He arched a brow at her. "I'm the duke."

She smiled. "There's so much to do!"

"Put invitations at the top of your list," he said, watching as she started writing. "Those have to be delivered tomorrow."

"I feel sorry for your secretary."

He let her complete the list with food and decorations and everything else a woman managed for a party. She discussed consulting Mrs. Theobald, and even planning her own costume.

But his mind was already turning back to the problem of Charles, and what Richard could say to antagonize the man so much that he would freely talk about his plot to kill a child.

Chapter 24

Meriel was so busy for the next several days that she could have gladly given Stephen the week as a holiday. But she was too worried to give him time to think on his father's death, or the fact that people were shooting at him. So each morning they had lessons, and each afternoon he completed assignments with Nurse Weston while Meriel worked on the masquerade ball with Mrs. Theobald.

The ballroom at the far end of the conservatory was thrown open for the first time in a year, the chandeliers were lowered and restocked with candles, the walls were washed and decorated. They settled on an Oriental theme and had Chinese lanterns and painted screens sent by train from London. Potted ferns and palms from the conservatory were moved in, as well as chairs and chaises to give rest to weary dancers.

And each night, Meriel welcomed Richard to her bed, or came to his. She no longer questioned this impropriety, only accepted it as something she could never deny herself again. The future—along with its dangers—did not exist. She had only these precious hours with him, for during the day he was far too busy. She sensed him finishing his business as the duke, in preparation for relinquishing the role to Stephen. She wondered how the staff would feel when they knew the truth—or if it would even be necessary to tell them.

But of course when the duke's body was returned, it would be obvious that Richard was not Cecil.

The day of the masquerade finally arrived, and the household was like a hive of well-organized bees. Mrs. Theobald oversaw everything and sent Meriel off to bathe and don her costume. Meriel had had little time to prepare, and had settled on dressing as a bouquet of roses. A green gown was sewn with hundreds of artificial red roses across her bodice and shoulders. Her headpiece and mask were festooned with live roses, put together by Beatrice, who was proving surprisingly helpful since she now assumed that the duke was halfway through with his current mistress.

Meriel had earlier said good-bye to Stephen as Richard and several armed men led him out into the darkness to travel by stealth into the woods. Tonight she was no longer the governess. She was playing her part as mistress to the hilt, the better to lure the constable into doing her bidding. Because if the man refused to follow her, then the entire plan was for naught.

Boldly she met Richard in the corridor outside the ballroom. Servants lined the walls, ready to do any guests' bidding. Meriel knew that she and Richard were the center of attention, and she struck a pose as he stalked around her.

"Hold still so I can smell the roses," he said, his voice taut with the seriousness of the evening, yet still having to appear amused.

He was the duke after all, and the duke enjoyed the challenge of a chase, especially during the masquerade ball.

She tilted her head toward him, then slyly backed away, glancing at him sideways through her mask. In his usual evening wear, Richard was dressed all in black, but for his waistcoat, cravat, and gloves. He wore a plain black mask that hid the upper half of his face, and left his sensuous lips bare and emphasized.

"I thought you would come as yourself," she whispered. "What a disguise *that* would be."

He grinned without amusement, obviously focused on the night ahead. Putting his arm around her, he pulled her close as if against her will and whispered in her ear, "Are you ready?"

"I'm ready. I won't let you down."

He kissed her hard then, his tongue in her mouth. She gasped and spurned him, as if such a public display was yet too much for the governess.

He laughed and led her into the ballroom to begin greeting his guests.

As the evening progressed, never once did he introduce her as "the governess." Many people seemed to think that Miss Shelby was a friend come down from London, and Meriel let them believe what they wanted. She needed to remain mysterious to lure the constable.

When Richard finally introduced her to the policemen, she was glad to see that the three constables had arrived together, two with their wives, and the third, Constable Leighton, clearly available. She smiled at him mysteriously and swept into a deep curtsy that highlighted her cleavage, left bare amid the roses.

Constable Leighton choked a little bit, staring down at her, wide-eyed. His red hair was slicked back against his scalp, and he wore the mask and flowing cape of a highwayman.

"Pretending to be on the opposite side of the law for the evening, Constable?" she asked.

He reddened and glanced apologetically at his fellow officers.

Meriel leaned near him, saying far too softly for the others to hear, "Would you care to smell the roses? They're very real."

"And r-ripe for the picking?" Constable Leighton stuttered, then went as red as his hair as if shocked by his own boldness.

"Only for a highwayman daring enough," she said, then turned and threaded her way across the crowded floor.

She cruised the perimeter of the room, drinking, laughing, and never remaining with one group for long. Always she managed to meet Constable Leighton's wide eyes over her fluttering fan.

When Sir Charles Irving arrived, the evening grew serious. She watched as Richard greeted Charles at the high, wide double doors that opened into the ballroom. The two men looked at each other, both smiling, both about the same height and coloring, though Charles was several years older. Charles, too, wore a simple black mask.

There was a tension between them, even though Charles must wish he could pretend otherwise. The man was too excited for a mere masquerade ball, his grin too wide, his superior air far too apparent.

Meriel hoped it would be his downfall.

For a half hour, she flitted about the ballroom, occasionally catching the constable's eye. When Richard and Charles finally met up again and began to talk, Meriel's insides grew a little tighter. She turned to look for the constable and found him almost immediately, standing alone with a drink in his hand, watching her.

She gave him a slow, secretive smile, and he stiffened. She pantomimed drinking, and he lifted a wineglass from a tray and brought it to her.

"Miss Shelby," he said, bowing low. "I'd be honored if—after you drink, of course—if you'd do me the honor of dancing the—"

"Constable Leighton," she interrupted, sipping her wine and batting her lashes at him, "I would love to dance with you, but first I have a slight problem. Would you speak with me in private?"

His eyes widened within the mask and he followed her dutifully, only to look disappointed when she stepped behind another potted palm.

She lowered her voice to a throaty whisper. "Constable, when I saw you, I knew you were the answer to our problems."

"Our?" he repeated, sounding wary.

"The duke would be outraged if he knew I came to you. He's a very proud man. But he could use your help."

The constable's chest swelled with importance, and he stood a little taller. "Of course, Miss Shelby. What is the problem?"

"Do you see him with his cousin, Sir Charles Irving?" She pointed between two palm fronds. "Sir Charles is . . . threatening His Grace."

He frowned. "Threatening? Why?"

She smiled as if nervous—which really wasn't a lie. "Sir Charles is next in line for the dukedom after Lord Ramsgate. He insists on being named the child's guardian, should anything happen to the duke. His Grace insists that Sir Charles means nothing by it, but I disagree." She sighed melodramatically. "If you could just come with me to follow them, and see how Sir Charles *talks* to the duke, the threat in his voice. I am quite frightened of him."

When he looked unconvinced, she gritted her teeth and played the silly female. "Oh, Constable, I know you can help me put my mind at rest. Then I'll be able to relax and enjoy the evening with you."

Again his face went scarlet, and he kept sneaking a glance at her breasts. She took a deep breath to bring them into better view.

Constable Leighton held out his arm. "Shall we move a little closer to the duke, then?"

Relieved, she led him through the crowd. When they got close to Richard, Meriel turned her back and smiled up at Constable Leighton.

He looked over her shoulder briefly, then resumed his cleavage watch. "I can just hear them. They're talking about horses."

"Well, of course. They're right where everyone can hear them."

"And now they're moving off," the constable said.

Meriel grabbed his arm and followed. At the last moment, Charles waved to someone and left Richard.

Though Meriel was disappointed, the constable didn't seem to mind. He asked her to dance, and she had no choice but to agree. It was another dance before Richard and Charles were talking, and then Charles wandered away again.

Meriel stomped her foot, but Constable Leighton only shook his head.

"Miss Shelby, Sir Charles doesn't seem to have much to say to the duke. And I have a card game that's beginning right now in the library."

"But Constable Leighton, the duke really needs your help!"

No amount of eyelash batting, lip trembling, or

bosom thrusting mattered. The constable bowed and left her.

"Meriel!"

She gave a little start as Renee, dressed as a medieval queen, called her name.

"I've been trying to get your attention," Renee said, pressing her cheek to Meriel's. "Ouch, thorns!"

"But there aren't any thorns in my—"

"Just teasing! I so love the roses. A bouquet is an excellent costume. But now the treasure hunt is beginning," Renee said excitedly. "What a wonderful idea Cecil had for this year's entertainment! Come with me! I saw the torches leading all through the gardens. It will be a magical night."

"Renee, you'll have to go without me. I promised Stephen I would visit and tell him about the ball. And he so wanted to see my costume."

"Well, then I'll come with you."

"But you'll miss the hunt! And to be honest, I helped organize it, so I already know where the prize is." The treasure hunt had been her idea to keep their guests distracted from the true purpose of the ball.

"I should have expected you would be the one behind the hunt," Renee said. "Oh well, I have my first clue. I'll tell you all about it when I get back!"

The ballroom crowd was slowly thinning out, and Meriel was able to catch sight of Richard again. He and Charles were at the far end of the ballroom, going out a door into the house. She picked up her skirts and practically ran, dodging servants and guests. She hoped that the men would walk past the library, where she could grab Constable Leighton.

But instead they went out into the night under the half moon, away from the torches lighting the treasure hunt. Charles picked up a torch from the path and lifted it ahead of them. It was still difficult for Meriel to see, and only because she knew the grounds so well was she able to follow them without turning an ankle.

They were headed for the old castle ruins, and she didn't have the constable with her. She was failing Richard, thwarting their plan. Her only hope was overhearing what they said, so she could testify on Richard's behalf herself.

"Enough of this!" she overheard Richard say. "We could have talked in the house."

Oh God, Charles was the one leading Richard out into the dark grounds. She remained behind a clump of trees and caught her breath when Charles finally stopped and faced Richard. The eerie sight of the ruins behind them made the scene look like something from a novel.

Charles smiled. "I'm so glad you gave me

another opportunity to see you, Richard. Perchance did you think you could kill me? Though murder isn't your style—you don't have the courage for it—I did plan ahead just in case. I'm sure you believe that Stephen is safe out there in the hunting lodge."

Meriel covered her mouth with her hand. Oh God, how could he have known where Stephen was? She wanted to run straight to the lodge, but she remained frozen in horror. Was Stephen alive or dead?

Richard moved closer to Charles, his hands fisted.

Charles laughed. "I've always been one step ahead of you, Richard. Your brother's steward has been in my employ for many years."

Jasper Tearle? Meriel thought, even as Richard said the name aloud.

"Don't be so surprised," Charles continued. "Cecil treated him abominably—hardly paid him what he was worth. I rectified that, and since then, he's been loyal to me. Cecil was too foolish to figure out how all his money was slowly being siphoned away. Jasper tells me he's been quite worried since you arrived, because you seemed suspicious of the account books almost immediately. Yet you allowed yourself to be distracted—by the pretty governess, perhaps?"

"Have you killed Stephen?" Richard ground out.

"Good heavens, no," Charles said. "I wanted to assess the situation first. Maybe, if he's a good boy, I'll let him live. For a while."

Meriel thought of the threat to Stephen, and realized the little boy was now her only priority. She would trust Richard to deal with Charles. All that mattered was bringing the constable to rescue Stephen.

Chapter 25

Richard fought his every impulse to strangle Charles, to see the life leave his eyes. The man deserved to die.

But Stephen was still alive.

Wasn't the constable out there in the darkness with Meriel? Why didn't he come forward, especially after Charles talked about letting Stephen live?

"Is something wrong, Richard?" Charles asked softly, his smile fading as he looked around. "Waiting for someone?" Charles pulled a pistol out of his pocket and aimed it at Richard. "Come out, whoever you are, or I'll kill him."

Richard let himself smile. "Ah, Charles, you've underestimated me. I guess you've been out of practice, dealing with Cecil for so long. Kill me if you want, but it's too late. The constable must have heard all he needed, and went off to rescue Stephen. You better hope he gets there before your men do something drastic to my nephew."

Charles betrayed himself by a quick look over his shoulder, and Richard launched himself at the pistol. He deflected Charles's hand just as a shot went off, and he felt a momentary burn across his upper arm. Charles kicked him in the face, the stinging blow glancing off his cheekbone. As Richard rolled to the side and back to his feet, he saw Charles disappearing into the night in the direction of the hunting lodge. His torch lay burning on the ground.

No constable had appeared to apprehend Charles. What had happened to Meriel? Though it was difficult to forget his concern for her, Richard had to think about saving Stephen. He took off after Charles, leaving the torch so he wouldn't be seen. In the darkness, he could only hope he was heading the right way.

Occasionally Richard paused to listen, and he still heard someone running ahead of him on the gravel path. Off in the distance, the formal gardens lit the sky, and he could hear the shouts and cheers of the guests. He left that behind and crossed the last open grass before the woods. Up ahead, he thought he saw a shadow slipping between the trees.

His relief was great—until he realized that Charles might be desperate enough to kill Stephen before Richard got there.

Richard pounded down the path, the light from the half moon only occasionally filtering through the branches. He tripped twice over exposed roots, but he was lured on by the flicker of light up ahead.

He came out into a torchlit clearing in front of the hunting lodge and slid to a stop, sweat running into his eyes, his chest heaving. Charles was already mounted, and when he saw Richard, he reached to the far side of his horse and dragged something across his saddle.

Stephen.

Facedown, the little boy flailed, proving that he was still alive. Richard swayed with relief. Then Charles put the barrel of another pistol against the boy's neck. They must have terrorized Stephen with it already, because he knew enough to remain still.

Where were Richard's hired guards? He saw three men motionless on the ground near the lodge, and he prayed that they were still alive. A flicker of movement caught his eye. A wide-eyed Jasper Tearle looked frantically between Richard and Charles before slipping away into the woods.

"Don't move, Richard." Charles's voice was a snarl, no longer polished and calm.

"You have one bullet," Richard said. "You'd better shoot me, because if not, I'm going to kill you." It was dark—he prayed that he could dodge in time and save Stephen.

"So arrogant, the lot of you," Charles said. "Your brother was no different—but I beat him in the end, didn't I?"

"You killed a sick man. Not very sporting of you."

"I beat him long before then. To think, I loaned him his own money! When he owed me more than he could repay—and he knew that if he died, I would make sure I controlled Stephen—he offered me a deal."

Some part of Richard already knew what was coming.

"Strangely enough," Charles continued, his pistol still on Stephen, "he guessed that I would harm his son to control the dukedom. But it was already financially unsound, so he offered a trade. He would get *you* to masquerade as the duke, and then I would be able to hunt you. Because of course, once you're dead, Stephen inherits all your money. Please tell me Cecil didn't lie about that."

Richard remained silent, still trying to comprehend that his own brother planned his murder. He felt almost dizzy, as if his whole life was not what he'd thought.

"Now, your poor, ignorant brother thought he was saving his son," Charles continued. "I'd agreed to let Stephen live, and control everything through him. But between you and me, Richard"—he laughed softly, and patted Stephen's back—"I'm changing the rules. I deserve to be the duke. My mother was the eldest in the family. It's only fair that the title finally come back to me."

For a moment, Charles's words echoed strangely. Hadn't Richard just considered remaining the duke, as if he deserved it? The lure of such power overtook so many people.

"You can't kill Stephen," Richard said, "because then he won't be around to inherit my money."

"I'll think about it." Charles slowly raised the pistol and pointed it at Richard.

For a frozen moment, Richard waited, caught between diving away and concern that Charles would just kill Stephen instead. The boy was the only thing between Charles and all the power he craved.

Suddenly, from around them three men appeared out of the darkness. Richard recognized the constables, one of whom was holding a pistol trained on Charles. Richard remained still, not wanting to panic his cousin.

But Charles barely blinked an eye. He pointed

the pistol up into the night sky and sighed heavily as if with relief.

"Thank goodness you've come, Constables. I was trying to protect my young cousin from this impostor posing as the duke. This man is the duke's bastard brother. He's already killed the duke, and I knew his next target would be poor Stephen. Thank goodness you've come to save us from him!"

"Stop!"

It was a woman's voice—Meriel. She walked into the torchlight alone, her hands raised. Her mask was gone, and the roses at her shoulders drooped. Richard's breath left his body at the danger she put herself in, all for him and Stephen.

She turned appealing eyes on Constable Leighton. "He's lying to you, Constable! I'll tell you everything. Won't you listen?"

Charles was watching her with sympathetic concern, as if Richard had fooled even her. One constable took the pistol from Charles and told him to dismount slowly. Then Charles lifted poor Stephen down and set the boy on his feet in front of him, holding his shoulders. Stephen turned wide, frightened eyes on Richard. Tears tracked dirty streaks down his cheeks.

Constable Leighton regarded Meriel thoughtfully. "You did come to me for help, and said that Sir Charles was threatening the duke."

"Sir Charles is right about one thing," she said gravely. "This is not the duke. He's Richard O'Neill, the duke's brother, and he's only here because it was the best plan I could come up with to protect Stephen."

"You'd better explain yourself," Constable Leighton said.

Richard thought the same thing—this wasn't part of the plan. What could she be thinking? He tried to warn her with his eyes, but she looked away.

"The real duke disappeared," Meriel said. "I knew that this would leave Stephen unguarded, ripe for any unscrupulous family member to exert his influence. By questioning the servants, I knew that Stephen's own uncle could be counted on to help him, to step into the role of the duke temporarily."

Stephen suddenly pulled free of Charles and ran to Richard, who bent down and hugged him tight.

"Uncle Richard!" Stephen cried. "That man tried to hurt me!" He burst into tears.

Charles shook his head. "The poor confused boy."

"He's not confused," Meriel said. "He knew about the masquerade the whole time. Do you think he wouldn't recognize his own uncle?"

Richard looked up at Meriel, knowing she held his whole life in her hands. And he trusted her with it, as he'd never trusted anyone before.

"Constable Leighton," he said, rising to his feet, yet keeping a hand on Stephen's shoulder, "my cousin Charles just told me that he's had the duke's steward in his employ for years. It will be a simple matter to get Mr. Tearle to testify to all that he did for Charles. And the falsified account books are at Thanet Court, in Tearle's own handwriting. He's the man who took Stephen away from his guards tonight, and Stephen will be able to vouch for that."

"That is ridiculous," Charles said, still sounding mildly amused. "If they've convinced their steward to lie, it has nothing to do with me."

Constable Leighton looked at him thoughtfully. "But I arrived here tonight in time to hear some of what you were saying, Sir Charles. You had a pistol to that boy's head."

Richard sighed and ruffled Stephen's hair in relief, then glanced at Meriel, who watched him, wearing a tremulous smile.

Constable Leighton strolled closer to Charles, whose smile had finally faded. "And you said you were in league with the real duke, but you were breaking your agreement."

"You misunderstood, Constable," Charles said, then stiffened when the other constable behind him put a hand on his shoulder.

"You can come with us into Ramsgate, Sir

Charles. I'm sure you'll try to talk yourself out of this, and it will be a long night."

Constable Leighton turned to the other officer. "We'll need to start a search for Jasper Tearle, and see to Mr. O'Neill's injured men." He looked over his shoulder at Meriel and grinned. "Thank you for the loan of your pistol, Miss Shelby. Might I keep it awhile longer?"

"As long as you'd like, Constable," she said. "You have my undying gratitude."

"It came from such a nice hiding place," the man replied.

Meriel blushed. Richard came to stand beside her, and he smiled as Stephen hugged her.

"So where was my pistol again?" Richard asked.

"Strapped to my thigh," she said haughtily. "You told me to find somewhere to put it."

Charles was led away, already trying to explain his actions.

Constable Leighton looked at Richard. "We'll need to ask you more questions, Mr. O'Neill."

"Any time, Constable. But might I get my nephew into bed tonight? It's a very trying time for him. Please ask Sir Charles where we can find the duke's body."

The constable looked sober. "I will. So you're certain that the duke is dead?"

"Sir Charles told me he was. He held hostage my brother's terrified valet, who verified that my brother was dead. That man still hasn't been set free."

"We'll find him. I'll speak with you in the morning."

Richard put Stephen up on his shoulders, and then he and Meriel followed the constables through the woods. By the time they got back to the house, Stephen was drooping forward with exhaustion. Guests were still milling about the grounds, and they stopped to watch the parade of constables and their prisoner. When Richard, Meriel, and Stephen brought up the rear, they received shocked stares.

Meriel leaned toward Richard. "They act like they already know who you are," she whispered.

"Maybe they do. One constable came back before the others. All he would have had to do was tell one person and then—"

"An explosion of gossip."

As they left the constables and headed back indoors, whispers and stares followed them. Meriel wanted to feel vindicated, but all she felt was exhausted and sad for Stephen, who had lost a father and now a cousin.

Mrs. Theobald met them in the conservatory, staring wide-eyed until she saw Stephen. She promptly burst into tears and grabbed the little boy. He sagged against her, blinking drowsily, and she allowed Richard to take him from her.

Stephen cuddled against his uncle and closed his eyes.

Meriel put her arm around the woman and whispered, "I told the constables that the masquerade was all my idea to protect Stephen until we could find his father."

Mrs. Theobald glanced at her shrewdly, then nodded with obvious relief. "You are good to Mr. O'Neill." She lowered her voice. "But then, you love him."

"Yes." Meriel felt like a silly girl as tears welled in her eyes.

They both turned to look at Richard, who cradled Stephen and watched him sleep.

"Meriel!" cried a voice.

She looked up to see Renee striding quickly through the turning paths, pushing aside ferns. "I heard the most dreadful rumor," she said. "It certainly can't be true that Cecil is—"

She came up short as she saw Richard's face. He looked at her with such sorrow, such resignation. Her eyes widened and flooded with tears.

"Oh dear, you're Richard, aren't you?"

He nodded. Her shoulders slumped, and she looked bewildered as Meriel put her arm around her.

"I should have known," Renee said to Richard. "You seemed different, but I thought you—he had finally grown up." Her voice trailed away, and when she spoke again, it was husky with strain. "Is it true what that constable said? Is Cecil . . . dead?"

Richard nodded. Meriel took Stephen from him and watched with sorrow as he went to Renee. Renee didn't seem to know what to do with him, but then she began to sob, and he put his arms around her.

"How horrible it must have been," she said, hiccupping with each unsteady breath, "to die like that."

"We don't know how he died yet, Renee," Richard said gently. "Consumption might very well have taken him."

"But you don't believe that," she said.

"No."

Meriel watched his face as he spoke about his brother. There was pain and heartache and a terrible knowledge. She hadn't heard everything Charles had said, but he'd implied that Cecil had betrayed Richard.

How would Richard, who had so few good memories of his childhood, ever forget this?

Within the hour, the guests were all gone, Stephen was in bed, and Meriel was alone in her room, hurriedly removing her costume. When she wore her dressing gown, she rushed down the private staircase and knocked softly on Richard's door.

There was such a long pause that she began to think he wasn't there. Then he called for her to come in.

She opened the door and saw him slumped tiredly in a chair near his writing desk. He was still wearing some of his evening clothes, although his coat and waistcoat were tossed on a nearby chair. A dark bruise had blossomed on his cheek. There was a small bloodstain on his upper sleeve, and she wanted to tend to the wound beneath. But he was staring at a piece of paper in his hand.

She slowly walked toward him, and he looked up with an exhaustion that made her want to cradle him in her arms and never let go.

"Hargraves just brought this," he said.

"What is it?"

"A letter from Cecil."

She would only have sat near him, but he pulled her onto his lap and rested his cheek against her shoulder.

"It just arrived today?" she asked.

"Several days ago. Cecil wrote that Hargraves should give it to me when everything was over."

"What does it say?" She found herself whispering.

"It's an apology for getting me into this mess," he said, laughing without any amusement. "Cecil said he knew he was dying, and that he'd made a bargain with Charles, doing the best he could to safeguard Stephen."

She stiffened. "And he expected you to receive this letter after you were dead, a death he practically arranged?"

"No, he never expected me to die," Richard said, looking bewildered and amused and . . . peaceful. "He put me in the middle of this situation because he trusted that I could defeat Charles where he couldn't. In his naive way, he thought I, his big brother, could fix everything for him."

"And you did," she said, near tears herself. She was so grateful that Richard would not have to live with the knowledge that his brother had wanted him dead.

"Just barely." He held up another piece of paper. "This is a document granting me guardianship."

"Oh Richard, how wonderful! Now you and Stephen will never have to be parted."

She put her arms around him, snuggling as close as she could get, letting him rock her. After several quiet minutes, she broached the subject most on her mind.

Looking up into his face, barely breathing with nervousness, she said, "Will I still be Stephen's governess?"

"No." He smiled down at her tenderly. "But would you be his aunt?"

The grin she wore almost hurt her face, even as her foolish tears started to flow again.

"I hope all this crying is a good sign," he said, "because I love you, Meriel. I never thought I could trust anyone the way I trust you. You not only saved Stephen's life—you saved mine, in every way that matters. You guided me when I needed it, you offered me your support when I didn't deserve it, you—"

"Just stop!" she said, laughing and crying all at once. "You have no idea what you've done for me, Richard. This last year has been so hard. I told myself I could never trust my emotions, that I would let logic guide me. I had only that. And then I met you, and I was drawn to you from the very beginning."

"Is that such a bad thing?" he said gently. "I couldn't stop looking at you from the moment we met."

She stared up into his face, feeling hot tears etch paths down her cheeks. "But I thought you were the duke! I thought you were the kind of man I should never be attracted to, that once again my emotions were leading me in the wrong direction."

He remained silent, stroking the damp curls from her face.

"I had lost so much, Richard—my place in society, my respect for my father, my belief in myself. I replaced it all with a need to control everything—and I don't believe we're so different there."

He laughed.

"But then . . . I discovered that my intuition about you was right. You were—you are the perfect man for me, and I should have trusted myself—trusted that from the very beginning."

"I hardly inspired trust," he said dryly, using his thumb to wipe away her tears.

"But you did. You proved all of my emotions right. You are a man worth trusting, Richard—and through you, I learned to trust myself again."

"Say the words," he whispered.

Her smile was wobbly with emotion. "Richard, I love you."

His kiss was soft and sweet and full of the promise of a future together.

He cupped her face in his hands, kissing her cheeks and her brow. "Will you mind marrying me and living in this old giant of a house?"

"As long as I'm with you and Stephen, I don't care where we live. We could take trips to Manchester, and show him where you lived."

"But he's the duke. He'll need to be with his people more than anything."

She nodded. "He'll need all their support."

"But not their indulgence. He can be a better duke than his father and grandfather."

"With help from his uncle," she said happily.

They kissed again, and he smiled against her lips.

"What are you thinking?" she asked.

"Cecil may have done a lot of things wrong, but he brought you and me together. Though I thought he was being his usual arrogant self, he always swore he would find the perfect wife for me. I wonder if he realized that when he hired you."

She snuggled deeper into his arms. "And he found the perfect father for Stephen. He created our family, Richard."

"I think we can take it from here," he said. "You're not going to leave me tonight, are you?"

"Never."

Meriel promised herself that Richard would know the joys of family for the rest of his life.

AVON TRADE... because every great bag deserves a great book!

0-06-052228-3
$12.95

0-06-088536-X
$13.95 ($17.95 Can.)

0-06-088229-8
$13.95 ($17.95 Can.)

0-06-089005-3
$12.95 ($16.95 Can.)

0-06-089930-1
$12.95 ($16.95 Can.)

0-06-077311-1
$12.95 ($16.95 Can.)

Visit www.AuthorTracker.com for exclusive information on your favorite HarperCollins authors.

Available wherever books are sold, or call 1-800-331-3761 to order.

ATP 0706